Joan Barfoot   Photo by Anne Noble

Joan Barfoot is a Canadian writer who has worked on a variety of
newspapers and lives in London, Ontario. *Gaining Ground*, her first
novel, won an award for the best English-language novel in Canada
when it was published there under the title *Abra* in 1978. Her second
novel, *Dancing in the Dark*, was published by The Women's Press in
1982, and has been made into a feature film, her third, *Duet for Three*,
was published by The Women's Press in 1986.

Joan Barfoot
Gaining Ground

The Women's Press

First published in Great Britain by
The Women's Press Limited 1980
A member of the Namara Group
34 Great Sutton Street, London EC1V 0DX

Reissued 1984

Reprinted 1985, 1987

Published in Canada under the title *Abra*
by McGraw-Hill Ryerson Limited 1978

British Library Cataloguing in Publication Data

Barfoot, Joan
    Gaining ground.
    I. Title
    813'.54[F]   PR9199.3B3715
    ISBN 0-7043-3852-1

Printed in Great Britain
by Woolnough Bookbinding of
Irthlingborough, Northants

GAINING GROUND

1

My name is Abra.

My name is Abra.

I had almost forgotten that; the naming of things lost its importance here, with no one to hear them named.

And so, until just now — you see I am remembering time as well — "Abra" was gone. Now she is here again, as are so many other things, memories, and I do not know any longer. I thought the struggling time was over. I had forgotten it. I had forgotten so many things.

Abra. An odd name. Today I have said it over and over, making the sounds, making it disintegrate into nonsense. The harsh "A" at the beginning, sliding away into softness. Abra. That is my name; it is what other people have called me. It loses its meaning with repetition. My name. Abra.

2

It should have been obvious one of them would turn up, one day. I am glad, though, that I did not think about it. It would not have helped.

The girl is pretty, very pretty. I can see her clearly from the garden, where I have been thinning the lettuce, checking growth, weeding; I do this every day, and it is going to be a fine season. She is walking slowly toward the cabin — is a car waiting for her somewhere, or can she have walked all the way from town?

She seems a very pale person, but then my own hands working among the plants are now so brown that I cannot really be a judge of pallor. She doesn't notice me squatting in the garden. I imagine she knocks very softly on the door, for she looks timid. I consider, at first, staying where I am, waiting, quiet, until she leaves. But she looks around and her face is frightened, so vulnerable, I think I must do something, for I am strong and think it can do no harm. I stand, brushing soil from my hands, wiping them on my jeans, wondering how to approach her so that she will not be more frightened.

I think to call out to her first, gently, not to startle her, because she looks so much like one of the deer I sometimes see here, senses darting, alert for signals of danger. But after so little use, because I have never become a person who talks to herself, or to animals, or to plants, my voice refuses to be normal. "Can I do something for you?" I call softly, but my voice cracks and comes out, I know, gnarled, maybe menacing. She is startled, whirls to see me and stares. I feel badly. I have tried to keep people away, but I have never tried to frighten anyone. It is sad to see someone look at you with fear.

The words are better the second time. I clear my throat, smile, carefully put down my hoe and begin to walk slowly toward her. I wish for something in my hand to offer her, a piece of food, a gift.

"Can I do something for you?" I say again. She is watching me. I approach her slowly, slowly, giving her time to realize my kindness, my lack of will to hurt her. One must do that here with the animals. The things of nature are filled with mistrust.

She watches me still and waits. She does not bolt, the way some animals still do, although I have been here so long. Her face puzzles me, for it looks as if she wants to run, there is a wariness, and yet there is determination too, and she will not run. Closer, I think she looks ill, and I wonder where she has come from. I feel no welcoming; but also, and I am surprised at this, I do not especially want her to go away. I cannot say why.

I stop a few feet from her. She must say now what she wants, give me some sign, for I cannot go further. We stand silently looking at each other. Several times her mouth moves as if she will begin to speak, but each time she swallows back the words. I think I do not look unkind, although I do not know what she may see in my face.

Until finally: "Are you Abra Phillips?" Her voice is very soft, girl-like and high, trembling a little as if it is not her real voice but has just appeared, like mine, unrecognizable to her.

The words mean something to me. Somewhere in my mind, "Abra Phillips" is familiar, and I consider it. "Are you Abra Phillips?" Am I? I think, finally, that I must be; there is no one else to connect with the name.

"I believe I am," I answer. I say it judiciously, for that is how I have weighed the answer, but she steps back a pace, and her expression tightens. I am puzzled; what is Abra Phillips that this girl, this slim person with large eyes, staring, should be so threatened?

Again there is silence. I cannot think how to reassure her; it does no good to say, "Don't be frightened. There is nothing to

3

be afraid of." The things of nature have to learn that for themselves. They take no one's word for it.

"Do you know who I am?" she asks at last, almost whispering, sounding older that way, not so girlish.

I do not know who she is, and now I, too, feel uneasy. Should I know? I feel pressure from her, an expectation that makes me uncomfortable. I recognize nothing about her, cannot recall meeting her, am sure she can be no one from the town. But still, and again I cannot say why, it seems important to be polite.

"No, I'm sorry, I don't recognize you. Have we met?"

"A long time ago, yes," and she looks at me, hopeful. "I suppose you might not recognize me now. I'm Kate."

It is evident that she expects me to know her by that, and to make some response. But I do not know her, cannot imagine what she wants from me, resent this unspoken burden of hers. I feel the beginnings of anger, for this is my place. I want her now to leave, and I am abrupt.

"Please go away," I say. "I don't know you, I think you must have the wrong person. I do not know anyone named Kate, I don't know what you want from me. I can't help you."

I start to turn away. The sun is very high, very hot, and I want to work in my garden, to pull the cool earth from underneath and spread it around my plants, to dampen and comfort them. In such heat they can feel burned.

But she does not go. I can feel her standing there still, watching me, and then I hear her begin to cry. Even so, or especially so, for I can think of nothing I can do about her pain and I want to be away from it, I do not turn back. I am still moving slowly, carefully away, when she speaks again.

"Kate, Mother," she says. "I'm Katie. Your daughter. I'm your daughter. My name is Kate Phillips."

I stop, but I do not turn back to her, not yet. Daughter? Someone from so far away, so far back that the time she comes from is no longer with me? A daughter. I consider the word, a strange word; I roll it in my mind, explore what it means, and finally I remember "daughter"; it is child. A nine-year-old, very thin, with enormous eyes, like this young woman who is here now. Daughter was that little girl. Can this person also be daughter?

4

I turn to consider her again. The eyes, yes. The slenderness yes also, although this person is not thin in the same way as the nine-year-old. Not a child's face, though, not the daughter's face at all. Much older, not lined, not older like that, but somehow tired. Not fresh, like the daughter's face. They cannot be the same person, the daughter was someone else altogether, a child. I have not thought about her for a very long time, and this person has no right.

"No," I say strongly, my voice supporting me this time, giving me timbre and strength and harshness. "No, you are not my daughter. I remember her, and she is not like you. Go away now."

She does not move. Her face is rigid, hurt and determined both, and it will not be so easy. I wish that I had kept the hoe; not to hurt her, but because I feel defenceless, naked, standing here against her.

"I'm sure I don't look the same, of course." There is a strain, as if she is making her voice reasonable against its will. "I was nine years old. Now I'm eighteen. You can't expect me not to have changed. You've changed too. I didn't recognize you at all at first."

Time. She was nine. Now she is eighteen? Nine years? It is possible, I admit. It is certainly possible that it has been nine years — it may have been twenty, or eternity.

So. Granted that it is possible, I still have perhaps a choice about whether or not to recognize her? Her body seems to be leaning toward me, and her face is concentrated on mine, willing me to accept. Her persuasion is silent and powerful, but I have to resist. I want to tell her again to go away, to refuse her. I can see more clearly now the nine-year-old in her. The hair, the hair has deepened, not so much red in it now, and not so soft. Waving, very beautiful, not curling and short as it used to be, so easy to run hands through when walking by the child. I had thought reddish hair would be coarse, but hers had been soft. Now it seems thicker, less delicate.

More flesh, on the body and the face. Her bones used always to be there, a hug was sometimes painful if bodies combined at odd angles. Now there would be no pain, even the bones of her face more covered.

5

Only the eyes are the same. Very wide, very brown, intent, serious. With that signal behind them, asking not to be hurt, that was there at nine, before anyone had considered hurting her. She was a child who seemed, already, to know many things.

I know her now, and it locks me to her.

"I'll make tea," I say, starting toward the cabin. Knowing, I cannot act against her, but I hope she will choose the other way, run back to the city and her home, whatever it is; but no, she follows me. I suppose there can be no choice now, for either of us. So many things have been like that.

I put on the kettle while she sits at my old round wooden kitchen table. I find a second cup, packed away on a high shelf, and although she is taller than I, she does not offer to reach it for me. She is still frightened of me, wary.

I am not used to being watched. I am clumsy with the tea, pour it awkwardly. I feel I am being asked to perform, to be someone for this person who is daughter. There is a familiarity about the feeling, a sensation shooting back into memory, although I can't say precisely where it was before. There is nothing to do then but sit down, so I do, heavily, longing for something different, wanting to be peacefully back in the garden, alone. She is looking at me, sad, expecting something. What?

"Why are you here?" I ask finally. There seems to be a rhythm missing from the question, as if I should soften it by asking it again in a different way, but I leave it as it is.

"I'm old enough," she answers. There is a pause, as if she thinks I will understand that. She is holding her cup with one hand, running the forefinger of the other hand around and around the edge at the top, looking down, watching the finger as if it explains everything. Finally she goes on.

"I wanted to know where you'd gone. I wanted to know why it happened. Daddy said to wait, he said to leave you alone because that was what you wanted, but I'm old enough now, I figure I have rights too, and they're as important as yours." This last is defiant, hostile, as if I might disagree and say she has no rights. But then, what else would she think, after all?

"It was hard to find you," she continues. "Daddy wouldn't tell me anything. It took me six months." She glances at me, asking me to appreciate her investment, her effort.

"I'm sorry," I say. "It never occurred to me that you would want to find me." I shrug. "I guess I assumed too much."

"Just what did you assume, Mother? What did you think you knew about us?" She is openly angry now, not frightened, but there is pain in her voice. "What the hell would ever make you think I wouldn't go looking the first moment I could for a mother I can hardly remember? I wanted to know why you left me. That's all, just the reason why you left me."

Stupidly, I can see, that surprises me, for I haven't understood how far apart we must be. She has taken it all personally, and it wasn't personal at all. Of course, in many ways she must still be a child, but I react fiercely against her anyway, protecting myself.

"Why do you assume I left *you?*" I ask, and she looks frightened again. "I didn't leave you. You had nothing to do with it. It was just me."

When she speaks again it is more calmly, with control.

"Then why did you go? If I wasn't important, and Daddy and Elliott weren't important, why did you go then? There must have been reasons."

"I don't know. I don't recall. I think there weren't really reasons." I pause. "You're eighteen, you say?"

"Yes."

"Then you've survived. Why don't you leave it at that and go on with what you have? That's the point, surely?"

Words are coming slowly, with great difficulty. I want to be emphatic, to make her go away, but I am not sure enough. It has been so long, there has been no need for words for such a long time; even my thoughts no longer seem to use them, but are sensations, flashes in the mind, and the remembering of words and the actual execution of them, forming my tongue and lips and throat so that they come out and can be recognized is an effort, and every part of the process must be painfully considered before a proper sound will emerge. I have not realized until now how far away from it all I have fallen. There has been no need to realize.

It is an unaccustomed exhaustion, a tiring intrusion. I stand suddenly, deliberately forgetting that this person opposite me,

7

whose head snaps back as I rise and whose eyes draw away into themselves, is still afraid of me, wants something from me, is terrified of receiving nothing. I move swiftly, harshly, to the door and out of the cabin. I need to put things back, feel myself free again. The sun is still beating down, almost directly on my garden; such a very few moments have passed. The hoe is still lying beside the rows of tiny corn plants. I want every moment for my work, the summer will go quickly and there is much to be done. I pick up the hoe and start weeding again, harder now, attacking the low-lying green plants that threaten, every year, to choke my food. I behead them, dig up their roots, and then I feel vengeful, regret having injured them when, if they must be destroyed, it is better to do it with gentleness. I become calmer, concentrate on digging them out carefully, just tiny baby growths, offspring, perhaps, of ones I have already taken away. I place them at the ends of the rows of corn, just three long rows this year, most of the cobs for freezing for the winter, and leave them to be picked up when I finish.

I think of the corn, when it is grown and giving food, and the soft silk surrounding the cobs, and I recall again the softness of Katie's hair, the daughter of nine years; and then I remember the young woman in the cabin and I can feel her waiting, the pressure of her waiting. But it isn't time yet to go back to that, my anger rises again at the remembering.

The plot of corn is finished, and I gather the weeds, there are only a few, and place them in a basket. I carry them to the compost heap, add them to the pile, turn it over. Rotting goes on swiftly there.

The cabbages will have worms again. Every year the cabbages are almost useless, and yet every year I try them again, and never learn what to do about them. But the tomatoes and the green peppers are doing well, and many of them, like the corn, I will freeze for winter. I have never been able to freeze vegetables so that they taste in any way fresh, but in the winter I need food and I eat what I have put away for myself, knowing that at least it is nourishing.

Occasionally while I move among the plants, crouching, checking them, for it is vital to me that the garden be good every year, I stand, bending backwards slightly, my hand in the small

8

of my back to ease the ache. I am no longer young; I can no longer assume that the parts of my body are in good order. I never go to a doctor, but I can feel things breaking down gradually, so that one might never notice if it were not so important to keep track of these things. When I stand I raise my face to the sun, because it is good to consume it while it is so intense.

The last time I stand and turn myself toward the light, I see the young woman again. She is standing now on the porch, watching me, looking into the sun but not shielding her eyes, so that she must only see the shape of me. Her arms are at her sides, her shoulders hang loosely, as if she has admitted defeat.

"Good," I think. "Now she'll go away." I bend again over the plants. There is lettuce enough for a salad for my dinner; just for mine.

She has come up behind me and is standing there when I rise, holding my handful of lettuce. I am startled, and that combined with the sad and silent way she watches me makes me angry again.

"Well?" I ask shortly.

"Do you want me to leave?" Her voice is high again, young and tense. My anger slips; I cannot hold it. I cannot put my finger on what it is about her that defends her against me. But there is some — bond. Why can I not understand?

The struggle and the confusion are beginning now in earnest; I sense the danger, but I cannot order her away. I can, at most, be brusque.

"You'll have to do what you want. I won't invite you to stay, but I can hardly make you leave. There is a hotel in town. You must have gone past it, getting here. I live alone. I don't think I can help you, truth is something I don't know much about, and if it's explanations you want, I can't give you any. In the end, you know, you'll have to go away and do whatever it is you do in any case."

I am harsh. I am not accustomed to giving. What she wants is something I long ago became incapable of being. It has been much too long to try again.

I feel she may be hurt, but will go away and get over it. Get on with things, which shows how little I remember. That she begins to cry again, leaves me at a loss. I turn back to the garden, and I suppose I really am avoiding her, because I find myself touching the green bean plants quite unnecessarily, to see how they are coming along. By the time I look at her again, the tears are drying on her face, she hasn't wiped them away, but she seems more composed.

"It won't be that easy, you know," she says. She is calm now, very level, decided. "You can't get out of it that way. As if you had nothing to do with it, as if it was all to do with me." She tosses a trailing piece of that lovely red-brown hair away from her face.

"I'll let you think about it for a while. I'm going back to town now, I'll check into that hotel you mentioned, and I'll come back tomorrow. I'll leave you alone, you won't have to talk to me if you don't want to." She is very pale, determined and child-like. "But I'm going to be here. I'm going to keep on reminding you that I'm your daughter, and that you don't get away from everything that easily. I'll keep coming back here, every day, until you want to talk to me.

"I'll see you tomorrow, Mother."

She comes closer to me now, stands quite near, looks into my eyes. I look back at her steadily, not challenging her, I think, and not encouraging her. Gently she puts her hands on my shoulders and bends a little. She kisses my cheek. Her lips feel like a flower brushed on my face.

I must confess, although I never will to her: as she goes I follow her, tracking behind, along the string of trees that line the lane, moving silently behind them, keeping glimpses of her between them, watching her look back toward the cabin until she cannot see it around a curve, and then slowing, confident she is out of sight, becoming sad again. I see her wipe a hand across her face. She seems pathetic, and I am angry; but this time I must be angry with myself as well, for it isn't she who has shown me this; I have made an effort to see it myself.

It is not that she is my daughter. I would be resentful of anything that tried to trap me.

But why, with her, am I letting it happen?

At the end of the lane, which is almost half a mile from the cabin, she stops. I always park my car there, in an impromptu

10

kind of lean-to garage, except on the rare occasions when I go into town to stock up on necessities I can't provide for myself. Then, if it's possible, I drive it right up to the cabin, balancing precariously in the narrow ruts, creeping along to avoid toppling into the encroaching ditches at the sides. After I've unloaded on those days, I return the car to the bottom of the lane. Several times in the winter I've been stuck when it has refused to start, and I've learned to get along without supplies I thought at first I needed. Eventually I've dug out and gone to a neighbour's for help in getting the car going again. The people around here don't ask questions, not any more. The man on the next farm comes and jumps the battery and goes home again, and I give him a few dollars each time it happens. In the first while I was here, that happened several times, both because I didn't know how to stock up properly, and had to keep returning to town, and because I didn't take good care of the car. I didn't realize how important it would be. Vital, like the vegetables. It's an old thing now, but the mileage is still low because the only place I go is town, which is seven miles away, and that not often. Because I'm on a back country road, the driving can be treacherous, if not impossible, which is another reason I've learned to be organized before the snow falls.

I see Katie looking through the windows of my car, searching, I guess, for some hint about me, but there is nothing in it. She herself has a small car, and I like the way she gets into it. They look awkward, those little things, and she is fairly tall, but she tucks herself in gracefully, swiftly, altogether accustomed to its size and to her own. I notice, too, that she is a confident driver, reversing and driving away as if the car were an added limb of her body, and the narrow gravel road utterly familiar. I must say, physically I approve of the girl; it is her appearance in my life that is disturbing.

I walk back to the cabin rather more slowly than I followed Katie down the lane. The visit is opening up memories and odd thoughts, and I am surprised to find them lying so close to the surface. If I thought in the last few years about the other life at all, it was only in passing, as of something quite vague and different. Now, confronted by Katie and her bitterness and curiosity, I am confronted, too, by a fragment of the old self. I

11

cannot pick out any incident that might be called a memory, but I can see forms, outlines, and it frightens me that they may come back, rushing at me, knocking me off my balance. Suddenly now I feel without confidence, the solidity I have grown accustomed to.

I do not think that I have ever suppressed memory, not at all, even at the beginning of what has become, apparently, nine years. It seemed instead quite natural that all the past should die, as the person who lived it did.

I do not want Katie to come back. I do not want her, bringing that past with her when she walks up my lane. I want her to go back to the city, to do whatever makes her feel content and right. But I do not want her here, questioning my content and my right.

It will not be dark yet for a long time. The light stays in summer until very late, so that long after I eat I can be outside, still warm, working again in the garden or the woods or simply sitting, listening to the life around me. We don't converse, that life and I, but we recognize each other, and the summer evenings are good.

Later, after dark, if I am not yet tired, I sometimes bake. Usually it's bread, which is useful. But this night, after I split some wood, which would have been done much earlier if it had not been for Katie, I am still wakeful. Almost tense, I think. I want to make something, not bread but something I don't need, something frivolous like a cake; and so I do, using too many precious eggs, which means I will run out before the man who brings them to the gate comes round again.

It has been a long time. The cake seems difficult, clumsy to make, messy, and it must be very late when I finish. The cake looks appetizing, appealing, but I am not tempted to eat any now. I do not want to spoil its shape, its symmetry, by cutting into it.

I do not think I made it for Katie. I certainly wasn't thinking of her when I decided to bake it. But it is there, the next day, when she appears, and when she leaves there are several pieces missing and I am pleased because it seems she has enjoyed it.

3

The first time I saw this place, I knew I had come home. I do not mean I knew it in a peaceful, comforting sort of way, the way one recognizes an old friend; that first time it was like an electric shock, sharp and abrupt, strange and terribly painful, and it changed everything. With it, the life I had disintegrated. From the first moment this was my home. How can that be understood?

But after that initial shock of recognition, after the first changes and the settling in, the shiftings in me came more slowly, took their time in rooting. I cannot say that I lost right away the sense of distinguishing myself from what was around me. I heard the birds, looked at the flowers, but always I was separate from them, someone listening and looking. I do not know when the distinction disappeared, but it must not have been for a very long time. Not until I became a part of it, which is a different thing from feeling at home.

It was spring then, which was a blessing because if I had arrived later, toward autumn, I most surely would not have been ready for winter. Odd — I see that remembering has separated me from it; that looking back at myself as an object of my memory has made everything I saw then an object as well, so that I have lost the unity. It is part of my confusion now, my disorientation. At this moment I don't belong, although the knowledge that I am home has not changed.

Of course it's a different season now, summer instead of early spring, but that does not make the difference. The rhythm of the seasons is quite natural to me now. Each year, I know, the same sensations, the same breaths recur; there is security knowing that in the spring I will feel the new life, my own joy, a wish to touch all young things, the crocuses and snowdrops, searching them out, walking, the tenderness of finding a cluster of small flowers hiding from still-chilly winds, waking in the mornings, hearing each day the return of more birds until the air is filled with them.

And in the summer working, caring for the garden, cultivating my plants, my food, inhaling the sun, seeing my skin become brown just as the flowers are also growing their colours, and my beloved garden plants are delivering their brilliant food. The long evenings, the sense of having achieved in each day what there was to be achieved.

The autumn, the yellow squash lying in the garden, waiting their turn to be picked; the one maple tree, not on my land but near the crest of a hill on a neighbour's farm, that turns such a radiant scarlet, the only one that is so dashing, so flagrant. On my trees the leaves change more softly, lighter oranges and yellows, until they fall and I gather them up, and although I know it is probably against some township bylaw I burn them, the ones I do not keep for rotting down for next year's garden, and the scent of the burning is a perfect day. It is my last rite for the dying year.

And then the snows fall, easily at first, sometimes then with fury, but mostly with huge soft flakes that stay white on the ground and are almost always fat, because, I think, they don't have to force their way through the black and the heat of the skies above cities; here, although I am truly not far from the city, less than two hundred miles, which is nothing really, it is clean.

The first time the snow comes, it is a surprise even to itself, it seems, tentative, not belonging, an advance guard set out to test the ground which absorbs it immediately and leaves no trace. But then the snow falls harder, more determined, clinging to the earth, unwilling to be thrown off or pulled in, and winds come too so that it is not silent, not this time, not yet, and quite suddenly it seems the earth is white, green and brown one moment and then in an instant white, and soon after that the winds slow, the snow slips down more gently, knowing that it has won, it is its turn, and there is no more need to be ferocious. I watch that first snowfall late into the night, the lights turned off so that I can see better into the darkness outside, and although it marks a change there is nothing unwelcoming in me.

I wake up in the mornings and look out at untracked snow. In the evenings I have my fireplace, my drawings, my self. Everything is very slow, very soft, and my thick quilts are like the snow, heavy and protecting. In the beginning it was a test, this hibernation of the winter, and I felt pale for a long time that first year, before my mind became as still as the whiteness outside.

One cannot regret the loss of a season. I do not feel sad because the snow melts and the time to leave my quilted womb has come, or because the last squash is picked, the last scarlet leaf gone, and it is time to retreat once more. Each time is right for its time, and it may be mildly astonishing to find that each season corresponds exactly with some rhythmic need of my own.

I know that in the next two or three months I will gather up my small harvest, pickle it, freeze it, preserve it. I will turn over and fertilize the earth, so that it will be rich in the spring. I will have my major fall expedition to the town, to find the things I need for winter that I cannot provide for myself. I will sweat over my stove, stirring and pouring, and my home will be filled with the odd, bitter smell of cucumbers becoming pickles, and I will see the freezer filling with the food I have blanched and bagged for the long time ahead. The wood which I have cut throughout the spring and early summer, and of which I will cut more in the next weeks, I will carry close to the house and cover with a weighted tarpaulin, so that in the snapping winter afternoons I can easily gather in enough for the evening and the next morning, to take away the chill. I will gather up seeds and put them in bags, ready to hand out to winter birds and squirrels.

At that brief moment, perhaps just a day, when I feel that autumn has ended and that winter must begin tomorrow, I will walk. It is the day I say good-bye to the season, and I do it at the end, the beginning, of each one.

In this autumn I will begin with my daily check of the garden, or what will be left of it by then. The soil should be moist, faintly acid smelling, from its infusion of decayed compost. It should be very soft, too, loose and crumbling, and I may walk through it in my bare feet.

Then there will be the slow progress down the lane, through all the great old maples, enormous trees that must have seen generations passing by. I know very little of the history of this place; farming families mostly, I suppose, not well off for the land is not good enough for prosperity. With my own past discarded, I wanted my home to come to me the same way. When I did learn a little of its past, it was inadvertent and did not matter.

I will sit in my car at the end of the lane for a few moments, warming it up. I have to admit I keep the car locked; it is one of my key possessions, and to have it stolen, unlikely though that is on the wilderness of a back country road (but farm boys are not so unlike city boys in their desire for adventure, although the maliciousness one sees in the city is generally absent), would be serious and so I take care to keep it, and them, from harm.

The ditches along my lane, and along the road that I will follow on foot for a way, will be almost dry. Only a trickle. In the spring, when the snow is melting and the springs that are high up in the rock cliffs some miles away are carrying it down full speed, the ditches overflow as does the little creek that runs near my cabin. They move with a rush then, their sound loud in the night; but in the fall they are quiet, almost dormant.

I will walk along the road a short way, then cross the ditch and climb the little rise on the other side. There is a fence there that separates the land that is mine from the land that belongs to the township, and I have not kept it up and neither has the township. It doesn't especially matter, since neither I nor they have livestock that may wander off, although I thought once of keeping goats. I decided against it, because I do not want to be responsible for the well-being of animals.

The fence, as I say, is not what it once was, when this land was truly a farm. It wobbles on its posts, the wire sags, and the only part of it that has kept its tension and purpose is the barbed wire across the top, which may be what holds up the fence posts.

The barbs make the fence difficult to climb because it is an easy thing to be caught on one as the fence bends under my weight. Each time I say I will come out one day and clip the barbed wire away from the top, but I never do. It belongs.

When I have edged over the fence, I will be standing in my own woods. Not a forest by any means, but a small woods where there are squirrels and chipmunks, probably snakes and skunks, rabbits and, now and then, passing through on some mysterious transient route, a deer or a family of deer. I will be very still; I will sit or crouch on a blanket of leaves, and the trees will be almost barren. If I wait motionlessly, carefully, the easiest of the wildlife, the squirrels and chipmunks, will go back to what they were doing before my disturbance, chasing each other, carrying off nuts, preparing for the next season as I have. Do they also recognize this last day, this moment of the break?

When I take this same walk in the spring, the first small flowers are just opening. In the fall different flowers, the last of the season, will be finally wilting. The trees will be almost skeletal then, and yet I do not ever have the sense of death.

After a long while, for I take the whole day for this walk and move only when the time comes, I will go on. At the other side of the woods the land dips into a ravine, the great trees end and dense bushes clot the bank. But I will go down, pushing through, and at the bottom, where very little sunshine penetrates, is my stream, the one that runs through the property, from other people's toward other people's, but here it is just my stream, and it passes from here close to the cabin. The sounds of the frogs that live around it dot my sleep, and the sound of the creek itself is always in the background of my hearing. Here in the ravine it is wider, narrowing farther along, and I must step carefully on stones to get across without wetting my feet. The water will be very cold in late autumn, is in fact cold all year around; it is not the sort of stream in which one paddles for long, as I have learned.

The water will be very low, and the ravine so dense that it will seem there is very little life; it will be more silent even than the woods, except for the gentle trickling. The birds that have not yet flown south will seem far away, far above, and there is no place on my land that is more quiet. One can drink here not only the water from the stream, but the silence.

Up the other side of the ravine there is another fence, much like the first, but without the barbed wire. Because I do not want to be the person to break it down entirely, I will climb it gingerly, testing my weight on it, finding the strongest spot. One of these years, I know, it will just lean over and not come up again, but not, I hope, in my time.

Over the fence is a pasture, rocky and rough, flat and unlovely. The land here is generally not good for crop farming; one would want to be grazing cattle here, not trying to plow it.

I know it's selfish to keep these acres to myself, not contributing by raising food. I know I could rent this land to a farmer who wants a little more for his cattle, but I don't because I want to be able to walk here undisturbed.

There are big rocks to sit on to survey my world. I will move among them, pausing, watching the tiny life of the pasture, toads, birds, insects, worms, everything is there except that it is tiny and if you take a step you must be aware that something is dying underfoot. In places like the woods, where everything is larger and grander, one is not so conscious of that. But in the pasture, with just rocks and grass and weeds, one must look down and see the little forms.

At the far side is a fence that is important, because it divides my land from the next farmer's and he has cattle that could stray. I keep an eye on this fence on my periodic walks, but he is the one who keeps it repaired. When I see that he has worked on it, I pay for half of the repairs the next time I see him. He is the same man who delivers my eggs and starts my car.

Eventually on this walk I will come to the end of the pasture and head back along a path toward the cabin. There are bushes along this path, wild flowers, a couple of maple trees. Ahead I will see the enormous willow that hangs over the cabin; one day, I think, there will be a winter ice storm or heavy snowfall and one of its great limbs will crash through my roof. Or the whole tree may just lean over, because it is already split naturally, and collapse on me. I would not cut that tree, though, if I could, so until it happens, I try to trust it and forget it.

On each walk, the sight of the cabin and the willow ahead

makes me eager to get back, to light a fire, put my feet up, think, perhaps, about what I've seen, be warm in my home. And so I will hurry along the path, forgetting already the creatures dying beneath my feet.

The cabin itself is very old, hand-built of stone, carefully, solidly made. It is not, however, primitive; it has electricity and plumbing, and I bought a freezer as soon as I came here. It is my home. It is not an outback, a wilderness; I do not have an interest in "roughing it." I am accustomed to comfort.

There are just four rooms, not counting the bathroom. The kitchen is large, modern appliances and ancient wooden counters and cupboards everywhere, hooks that I have put up myself to hold the pots and pans. I have painted the room in black and white, except for the counter tops, which are plain wood. The colours do not sound warm, but they are. I have a small table, round, some heavy kind of wood that I refinished, and two chairs, one of which sits empty. I eat breakfast at this table, and often lunch, but rarely dinner. I did not used to eat so many meals, but here the work is different and I need more food.

The refrigerator and the stove are second-hand and white. The kitchen is the first thing that happens when you walk in the door. There is only one door to the outside in the cabin.

It is pleasant to sit at the table in the centre of the kitchen and look around this room, which has no curtains on the window above the sink. Often kitchens are the best rooms for sitting. Certainly mine is welcoming; I would find it difficult, though, to say that I have a favourite among the rooms; each one is different, and each serves its purpose with, I think, a certain grace.

Past the kitchen, through a short, low hallway, is the living room. I eat the evening meals here, because it is an evening room, dark, with just two narrow farm windows, at its best at night. In daylight, it can seem oppressive.

I covered this room when I came in an old-fashioned cream wall-paper with deep red feathery patterns. I had never done such a thing before, and will not attempt it again, for I am not good with my hands. I spent several painful days doing it, trying desperately to smooth out lumps, make edges meet, cut the paper away from the obstacles of doors and windows. When it was finished, I felt tired, discouraged, incompetent, for there were gaps between sheets of the paper, wrinkles on the walls — nothing too obvious, but mistakes nonetheless. I look at it now and do not notice the mistakes.

The furniture I bought at a second-hand store in the town, just an old couch, a deep chair with relaxed springs, three small tables, two table lamps, a floor lamp, a footstool. I bought many yards of material and re-covered the couch and chair myself.

I chose a quiet flower print, all muted blue and rose, and the rose blends more or less with the wallpaper. But actually covering the furniture with it was another struggle, with tacks and corners, and even now, sometimes something will come loose and I have to repair the damages I did. It is, however, comfortable.

The tables I sanded down, because they are made of fine wood that had been painted over. Again I spent days on it, but for that I was able to work outside, in the sunshine. Now and again I rub oil into them and they have a deep, quiet glow. They are the one part of the living room that has elegance.

Later I made curtains, a dull blue shade to match the couch, but only after I had experimented with making some for the bedroom.

The vital feature of the living room is the fireplace, which is enormous and I suppose must once have been used for cooking. Now and then I use it that way, too, in the long winter evenings when there is nothing but time, and in front of it, a few feet from the flames, is a good place to set bread to rise. I have never yet run out of wood, nor had to buy any. Every day except in winter I chop wood, sometimes taking down dead and dying trees, sometimes stripping the limbs and bundling twigs for kindling, other times cutting the trunks into smaller pieces, so that there is always ample by the time the fireplace is needed. It is built into a wall, and the furniture is arranged around it so that it is the focus of the room.

It isn't for warmth that I take so much concern for it. The cabin is kept comfortable by electric heaters in each room, and often in the winter I find myself turning off one or two of them because it is too warm. I think just that it is a great pleasure to sit in front of a fire, and even the labour is, now, part of the pleasure.

The bedroom, which is next to the living room, is also full of second-hand furniture, wooden, and it, too, would probably look elegant and fine if I sanded it down and refinished it. But I have never gotten around to that, and I don't expect I will, now.

It has been painted white, not by me. There is a huge old dresser with a place, a kind of broken-off stand, for a missing oval mirror at the back. The mirror was not with it when I bought it.

The bed is a double one, with a plain headboard, and I have set it up by the window so that in the mornings and at night I can lie in it and look out to see the dawn and the wakening birds, or the stars. I painted the walls blue, but not an ordinary blue, a kind of sea blue-green, and the curtains are also a blue shade with a pattern of deep green flowers.

They are lopsided. I cut the material carelessly, hemmed it badly, and this is the result. But still there is a feeling of resting peacefully on the sea, looking into this fragile colour of my bedroom.

The bathroom is only a bathroom. I have done nothing with it, apart from putting up a new towel rack and shower curtains that are an unattractive pink but were the cheapest I could find. The tub, toilet and sink are all white, shining more or less, and the room has faded bluish linoleum on the floor and tired, dirty-pink walls. I pay no attention to it.

But the other small room, which is only slightly larger than the bathroom, received the most thought if not the most time, and is certainly the most intimate. It was once a second bedroom. Now it contains a desk, a swivel rocker and some of my own sketches on the wall, which are not good, but mine. The desk is very old, pine, and it is the only thing on which I spent much money. It has huge drawers, and in two of them I keep a careful record of my getting-and-spending, as my grandmother used to call it. In the others are my journals, the books I have kept of my travels through this place. I write here, fill in sketches. It is where I come least frequently, but with the most thoughtfulness.

After Katie leaves, after the wood is cut and the cake baked, I sit in this room. Bewildered by her and by my own reactions, I come here to write about it, to try to clear it up in that methodical way. But I can't. It is a jumble in my mind. I wonder

21

for the first time since coming here how I look, how I appeared to her, and it bothers me that I seem to care.

I know for certain that my hands have aged. I see them every day, and I see their thinness, their callouses. The veins stand out in them, and the skin is remarkably transparent; it is a shock to first realize how thin the covering of skin actually is. I have moved that tiny protective layer back and forth and seen through it clearly to the veins and arteries that do not move beneath, and realized how little there is to protect them, how very frail and vulnerable I am, just being human.

I know that my body is trim; when I look down at my belly and legs I can see that they are tight and muscular, without extra flesh, even in the winter when I had thought I might be plump. That is the time when my body pales, but in the summer it becomes a deep brown and tough, not as fragile-looking as the winter translucence of it.

I do not know about my face. I began to cut my own hair soon after I came here; the first time chopping it off short, almost in anger against the long darkness of it that I kept in coils, or braided, around my head, or pulled back and falling loosely down. I remember now that people used to tell me it looked gracefully old-fashioned, but I cut it all away. Now when I run the scissors through it, I see much gray in what I cut, and I assume that that is now the predominant colour, although I am not so old. Only forty-three or four, I think, if it has really been nine years.

I know I have a habit of running my fingers through my hair, which likely makes me look still more odd. I wonder now what Katie saw, and am not surprised that she may have been frightened.

The hair, I can feel, is uneven. It is still cropped short. I do not have a mirror.

Two things I have been without here: mirrors and clocks. At first it was so hard. It was an instinct to want to know how I looked; or perhaps I wanted to be able to catch glimpses of myself, just in passing, to reassure myself that I existed. That is what mirrors do; and also, I have decided, what clocks do.

Now I prove my existence by what I do. A growing pile of wood that is larger than yesterday's tells me that this is what I

22

have accomplished, that progress has been made, which is what time is.

I remember now that in the old life, I watched clocks. They told me everything: when to do each thing, waking, cooking, laundering, watching television, reading the newspaper, even having a cigarette. And sleeping. Time was how I counted off my life.

Now I see that it was time I was accomplishing. I was not timing my tasks, but making the tasks into time; and all that is gone. A job now takes simply what it takes, a season is something in which a certain amount is done, but not according to any schedule of mine. I do what I can and for the rest I have no further responsibility. I have been absolved.

I learned the hard way. When in the first enthusiasm and energy I tried to push, to do more than was necessary or possible, nature took no notice. After I finished with the inside of the cabin and went out to work the garden, I learned that I could not make it hurry. Elementary, obvious — but for me it was a revelation, and so I learned to let each thing have the time it needs.

Slowly, in those first weeks and months, and painfully because so many things went against the nature I brought with me, I learned.

4

The memories collapse on me, striking me, and I have no protection against them. I think, "I do not want to cross over into this, it cannot be of any use," and then I am into it anyway, quite helpless. "Look," the memories say, "this is what it was, this is what you left, look at it, see the way it was." Why is it happening now, when so many years ago, when everything changed, there was very little reflection, or thought, or confrontation, or regret?

It is strange, although I do not see this right away, that what I recall are only the rhythms of the life, and later the lack of rhythms. There is a coldness, a distance about them, an unreality and a lack of substance, as if they come from someone else's life. Perhaps that is a fault of the memory; or maybe it is that I was then unreal and without substance, and so am helpless to remember any other way. I cannot tell. I know, however, that the memories are painful now. I am unconnected with them, and yet they hurt me.

But this is what I remember; this is how it was.

Elliott was eleven; Katie nine. My husband's name was Stephen. My name was Abra.

Those were the labels we used for each other.

And of course there was the dog, Fletcher. We got him from the Humane Society for Elliott's seventh birthday and let him name it. He chose Fletcher, after his first grade teacher, Alice Fletcher, because he hadn't liked her, and he knew that although he loved the puppy there was an insult in naming it after a person. He said he was going to tell Alice Fletcher what he'd done, but he was neither so brave nor so cruel. Stephen and I worried for a while, though, about such a curious, inheld hatred in the child.

(I considered, when I was leaving, bringing Fletcher with me. He grew to be a big dog, part German shepherd, and I thought he would be not only company but also protection if it turned out that the new life was frightening. In the end, of course, I couldn't, not just because he was Elliott's dog, but because I knew that if the thing was to be done at all, it must be done alone. I was fond of him, though; I should ask Katie about him. I expect he's dead by now.)

We had a big house. Stephen was (is) a stockbroker, very successful, unusually successful, I was told, and we were, I suppose, what was called upper middle class. Still we had fairly simple tastes, accustomed to comfort but unused to luxury, and the house was the biggest thing we ever bought, quite extraordinary when I think about it.

It was close to the centre of the city, on a little-travelled street, with a luxurious acre of land all on its own. It had trees and hedges and gardens, and the people who lived there before us had had a gardener come in to look after it all. I believe they also had a cook. We did not live like that, although I had a woman in once a week to clean the house. I mowed the lawns, the gardens went wild, and now and then Stephen would clip the hedges. It seems now that there must have been something very out of kilter with me then, for I rarely bothered with the gardens, did not enjoy them; and yet now the garden is the centre of my life.

But then so many things were different.

The furniture we bought was sturdy and simple and not especially elegant. We said it was practical, while the children were young and tearing around, pursued by a large and never very clean dog, and that things would change when they were grown. I don't mean to imply that we were shabby; we were not that, by any means. We were a family. We were simply — lived in.

Stephen seemed to me a kind man and gentle. I learned from his friends that at work he was crisp and efficient and intolerant of mistakes, but at home he was loving, and extraordinarily good with the children, for I knew other men who were too tired for theirs. But Stephen tried always to have time for them, and on the weekends, when he could see that I needed a break, he would take them out, to the park, to the zoo, for a swim or just a walk. He enjoyed them, and they were comfortable with him.

Perhaps now he is like me, almost gray. But then he had dark hair with tinges of deep red, and he was tall and straight. He wore suits and patterned shirts and ties to work, and slacks and pullover sweaters at home. I remember he wore some distinctive kind of after-shave, but I can't recall now what it was called. I know that whenever I went somewhere in those days and smelled that after-shave, I thought of him.

I think I loved him, although I do not know, now, what that means. Other people, whose marriages were disintegrating around us, envied us because we seemed to enjoy each other's company. I remember believing then that I loved him, so I must have.

Elliott looked like me, Katie like Stephen. Elliott was short for his age, dark-haired, without the reddish tints of his father that Katie inherited. His features were small, and he had blue eyes, and when he smiled his face crumpled upwards and his eyes were blue half-moons. The smile was special for being somewhat rare, for he seemed a shy child; after he got to know people, they liked him well enough, but it took him a little longer than others. I thought he was happy. I remember loving him, too.

Katie. Beautiful Kate with the big brown eyes and the long thin body, who danced almost before she walked, for whom music was an invitation. We gave her lessons, both in music and in dance, for a while, but it took the edge off her enjoyment when she learned that there were rules. It was hard to decide to let her quit the lessons, because we thought, the way one does, that maybe if she kept on she could do them professionally one day, but we saw her enjoyment fading, her movements becoming more stylized and conscious, and knew we were ruining it for her. After the lessons stopped, she went back to simply loving to move and sing.

I told them stories and we went for walks, and I always tried,

26

sometimes failed, to have enough time for them.

In our huge house they each had their own bedroom, plus a guest room that they used for playing unless we had company, and Stephen and I had a large bedroom; and the other rooms, the dining and living rooms and the kitchen, were all big and bright, with huge windows, and as well Stephen had a smaller room, a den, where he did extra office work.

It was, I thought, the best life I could have hoped for, better than most people dare to hope for. Healthy, happy children, a loving husband. Even Fletcher. A portrait of happiness — it could sit on a mantel. And I swear I loved them all, and I did the best I could.

And then I left them, left all of it.

Nothing in particular, but something began to happen, and it ended in the spring I came here. The ending was clear and distinct and cold and final; I search, but I cannot find the beginning. I have snapshots in my mind, but there are no answers; only labels on the back.

Mornings: the children and Stephen gone to school and work; me drinking coffee, smoking cigarettes, still in my housecoat, feeling — a restlessness, an uneasiness, a spell of ennui, nothing more.

Afternoons: worst in the winter, for the city was slippery, greasy, and cars coming down the slope and around the corner just above our house often slewed dangerously. I spent hours terrified for the children, picturing some fool careering down that hill, missing the curve, gliding gently, always in slow motion in my mind, sliding irrevocably into them. I watched for them from the living room window in the afternoons, grateful almost to tears when I saw one, then the other, struggling up the street; holding my breath until they got to our walk, running to open the door for them, helping them get their winter clothes off, hugging them. Sometimes if friends were with them or they were in a hurry they would be impatient with me, and I tried to let them be, I truly did. But they seemed so precious, so delicate, so very fragile that it was all I could do to keep myself from holding them, guarding them — against what? Sometimes I did hold them tight, squeezing them, as if something were trying to tear them away; and other times I was

27

almost afraid to touch them, for fear they might break.

Evenings: warm inside and safe. The children home, and Stephen too, unless he had a meeting. If he did, I would sit in the living room after the children were asleep, reading, enjoying the solitude that was a treat, a luxury. If he were home, which was most often, we would sit together, both of us reading, and have a drink and listen to soft music on the stereo, and now and then we might speak, the quiet easy conversations of people who are accustomed to each other. Sometimes if we felt especially lazy we would wheel in the portable television set from Stephen's den and watch terrible programs. If there were a really dreadful horror show on the late movie, like a Japanese monster picture, we would giggle and make popcorn and stay up very late with it. Occasionally, but only very occasionally because one of the children might get up, we would make love on the couch, and the Japanese monsters would howl and lunge and the people would scream and run in terror and we would laugh and hold each other. Stephen had a fine body, very lean, and he liked to laugh in bed; I am sure he was not lonely in that way after I left. There are many women who like to laugh in bed, and many who must still find him kind and handsome.

Friends: there were some, I suppose. I got to know vaguely the women in neighbouring houses, well enough to ask small favours and return them, not well enough to care or be cared for. And in a similar way I knew the mothers of Elliott's and Katie's friends, well enough to talk about the children, not well enough to talk about ourselves apart from them. Occasionally, too, we would hold dinner parties for people Stephen worked with; we took these things for granted, as part of his job, and mine as his wife. We invited Stephen's bosses and their wives, a couple of tactical underlings and their wives, and the business of seating them all properly, steering the conversations to different interests and abilities, making sure that awkwardnesses were turned aside, fell largely onto me. I think I did it well.

Those dinners were the only demands Stephen's career put on me, and I was grateful for that. I never drank too much or talked too much, or said things that were impolitic or unkind or cut too close. And in a curious way, although they were unnatural and required me to look and be a different person, as they required everyone there to look and be unnatural, I must confess that I enjoyed the dinners, even looked forward to them. They gave me a role I could play with, took me out of myself, as they said in those days, and as long as I didn't bungle it, I could consider it a game.

(Those snapshots flash before me, and I try to see what kind of person all that made me, as I came close to the last years of that life. Loving, worried, caring, and given to play-acting? Happy with a family that was secure because each member knew I would always be there, always have time, for each of them? A woman with a fine home and a fine husband and fine children, of whom nothing better could be expected, and it was I, Abra, mother, wife, who kept them all together, all secure, all loved?

(I feel nothing of that person now. But from the pictures, I can say that I was not unhappy then. I was relatively comfortable and, I thought, a success at what I had set out to do, which was to raise my family and attempt to have a happy marriage. But all that was in one compartment, an objective one, and in another, where I could not reach it, a vague uneasiness was growing. How could I have guessed then what it meant? How could I have changed what happened?

(I am guilty. I know those people found me guilty, pitied Stephen; and certainly those people I loved, that family, were hurt and found me guilty. And I have no explanations to give them. I accept the guilt, I understand that I have given them grounds for judgement. But it seemed to me then, and it seems to me now, that it could have been no other way.)

5

Katie can't understand any of it.

She returns, as she has promised, the morning after her first visit. She looks haggard, sleepless, but determined — apparently she has come to some kind of resolution. I am still drinking tea in the kitchen when she arrives, although it is late morning. I, too, have slept little; the night has been full of memories, and yet so few, only a beginning.

In the midst of the past, I have forgotten she will be back, and the knock startles me. I look around, recognizing where I am and what it means, and I rebel, for a moment, against having it disturbed. But then she knocks again, and of course I must answer.

She is wearing a long light blue skirt and a halter top, carrying a white shawl against a change in the weather. I run my fingers through my hair, the old habit, then remember how she must see the gray and grizzled effect, and try to pat it down again. "May I come in?" she asks.

I stand back to let her by. She looks lovely; I feel awed by her youth, and struck by the knowledge that I had something to do with creating her. There is again the feeling of a bond.

"Tea?" I ask. She is standing by the kitchen table, tentative about whether she is welcome at it. I gesture to the second chair and she sits, folding her hands in front of her on the table. She has very long fingers.

"Please," she says. I pour two cups, and we sit in silence for a few moments before she breaks it finally. "Do you mind that I've come back?"

I wonder now, after the first doubt, do I mind? It comes to me that I am glad to see her, am curious about things that returned to me during the night of remembering. I suppose the curiosity is the first sign that I can be drawn toward a life that is gone. That is the way she sees it, and I should cover it from her, should keep her from knowing that I am interested. But I am unused to dissembling; there is no need for it here, and I have forgotten the ways.

"No," I say slowly, "I don't mind." There is something I want, some defence. I remember. "Do you have any cigarettes? I gave them up, but just now I think I'd like one." She reaches out a package and I take one. She lights it for me, and I see that her hands are smooth, but the nails are bitten to the tips of the long fingers. "Thank you. It's been a long time." I sit back, holding the tea and the cigarette, which makes me dizzy; she notices there isn't an ashtray and gets up to find a saucer.

"I think I'm pleased you came back," I am saying as she sits again. "I was wondering, what's happened to Fletcher?"

"Fletcher?" she says, her voice high and astonished and wounded. "You want to know about the dog?" She catches herself, remembers what must have been her resolve, and quietens.

"Fletcher's very old now, and he's a little crippled, but we still have him. Sometimes we talk about having him put away, but none of us can bear to do it. I don't think he suffers particularly, he's just stiff and can't get around much."

"Oh." I think of all the other things that might be asked, and hesitate. I want to know something about Katie first, how she is now and what her life is like; I want to know how far she may understand. What kind of person is she?

"I made a cake last night," I say. "Would you like some? I think it should be good."

"Yes, thank you, that would be nice." She is nodding politely.

I cut her a slice, but don't have one myself. I have never cared much myself for sweet things. She takes a bite, nods again. "It's very good," she says. "I like plain white cake."

31

I lean forward, watching her face intently. "Tell me what other things you like. Tell me what you do now."

She settles into the chair, more relaxed; she must feel the advances she has made, must know that questions mean I am breaking down in her favour.

"Well, I'll be going to university this fall. I'm planning on majoring in archeology, and maybe next summer I'll be going on a dig in South America, but I don't know yet. I've applied, but it depends how well I do in the course."

"Why archeology?" I wonder at the kind of interest in the past that consumes such people, the painstaking care with which they resurrect some dead artifact and try to breathe life into it again. I try to lighten the awkwardness between us, but it's been a long time since I've made a joke, and I feel her pull away from me as soon as I say it:

"You enjoy digging up old relics? Like me?"

She looks hurt, then recovers and answers. There is a trace of metal in her voice. She is lecturing.

"Old relics are clues to how the present has evolved. They tell us things about why we are the way we are. That's why I'm interested in archeology. There can't be a present without a past that formed it, not for civilizations and not for people. Old relics have a place."

She leaves it there and I am grateful and rebuked. Of course I know why it has been important to her to find me: she has discovered mysteries in herself, and thinks I am the root of them. I can understand the reasoning; I also understand its futility. I want to tell her that, but who am I, after a night of past-flashes, even unconnected and unanalyzed, to say?

I sit and watch her, trying to see what the connection is that I feel, but there is nothing to see. She is a young woman sipping tea and eating cake, a very beautiful, graceful young woman, but a stranger to me.

The silence has become intolerable. She is waiting for something and I have nothing to give, yet.

"I wish you wouldn't," I say in desperation, knowing it is useless but feeling something must be said. Yesterday silence was my friend, and today I cannot bear it — what is happening to me?

"Wouldn't what?" she asks curiously, looking at me, eyebrows lifted.

"I wish you wouldn't depend on me for what you want. I can't tell you, I don't have any answers. I wish you could see that I didn't come here because of you, or your brother or your father either. I'm just here, and I don't have any answers for you. I can't help you. I truly can't." I would like to weep, as she did yesterday.

She looks at me solemnly for a moment, then apparently comes to a decision, sighs and shrugs. "If that's what you want, then. We don't have to talk about anything you don't want to talk about. I just wanted to meet you, and I've done that. I won't keep you from whatever you do. Is it all right if I stay, though? Do you mind if I just hang around for a while? I don't want to make you tired of me, but I'd like to be with you for a while. We could maybe just get to know each other."

I am touched that she is so willing to let what she wants go. She is giving me time, and it is at some sacrifice to her and what she has come for.

"You're welcome to visit, of course, but I'll have to leave you to entertain yourself, because I have things that have to be done." The words are working better now, both in my mind and in my mouth; it has been such a long time, but they, too, like the memories, seem to have lain close to the surface all these years, and have come back surprisingly easily.

I rinse out my teacup and head for the door. "There are about seventy acres on the property, if you feel like going for a walk. Apart from that, there's not much for you to do."

"That's all right. I'll have a chance to relax." She smiles at me, and I find myself smiling back. The muscles feel stretched, unaccustomed, and yet it is natural to return her smile. There has never been anyone here before to smile at, or anything, really. It is pleasant, as a change.

On the porch I pick up a basket and the hoe. The early lettuce needs thinning and I will pick enough for a salad for two for lunch. The rest of the garden is still in the earliest, greenest, swiftest time of growth. Almost I can see it changing from day to day, and unless the weather turns it will be one of the best so far.

Quite apart from my need for their produce, I have a tender relationship with the plants. I like to touch them, knowing I helped bring them into being. Today, however, I am distracted, my mind wanders, and now and then I am startled, realizing that I have been touching, picking, weeding by rote, unconsciously. That frightens me, for it has been one of my main pleasures here, the relationship with the garden and the care I give it. To lose that, to do it like a machine, would be to lose everything.

And yet it is an effort to concentrate. I keep recalling the girl in the cabin, my daughter, what she wants from me, what she has brought with her. My hands do the duties of the present, and my mind scatters over the past, wondering about the questions this girl is raising. The memories are clearer now, the portrait of that Abra has some movement and order. But still so little detail.

The order, attempting logic, makes a stab at childhood, but is balked. There are only the faintest of impressions there, forms and images of protected times. With an effort, I suppose I might harden those forms into memories, but there is no need. The impressions are of sunshine and green, smiling and safety, questions and fear, acceptance; a sense of being removed, an observer — but observing what? Of feeling hidden, a secret, unique and alone.

I know that I was not unintelligent, but I did not control. I was not insensitive, but I could not see. I was, perhaps, simply too young, and so I committed a capitulation, an aberration. I lacked courage, but in general I have always lacked courage. It was not courage that brought me here. Now I am old, and I see.

The wedding. Everything about it hazy, dreamlike, faces floating, smiling, words coming from a long distance, from me, to me, dancing, smiling. I think I was happy that day; but everything was murky, unreal, and I don't really recall.

The night before, my mother and I cried. Suddenly I didn't want to be married, I wasn't ready, I wanted to stay home and be safe and alone; I was filled with panic. I can feel the beginning of tears, a tightening in my stomach, remembering.

I was nineteen. A year older than Katie is now, think of that, and is she ready and does she need me to weep with her?

Stephen was already at university; we'd been together for almost three years, and we didn't want to wait any longer. We were too much apart, with him away at school, and so we were getting married. He asked me in April, a chilly evening; we were in my parents' living room and they were downstairs playing cards and we had nowhere that we could go, felt trapped, and Stephen said, "It's stupid to go on like this, let's just get married and the hell with it."

I said yes and was frightened. My parents asked us to wait, we said we were tired of waiting, and they didn't seem to really object. I think, actually, that they were pleased. Stephen's parents, too, when we told them.

We couldn't afford a ring, so Stephen's grandmother gave us hers. We would rent an apartment in Toronto, be married in July, I would find a job, and by the time Stephen's classes started in September we would be well settled. It was all so clear.

It was what I had always expected for myself, what I had, I suppose, been taught to expect, although I cannot tell just when or how. I know I never doubted how it would be, although I am unsure how I saw the self I knew fitted to the life I saw. The vision I had, unquestioned, what was it?

No, not a vision but an assumption. A vague, undetailed picture of me, children, husband and house, comfort, security. But none of it, I see now, had any shape or form. I didn't think about what it would mean, what it would be like. I was a character in a movie of my future, and it was a very pleasant movie and it was unconnected with myself. I had never thought. I find that extraordinary now, but not surprising.

I got lost in the fantasy. I made up guest lists and revised them and thought about what colours would be nice in a bathroom. Until the night before, I had only dreams of being married, but I was still a child, dreaming.

We were to have eighty people, and my dress was white. The wedding would be held in our Anglican church, to which none of us had gone for years, and the reception would be afterwards at a restaurant with a banquet room. Probably we were all living in this dream.

A month before the wedding we drove to Toronto, Stephen and my parents and I, and found a one-bedroom apartment over a store. It wasn't far by bus to the university, and the rent was eighty dollars a month, which seemed like a fortune to us then and was. I might earn, we thought, about seventy-five dollars a week. Stephen's parents said they would pay his tuition fees so long as he kept his marks up, and he would get jobs in the summers. He had three years left at university. My mother said only, "Be sure not to have children, it would be impossible then."

Our parents got together and bought us a bedroom suite for a wedding gift. For the rest we went to second-hand stores and bought a table and chairs, two lamps and a couch, and that was the total of the furniture we ever had in that little apartment. The colour of the bathroom was not what I'd had in mind.

The wedding invitations were sent, and three people had showers for me. It was exciting and romantic, and above all that I had dependable, solid Stephen and his love. I was the first and the others were filled with envy. We fussed over each other, my friends and I, and we cried together because we knew it would not be the same again, and it was very sad, but a proud time, too. I was putting away childish things.

Until the night before the wedding, when I saw for just a moment. We would be in our apartment on our wedding night because we could not afford a real honeymoon. Tomorrow, twenty-four hours, so close, I would be in that apartment with this young man, and how well did I really know him anyway? with the shabby furniture and the need to find a job and keep a home together while he went to school, and that would be my life for the next three years. I was horrified by what I had agreed to. I was bewildered that I had not seen it before.

And yet the next day, when I woke up, the wedding day, I thought, "how foolish of me, I love this man and we will be happy," and all the weeping of the night before had been silly, only nerves. And it had blotched my face, made it puffy, and I was angry with myself for being ugly. By afternoon, though, the puffiness was gone and the dress was perfect; my father came to my bedroom, put his hands around my waist and kissed my forehead, wished me happiness, and he had tears in his eyes; but I was back in the dream and could not cry with him. We drove to the church and I got out of the car carefully, hating to have any marks on my perfect dress, and inside the music started and I took my father's arm and we were walking down the aisle, Stephen's white face far away, other faces turned toward me, smiling, nodding, familiar faces now unrecognized, and then the sonorous voice of the Anglican priest and Stephen's voice, faint, trembling, and then my own, and signing my name on the register and having pictures taken and the music again, following us out of the church, and being hugged and kissed by the familiar faces that were still unrecognized. There was no happiness or sadness in me; I was inside the wedding and watching it at the same time. I was — I was not myself.

And then later at the reception, dancing, still vague, hearing myself laughing and talking, no idea of what I was saying, no memory of it, did people know I was not there?

I slept most of the way to Toronto in the car beside Stephen. I knew that it wasn't the way a new wife should behave on her wedding night, but I was exhausted, a vast sense of something finished was on me, the event was over and reality was ahead and inconceivable. I wasn't sad, it wasn't the terror of the night before; it was simply done. There were no more tears.

Stephen woke me up as we parked behind the store. We unloaded our bags from the trunk, Stephen tired now too, and walked up the stairs to our apartment for the first time together. We turned on the lights and it looked cosy, and suddenly we were at ease with each other, and simply went to bed, without unpacking or showering, just falling into bed, holding each other, filled with pleasure that it had all happened.

There were four weeks before Stephen's classes started. We went to Hanlan's Point for a picnic, bicycled through High Park, held hands at the museum and made love. But I was also applying for jobs, and in two weeks I had one and was going out to work. We hadn't thought it would happen so quickly.

The dress store was small, just the owner and one salesgirl. Stephen and I were walking along Bathurst Street when I saw a dress I liked in the window, and although I knew we couldn't afford it, I wanted at least to wear it for a moment. We stepped in. I tried on the dress, loved it, and while I was changing back into my own clothes, Stephen bought it for me as a surprise. When I came out, Mrs. Kopalski, who owned the store, was wrapping it up and Stephen was looking pleased, and we ended up telling her we were just married and I was looking for a job, but so far we were still on our honeymoon and I hadn't found anything yet. She asked me a few questions, then said her salesgirl was leaving Friday and if I wanted I could start Monday. I was to go in Friday and watch and learn to use the cash register.

I rebelled, for a moment, at having duty thrust on me so abruptly, but there was no question of refusing. Three days later I was watching Mrs. Kopalski and her salesgirl, listening to them tell customers "It's you," and swearing I would never say it. And on the Monday I was there and saying it and ringing up sales, and Mrs. Kopalski told me I was going to be fine, dear.

And it seemed fine. Stephen and I could relax about money, and all we missed were two weeks of our honeymoon. When I went to work in the morning, Stephen was still in bed, and during the day he said he read and went for walks. He did the grocery shopping and when I got home from work at night he had dinner ready. It might have been a loving time if I had not been so tired; but every day I met new people, was kind and courteous and efficient, and every night I was exhausted. I changed, he said. I was distracted and he didn't like it; my thoughts were always on the next day, going back to that store to be kind and courteous and efficient, and he lost part of me to that and resented it. In my turn I was angry with his resentment, his pressure on me to be something I couldn't, at that moment, be; and underneath it all, although I never said it, were the words, "but I'm doing this for you, if I didn't have to support you I wouldn't be like this, what right have you to complain?" When I came home at night, tired, he would want to go to a movie, or for a walk, or to visit friends, and I would refuse because I was tired and wanted to brood about the next day. We fell apart those two weeks, and we must both have wondered, I know I did, if we should have put ourselves in this position.

But things evened out when Stephen went back to school. We shopped and did laundry together, but I took over the cooking, and I think it wasn't an unfair arrangement, really. We developed routines, duties, Stephen's energy for things outside school dropped and we were contented. We would both read in the evenings, he his school books, me my novels, and we could feel close and comfortable without having to talk. My job still drained me, and Stephen's courses worried him, but we had each other to turn to, and we became each other's refuge against the outside. We were careful to follow my mother's advice against having children.

I remember wondering sometimes if I ever did want to have children, although I knew of course I would, for the assumption of my life was always there, more rooted than any doubts. And yet it seemed then that things were comfortable as they were, and I was afraid of change. Children would be abrupt, would take so much concentration, so much love, and I felt weak and frightened. But I never mentioned it to Stephen, for I had to doubt the doubts. The whole vision of my life said they must be wrong. If I spoke of doubts, would it not seem odd and terrible?

And besides, I did not want to go on working, and what else was there? Stephen would sometimes say, "Won't it be great when I get going and you can quit work and we'll have babies — three is a good number, don't you think? — and buy a house and live happily ever after?" He was making fun of it in a way, but underneath he was serious.

We were never really short of money. At Christmas and birthdays our parents would give us small gifts of cash, and Stephen did well and so his parents continued to pay his tuition. We couldn't do anything extravagant, but we had enough to buy food, pay the rent and occasionally go to a movie. Now and then we would buy a case of beer and have some of Stephen's friends for an evening, and that was enough.

They were always Stephen's friends because I still knew no one. In my days I met customers, not people. In a way his friends became mine, and I listened to them talk about university, about courses, about people there. They were kind, but they did not ask about the dress shop. Sometimes, if I had a funny customer or something unusual happened, I would think, "next time they come over I'll tell them about this, they'll enjoy it," but I never did. The dress shop and what I did there seemed too far away from them to be properly shared. Still, what they talked about was interesting, and a change.

When I turned twenty-one, we became rich, thanks to my grandmother who died when I was thirteen. She was my father's mother, and an odd, secluded old woman, the family thought. She had money but disliked spending it; a widow, she lived in the home she and her husband had built, and when she died she left the house to my father, her only child, and her money to me, his only child. It was in trust for me until I came of age, but Stephen and I talked about it then and decided it wasn't mine, not really. It amounted, with accumulated interest, to fifty thousand dollars. It was a fortune.

Stephen suggested we invest it for the three children we would have, and when they were old enough to choose their futures, it would be a gift to help them. Divided among them, he said, it could be more than twenty thousand each.

It seemed to me an enormous gift, more than I had ever thought of, and then of course I realized it was much less than I had gotten, that I now possessed fifty thousand dollars, and somehow, illogically, it became right in my mind that I should pass it on. Although I found it difficult, more difficult than Stephen, apparently, to picture these phantom children who would be going off to university and getting married, who would finally receive this phantom inheritance.

The real reason Stephen argued against using the money, I knew, was that it was not his, was not something he had earned. It was a matter of pride. We did not discuss that.

Still, against his pride, I kept the money, in a separate bank account. I refused to let him invest it, even though as a stockbroker and a sensible man, he would have done it wisely. It was a cushion in my mind; not knowing why, I knew it was important, and I held out stubbornly until Stephen, annoyed and uncomprehending, conceded. Neither of us understood.

And although we were left a little puzzled about each other and ourselves and what had happened, nothing changed. The memory faded and we went on.

The following year, when we knew Stephen was going to graduate with first class honours, we invited our parents down for a weekend on us at a hotel, and organized a party for them and a few of Stephen's friends the night of graduation. I bought a new dress at a discount from Mrs. Kopalski, and we got in wine and cheese and worried a little about mixing friends and parents.

The night before graduation, our parents all arrived together and we went to their hotel for dinner and drinks and talked, mostly about how proud we all were of Stephen and how well he had done. The next day was a flurry of things to be done, and the graduation ceremony, and afterwards pictures and people kissing and smiling, and then back to the apartment where some people danced to the radio, although it was terribly crowded. Our parents sat on the couch and watched and smiled and said how nice it was to see the young people enjoying themselves, and how wonderful it was that everything had worked out so well.

They said, "These are the best years of your lives," and their eyes shone with their own nostalgia, and something in me tightened and silently said, "no, that can't be right;" and then I shook myself and realized that it might be, for I couldn't think of anything that was wrong. Except that I was lost.

Stephen would get a job easily, that was no problem in those days of hungry employers, and a decision would be upon me. What would I be? I was sure of nothing except that I could not spend my life in Mrs. Kopalski's dress shop, although she had been kind and would be disappointed when I quit.

What would I do? I did not feel it could be my choice; I did not know how to make a choice. That was how I was lost.

Stephen was working almost immediately. He started at a hundred and seventy dollars a week, and was promised much more as he progressed. We discussed our finances, decided that I would continue to work for just a while, until we had a down payment for a house. I was absolved, relieved.

Stephen ate up his work, loved it, brought numbers home with him and read the *Globe and Mail* every morning, analyzed, was excited by numbers that got bigger and dismayed by numbers that dwindled. He was well liked. The friends who visited us now were from his office instead of his classes, and everyone said he was doing beautifully and would go far. He glowed.

(I am weeding the tomatoes; they are still tiny and green and hard; it will be a good crop, and when I finish, I stand, bend backwards with my hand in the small of my back, and let the sun absorb into the skin of my face. My skin probably looks like leather now, wrinkled and brown and tough. An invitation to cancer. But the sun, it is so warm and I am alive.)

We found our house: a smallish three-bedroom place that cost, then, twenty-four thousand dollars. With care we had managed to save almost six thousand, which we used as a down payment. Stephen got a raise. We spent several hours working out a budget, and at the end Stephen said, "Well, you can finally quit. We're going to be in the clear."

And there is was. He bought a bottle of champagne the day I resigned from Mrs. Kopalski's, and we toasted my freedom that night. He told me I was beautiful, that everything that had happened in the past four years had been because of me, and that he was very grateful. I was twenty-three years old.

We bought new furniture for the house, to mark the end of poverty, and for a while I felt a little free. I slept in while Stephen went to work, rearranged furniture and shopped and cooked, was able to sit and have a coffee, read a book when I felt like it.

I began, also, to understand how Stephen had felt when I first started working. I tried to hold my tongue, but I was restless, bored, tired of my own company, and he was tired from working, although he loved it. I saw the parallel, but I couldn't help the discontent.

I wanted — activity. Once the house was settled, I was filled with a smouldering energy that demanded action, something, and Stephen would say, "Look, why don't you do something during the day, go bicycling or walking," but I could not do it alone. There was nothing I could do alone. Alone frightened me. If I were alone doing these things, no one cared and I ceased to exist.

Stephen saw and tried to understand, and was kinder than I had been in his position. "Do you want to get another job?" he asked, gentle, not angry. "It would give you something to do. You're so used to working, it must be hard to adjust." But I turned listless and said no. I did not know what was missing, but I could not give in that way.

Somehow, without discussing it, we must have agreed on the

42

answer. Within a couple of months I was pregnant, the decision had been made, and everything was settled and full again.

It was like the wedding again, all preparations and anticipation. I bought maternity clothes and baby clothes and a crib and bottles and redecorated a room for a nursery. I spent two weeks visiting my parents, who were thrilled and pampered me. I saw old friends, and although some of them had children now, and I wasn't the first this time, it was exciting, almost theatrical, to be pregnant and showing it. Once again I didn't see the reality, was carried away by the dreaming, and was comforted.

(I cannot remember precisely how I felt about Stephen then; perhaps by that stage he had slid into place in my life, and I did not think about him, took his existence as given in much the same way it seems I took my own. I recall only an image that is just a form, no features, and an impression, almost constant through all the years I was with him, of patience and kindness, a gentleness that did not seem imposed or forced, of understanding.

(Of myself I remember even less. A void, a blank. An impression of a vacuum moved by outside sources. Characterless, faceless, in any essential respects. I do not feel related.

(It is lunchtime. I am in the kitchen, and Katie is helping me make a salad, and we will have cake with it and, I think, soup, and it should be enough. I am dazed, thrown by being in two places at once, back in that first early house, waiting for my first baby, and here, gray and in a different world, making lunch with my second baby who is a woman. Katie is chattering, filling the spaces I am leaving, talking about boyfriends and school, no mention of the family, waiting for me to ask, leaving a blank that will draw me into it. She is right.)

Stephen and I both panicked when I went into labour. Again, we were unprepared for the reality.

The pains in the beginning were slow and far apart, and we laughed and hugged each other because it was finally happening and it didn't hurt so much. But after a while the pains were sharper and faster and nothing was funny. We wanted to call the doctor, and didn't like to bother him because it was very late. I was sweating, terribly chilled and then terribly hot, and the sheets were wet and Stephen's face was dead white, and he was crying and I think I must have been too. Finally, when the pains were so close we knew it couldn't be silly, Stephen telephoned the doctor and we tore off to the hospital. We thought it would be soon then, and the need to hurry became part of the panic, for what if we didn't get there in time?

It was another seven hours before the baby was born. I sent Stephen away after a while, because he only made the pain worse by being there, worried and frightened and weepy. I was separated from everything except the pain, lived in it, felt nothing else, until finally they numbed me with a needle and it was over. Some time later, back in my room, almost aware and beginning to understand things other than pain again, I saw a nurse and was able to ask about the baby. "It's a boy," she told me, "and he's perfectly healthy."

Soon Stephen was there by the bed, beaming, forgetting. I remember him grinning, saying to me, "Well, it was worth it after all, wasn't it?" and I hated him because for me nothing, then, was worth what I had gone through.

I slept again, and by the time I woke up and saw my baby, the memory of the pain had faded, was unclear, and I, too, felt that it had been worth it. Whatever it had been.

He had dark hair, lots of it, and blue eyes, but I couldn't see then that he looked particularly like anyone I knew. I hadn't known before that he would be real, and I looked at him with wonder. Here was another human being who existed only because Stephen and I existed and had given him his particular uniqueness; I must be perfect, I thought, and help him and protect him, because this business of a new person in the world was very sacred. I felt a huge desire to take him away, keep him to myself, because he was mine and he would be the result of me. Stephen complained that he wasn't allowed to touch or hold the baby, wasn't allowed past the glass of the nursery, and I was pleased because the baby was still mine, should be all mine, and I resented the nurses who brought him to me and took him away because I had to share him with them. I wanted him to be just mine.

We named him Elliott; I can't remember why.

It was a strange period that began then. When we took him home and Stephen held him, I watched them together and cried out when Stephen shifted him, afraid he would drop the baby or wouldn't recognize one of his needs. I knew. I knew everything about Elliott, when he was wet or hungry or had gas or needed just to be held. I didn't think Stephen noticed enough, he didn't know the baby well enough, didn't watch carefully. Neither of us could let the baby cry, rushing to the bedroom when we heard him, each eager to pick him up, but Stephen deferred to me, convinced of the mystique of mother and child, and almost always I won and comforted Elliott; but sometimes, if I were susceptible to the pleading in Stephen's face, I would hand the baby to him, very carefully and gingerly, and watch them with worried eyes until I suppose Stephen became uncomfortable, or weary of not being trusted with his son, and handed him back to me.

Much worse, though, were visitors. I was tortured by people who wanted to hold him, jiggle him, try to make him smile or make sounds, and they didn't notice, or didn't care, that I was in agony. Our parents visited, and I was barely allowed to touch Elliott, they took over, assumed I knew nothing about him, tried to teach me, when it was I, only I, who knew exactly what to do, because I knew this baby as if he were myself, and they couldn't know. I was his mother, and I was full of rage.

They told me how to feed him and when, and suggested it wasn't a bad thing to let him cry for a while sometimes, and I hated them for wanting me to hurt this little human being, mine, when he was helpless, and I was all he had to defend him. They must have seen something of my crazy anger, because before she left my mother took me aside.

"Let him breathe, dear," she said. "They're not as fragile as you might think, or they wouldn't get this far, so do try to relax a little. I know it's hard, especially when it's the first one, but remember that nobody can be a perfect mother and nobody can have a perfect child."

She smiled at me as if we shared some knowledge. "I thought when you were born that we could both be perfect, but of course it didn't work out that way, and I thought I was a failure. But we both got over it, didn't we? I made mistakes with you, you'll make mistakes with him, you can't help it. None of us can."

She put an arm around my shoulder. "You know, I'm telling you this because you're my child, and I don't want to lose you any more than you want to lose him. I've often thought that if we just put all our energy into raising the next generation, and they do the same and so on and so on, it makes us no better than ants, really, or bees. Save something for yourself. Good-bye dear, be well."

She kissed me on the cheek and left then, and I hated her, too, for a while. No one understood. I cried. No one else must come near him, I thought, and was fierce, for they would hurt him and make him less than I knew he was. Only I understood.

For months I went nowhere, because I couldn't leave Elliott, could trust no one else to look after him. I refused to visit friends, and when people came over, which they did with less and less frequency, they fussed over Elliott and I grew gritty, and they didn't stay long. I was lost to conversation, for always most of my attention was elsewhere with the baby, tuned to any sound, any whimper, any cry, probably even any sigh. Elliott was my world and I wanted just to be left alone with him. I didn't even want to talk about him, although he so completely occupied my mind, because I felt somehow that talking about him took him a distance away, made him separate, gave a piece of him to someone else.

Stephen must have grown more and more disturbed, although I didn't notice it. I was noticing nothing but Elliott, had seen nothing else for months, and there was no space in my vision for Stephen any more.

Finally he spoke. (I wonder now at the awesome patience that made him be still for so long.)

"Listen Abra," he began awkwardly, "I think there are a couple of things we need to talk about, about the way we're living." I looked at him vaguely, not knowing what he meant. I knew how we were living and it was all right; what did he want to talk about?

"I'd like it if we could go out for dinner," he said. "We'll make a night of it, we haven't been out for months, and we'll have a chance to talk and maybe get some things straight. It'll give us a break, I'm sure you must need one. You've been cooped up for months."

46

"No," I said. I was flat, surprised, harsh. "I can't go out, you know that. There's Elliott."

"We'll get a sitter. He's almost six months old, he isn't going to break." There was anger now in Stephen's voice, and yet I felt adamant, that there was no choice.

"Who?" I asked sarcastically. "Some teenager from down the street who doesn't know how to change a diaper? Just who do we know that you'd trust with Elliott?"

I thought the point was made, but I hadn't reckoned on his determination, his sense, now that he was aroused, of how serious the problem was.

"I stopped in next door on my way home and asked Jeannie." Jeannie was blonde, too plump, had four children and I didn't like her because she let her children play in the front yard and had to yell at them to get away from the street, and I thought, "What if someday she isn't looking and one of them gets hit, just because she had her back turned and didn't yell." I thought she was irresponsible about her children.

"She'll take care of Elliott tonight. We'll just drop him over there on our way out," Stephen said, "and pick him up when we come back. It's no big deal, she's got enough kids to know what it's all about. You don't have a monopoly on motherhood, you know."

I fought, fought hard, and in the middle of it Elliott woke up and cried. I started to go to him but Stephen caught my arm, made me stay with him, and for a moment we both stood there, rigid, listening; and then he stopped crying and Stephen took his hand away, and I looked at him as if he had betrayed me, which at that moment I thought he had.

"Go and get ready," he said, and his voice was hard. I had never heard him speak that way before. I was too startled, and frightened also, not to do what he said, but I didn't do it gracefully, slammed around the bathroom and the bedroom getting ready, and I refused to go with him when he took Elliott to Jeannie. "It's your responsibility," I told him, stony and furious.

Once we were on our way, just the two of us, Stephen tried to be entertaining and amusing, but it made me more angry, that he could be light-hearted even knowing that something terrible might be happening to Elliott at that very moment. I was

47

sullen, withdrawn, slapped my menu on the table and told Stephen that since he was in charge of the evening, he could order whatever he thought I should have. But I was surprisingly hungry; I remember he ordered a steak for me, and when it came I thought I couldn't possibly eat it, but I started and then I didn't stop until it was gone.

He waited until the meal was finished before he asked. "Do you see what's been happening to you?" I took a breath, ready to defend myself, but he left no opening, attacking now.

"You're obsessive, you're completely neurotic about the baby. Now I know it may not mean much to you, not in comparison with having a son all your own, but you are in the process of losing a husband at the same time." He was bitter, so bitter; he had stored it all for months, and he sounded venomous and foreign. I couldn't answer him, just stared. I had not realized.

"You don't see it, do you," he went on, a little more gently but still accusing. "We don't have a marriage any more; *you* do, you and the baby, you're a marriage and you and I don't have anything. You hang over him as if he's going to disappear if you're not around. Well lady, I'm going to be the one that disappears, because there's no future for me in this kind of arrangement. Let the kid grow up on his own a little. It's not going to hurt him and if you don't he's going to turn out to be a freak." A freak, my Elliott, I opened my mouth to argue, to protest, but again he didn't let me.

"Obviously things are going to have to change, and obviously I'm going to have to be the one to force it. For a start, you and I are going to go out at least one night a week, just the two of us, and we'll find a regular sitter. When Elliott starts to cry we're going to leave him for a few minutes, to see if he stops the way he did tonight. I'm not suggesting we neglect him, but let's try to keep things in perspective."

I loathed him. I wouldn't talk to him. But still it was almost a false anger, because I did not think he could be serious. No, I amend that. I knew he was serious, but I did not imagine that he could maintain this firmness. We had spent years together, and I had not seen him stubborn, holding out, fighting. There had been nothing until then, I suppose, worth fighting for. I did not realize that he was strong, and I thought that soon my anger would defeat him. It was in that way a false anger, magnified and conscious of manipulation, although there was a real rage there, too.

When we got home I ran next door. I barely spoke to Jeannie, sure that at some point in the evening she must have done some damage to my child.

He was fine. He was asleep when I got him, and he barely woke. There was nothing I could point to and say, "There, see, I knew we shouldn't have left him."

We went to bed in silence, Stephen stern and unyielding, me rigid and angry. In the morning it was the same, and after Stephen went to work I held Elliott and rocked him and promised I'd make sure nothing ever hurt him. I must have been holding him too tightly, for he began to cry and I had to walk the floor with him until he stopped.

I thought I might wear Stephen down with the anger, but to my surprise he held out, and the next week we went to a movie, leaving Elliott with Jeannie. I wanted at least to call, to see if anything were wrong with the baby, but Stephen wouldn't let me — I was astounded by the power his will had over me — and when we got home everything again was fine. The following week we went through another cold, unhappy meal, but then Stephen said there was a business dinner coming up, and I would have to be there with him. The next week, he said, we would go out one night by ourselves, and another night to the dinner. We would, he said, have to find a proper baby sitter from now on, because it wasn't fair to keep asking Jeannie when she had her own family to look after.

I attempted limp disobedience. I did not try to find a sitter, refused to consider it, but Stephen sabotaged me again. The seventeen-year-old daughter of one of the men he worked with would sit for us, he said firmly. There was no problem, she was experienced, knew about babies and would be fine. She was available until eleven o'clock on weeknights and indefinitely on weekends. She would be perfect, he said. There was something chilling and impersonal in his voice, as if he were announcing a new policy to an employee, that frightened me. It did not sound to me like Stephen, and I wondered at the difference.

I had to admit Karen was a nice girl, if terribly young, and she listened patiently while I told her everything I could think of about Elliott's habits and needs. I let her carry him, holding my breath, but she handled him competently if not as lovingly as I would have liked, and I left with Stephen less anxious than I had been before.

That night he allowed me to call home. Elliott, said Karen, was fine, had eaten well and was asleep. I asked her to please check him while I was on the telephone, make sure he was all right, because one of my biggest fears, although I did not tell her this, was that I might walk into his room and find him not breathing. Sometimes in the quiet of the night I would stand beside his crib, not breathing myself, trying to hear the tiny catches of air in and out of his lungs; or I would put my hand flat down on his back to feel the rise and fall. Karen sounded puzzled, but she did as I asked. He was well, of course.

Three nights later, at the dinner party, the end came, quietly, oddly and finally. I found myself watching the people and listening, and it seemed too remote for me to take a part in it. I did not care. I heard Stephen, confident and brisk, talking business with the other men. It dawned on me at last that there was more in his life than what I saw, and more places in him than those I knew. I was not in this world of his; I was far away from all these people; I was very quiet.

Afterwards, when Stephen asked me if I were all right, I said I was. I did not know how to tell him how it felt, being so far away — confusing, frightening, and very much alone. I could not describe to him how, even with the fear, the aloneness, I had felt a spark of freedom. As if I had lost a weight in knowing that he was more than I knew, and I wasn't responsible for all of it. There was lightness about it, an atmosphere without pressure, a kind of invisibility, and I would have to think about that.

At home, we went together to check on Elliott. He lay quiet in the crib, breathing gently, and I saw that he was alone, just his own small body in that crib, he was asleep, and I could not be there with him. Such a small moment snapped in me, I saw clearly, and it felt just then like a loss and I wanted to cry a little for it, but could not.

The next day he was still alone. I helped him but I was not him and I knew it. *Knew* it. I saw that I could leave him safely

50

with Karen; that when he was asleep it could not matter who was in the next room, watching television or reading, looking in occasionally. What had been unthinkable a few days earlier was now just there, through some mysterious process of withdrawal. It seemed to me then like a lesser love, less consuming and giving — less maternal? — but there it was. It felt also as if some intensity had gone out of my own life, something very real and clear was muddied now and I was a little lost again. I thought, "I really must sit down and think about this, figure out what's happened and how it came about, and whether it's good or bad," but I never did.

Stephen and I didn't talk about it. The change was mentioned only once.

"You seem a lot more relaxed these days," he said casually a few weeks later, and I told him I felt more relaxed, which in its way was true. But it was more than that. There was almost a hole, despair. There was no — passion. But there was a freedom, a relaxation, a kind of relief, so the passion must have been a burden.

Stephen and I grew closer again, in a way. We shared Elliott, and I think I was even grateful as things changed that I wasn't necessarily the one the baby turned to. I almost forgot about the other Stephen I had seen, the glimpse I'd had of other possibilities.

He no longer insisted that we go out together every week, and sometimes we just stayed home, the way we had done before Elliott, and read and talked. Early in the evenings he played with Elliott while I watched, listening to them laugh. Stephen said Elliott was starting to look like me, and by then it was true; he was leaving babyhood, becoming a person, developing a character and a look, and yes, he was like me.

He was happy, laughing, full of joy and love. I could not have hoped for more, and I knew he would not have been that way if Stephen had not stepped in. I was grateful to Stephen, too, because I could see that I, also, might not have survived without his strength.

(Over coffee, after an almost silent lunch, while I remember, I ask Katie about Elliott. He will be twenty now, a man. I can see by her face that she isn't fond of him; it wrinkles in quick distaste before she catches herself and tries to speak of him objectively. She seems to choose her words carefully, whether to be kind to him or to spare me from what she thinks I will feel as guilt, I don't know.

(She says he seems — bitter. Cynical, she says, in a way that makes him need to win. She starts again, says she hasn't explained that well; she meant to say that he doesn't seem concerned with people, that he has no love for anyone, not even for himself; that it is as if he sees living as a race for the top and security. He is at university, taking a course in business administration, his marks are high and he talks with his father about things he is learning and new ways of running businesses. She says she asked him once why he was interested in business, what he wanted from it, and he told her money, enough money so that he would never have to worry about anything, so that he would be secure. He didn't ever want to feel insecure, he wanted there to be nothing that he couldn't have. "It's strange," she says thoughtfully, "that with all that's happened, he's decided that everything he wants can be bought, if only he has enough money. He has such an odd sense of what security is, when he of all people should know." She stops, looks at me shyly, aware again that she may be hurting me, but I tell her to go on.

("It's just," she says, "that he seemed to miss you the most of all of us. He used to yell a lot; I remember that, but he never said anything. Once after you'd gone" — another glance to see if she should continue — "I went into his bedroom to borrow something, a catcher's mitt or something, and I found him crying. He was so angry that I'd seen him, he hit me. I know he was crying about you, or something somebody'd said about you, but he would never talk about it. Daddy tried a couple of times to talk to both of us, to see how we were taking it, because I guess neither of us really showed what we were feeling. I remember him saying it wasn't our fault, it had nothing to do with us — you said that too, didn't you?" — she looks at me with surprise, as if she is just now considering that it might be true. "We asked him why, then, and he said he didn't know, but he knew it wasn't Elliott or me. I've talked to Daddy about it sometimes, but Elliott wouldn't. He'd listen to Daddy and then

52

he'd walk out of the room, but he wouldn't say anything. Just that one time crying.

("I know a couple of years ago, I guess when he was about seventeen, he went to Daddy and said something like he knew Daddy knew why you'd gone and where you were, and man to man, what had happened, what was it all about. He was really tense, white, you know? because I saw him going into Daddy's den to talk, and I knew it was something important. I was only fifteen, and I eavesdropped, I know that's wrong but I wanted to know what was going on and Elliott never told me anything. I almost got caught, though; Daddy told him he honestly didn't know why you'd left, he'd never found out, and I guess Elliott didn't believe him, because he didn't say a word, he just stormed out of the den again and he never said another thing about it. He just decided to go to university, study business and get rich and be secure."

(Neither of us speaks for a few moments, and then she smiles at me, a funny twisted kind of smile that means I'm not to take personally what she is saying, that she is just talking of a reality, not what might have been if I had been different.

("It's so strange," she says again, "because of all people he should know that the one thing he really wanted, that might have made him feel secure, was something he won't ever be able to buy, no matter how much money he makes. I think it's sad. But you know, I don't really like him. He keeps you away, you know? He doesn't let anybody come close, he doesn't share anything, he won't let anybody help. He's really straight. He has all these standards, I don't know where he got them because they're not the way Daddy wanted us to be. He must have read them or something, and everybody has to conform to them. He's very big on proper behaviour, being polite, doing the right thing with the right fork, that sort of thing. He never seems to be with you, if you know what I mean. He's always *behaving*."

(She is upset, and is silent for a moment, struggling to be calm. "I just feel so sad for him," she continues finally. "It's all such a waste."

(Katie, I can see, is different in many ways. She wants to understand, which is why she is here; she is more open, ready to talk about how everything has affected her, hesitant only in

53

how what she says may hurt me, kind in that way but stubbornly unkind in others, ruthless almost, perhaps more like her brother than she realizes; but with different goals, wanting to be herself but not knowing what that is. I am only one of her first steps.

(She does not look ahead, she says, does not want to know how her life will move, cannot conceive of actually planning it. More flexible, obviously, than Elliott, seeing him and deliberately taking an opposite route, surely more likeable, more approachable. Determined, with the same determination as her brother, but their ends are different and so she doesn't see it. After lunch we do the dishes, and I am remembering again and she lets me be. She says she has brought a book that she wants to finish, and I go back into my garden, where everything is the same and full of changes.)

Everything was quite different with Katie.

When Elliott was almost two years old, Stephen and I decided it was time to have another child. Everyone then said it was unhealthy to be, or have, an only child and the experts we (or I) read so assiduously recommended that children be spaced apart by two or three years.

There were no romantic dreams this time; I had a child, another would come, and meanwhile I cared for Elliott and carried Katie as obliviously as a kangaroo with its young in a pouch. I think that at the time both Stephen and I wanted this second child for Elliott more than for ourselves. Not that we didn't want a second; but we did think of it as a companion for Elliott, a sort of second-string team.

Somewhere in my memory was the pain of Elliott's birth; I could not summon up the reality of it, but I remembered the thoughts, the blinding hysteria, and I did not want to think of going through it again. I sighed; it seemed inevitable and cruel.

But it wasn't that way at all; Katie came easily, swiftly, and there was pain but it didn't go on forever the way Elliott's had, it was over soon and easily forgotten, and I was smug with satisfaction.

She looked as Elliott had, like a baby, no resemblance to anyone. I fell in love with her as soon as I saw her, was grateful that we had decided, for whatever reason, to have another child.

But the wonder I'd felt seeing Elliott for the first time was not there; she was a baby, beautiful, and she was mine and Stephen's and we had created her, but it seemed natural now. Elliott had been a miracle; Katie was a child.

We named her after my grandmother, Kathleen, but we never called her that. Most often she was Katie, sometimes Kate, without any particular reason for the difference.

She smiled easily, laughed early, went without hesitation to new people, and I watched her and was proud. I felt none of the compulsive protectiveness I had with Elliott; I was pleased that people were attracted to her, that they wanted to touch her and hold her, and that Stephen was enchanted by her and would help take care of her; time was short for me now, there were two babies, and I appreciated whatever he could do.

Elliott was resentful of her for a long time; perhaps still. We had told him there would be another baby, but of course he couldn't have understood what that would mean, any more than we could. He was shy, and it pained him to see how she met people with joy and they accepted her in the same spirit, because it was something he could not do. I watched with my own pain as his face grew more and more shut. I held him and told him softly that I loved him, and he knew that that was true, but it couldn't make up for the fact that everyone else seemed to love Katie.

I did what I could; but oh, I was so tired. Stephen, the understanding grown-up Stephen, knew and did his best. But he was weary too, and overworked, and his mind was divided among us all; there was a limit to how much he could help, and he needed things from me too. He needed gratitude and reassurance and love, and I felt sometimes there must be three of me, one for each of them.

My life flattened. I was busy, constantly busy, for although the spark of freedom, the hint of aloneness I had felt still waited in my mind, I was responsible to my children. They were my work. I read to Elliott or played with him when Katie was asleep, talked vaguely to him while I fed or cuddled her, and let Stephen take over for a while in the evenings, while I got dinner and did dishes. And then Katie would sleep and Elliott would have his own time with his father while I might read, and then

Elliott would go to bed and Katie would wake up to be fed and finally Stephen and I would have a little while together before it all started again. I loved them all, I did my best, I did everything I could, and I was exhausted.

The children grew and changed, and Katie was more than a year old, Elliott almost four, when one night Stephen brought home champagne, beaming with a secret. After the children were in bed, he told me why and his face was young and proud. I saw then it had gotten older, while I had not noticed.

He'd been told, he said, that within six months he would have another promotion, a major one, and he would have gone as far as he could reasonably expect for a long time. We would be exceedingly comfortable financially. His idea was to "settle down" as he put it, as if we weren't already as settled as it was possible to be. We would buy the "dream house" that would give us plenty of space and privacy and we would get a cleaning lady and I would not be so tired and everything would be the way he had always wanted it to be. It sounded wonderful; it gave me enough hope to keep going.

We found the house, although it took a year of intermittent searching. I was assigned to that, and when I found something promising, Stephen and I would look at it together. There was always something wrong: ancient plumbing or the wrong kind of heating, or not enough privacy, until that last one, with the acre of land and the hedges, and if it seemed to me to be simply too big to be manageable, Stephen thought it would be just right. And it would set the right tone for his job, which was something we had to think about. We were buying a setting for a career play, along with everything else.

There was no reason for me to dislike the place, and I did not, in fact, dislike it. It just was not a home, and no matter what we did, it never became one to me. It was always "the house."

Katie and Elliott had never moved before, and they were both excited and hesitant, uprooted for the first time, taken away from their friends, but also the ones to be leaving, so that the gain was all theirs. They ran joyfully through the new house when we showed it to them, and because the house was empty it echoed with their shrieks and their discoveries. We let them pick out their own bedrooms.

It was too much change for Elliott, who had been looking forward to going to school with his friends and now was on his own. He began to have nightmares, both before and after we moved, almost every night for several months. I would hear him calling me, "Mommy," he would cry, "I had a bad dream." So I would get up and cuddle him until he went back to sleep, although sometimes Stephen said I was foolish because he must be having the dreams to get more attention, more security; but I thought that was a good reason to go to him, and continued until gradually the nightmares dwindled, then disappeared, for by then he had made friends at school and was too busy and tired to be bothered with bad dreams.

Elliott only went to kindergarten in the mornings, and during those hours I had time, new time, to give Katie the attention that Elliott had had, all the reading and the walks and the discussions that had slipped by me with her because Elliott was always there.

My days were filled with the smallest of concerns, significant to me. Ought I to do a laundry or take Katie to the park? Was Elliott happy at school, was I giving him enough attention so that he wouldn't feel cast off into the world, replaced at home by his joyous little sister? Would Katie be spoiled? Was I giving her less attention than I had given Elliott? Were a few minutes alone with Stephen in the evenings enough, or should I somehow reorganize myself so that he could have more of my time? Did he feel I paid too much attention to the children? He said not, he said I was doing beautifully, wondered how I kept it up, where I got all my energy, but sometimes I wondered if he weren't going through more than he talked about, weren't holding back something to protect me from more pressure. Perhaps he felt I was not strong. He seemed content enough, said he enjoyed his new position and thought he handled it well, but still I wondered if I were not failing him somehow, because he was good and I did not think I could ever be so good.

Each day was the same, or so it seems in memory. Katie woke up about six-thirty in the morning, and I would get her started while Stephen got ready for work. Elliott and Stephen always had poached eggs on toast for breakfast, Elliott with juice, Stephen with coffee. I would put the eggs on and Stephen would make the toast and by the time I got Elliott to the table, it was ready. Stephen drove Elliott to school on his way to work, and Katie and I were left to our mornings.

Her breakfast was simultaneous with my first cup of coffee. I never ate breakfast; I just wanted to sit for a few minutes, because those first hours of the day had gone by in a mist, me a robot grinding through them, and this was my first moment of relative peace, although Katie rarely stopped talking, even while she ate. (I am pleased to see that now that she is an adult, she has learned the art of silence.)

While I did the dishes, she would tell me a story she had made up overnight. They weren't always great stories, often the endings were flat, but always they were new and original, and I was proud of that.

"Guess what Mommy," she'd say, her legs swinging under the kitchen chair that was too high for her, her hands fidgeting with something, her eyes following me while I washed and rinsed the dishes.

"What?"

"A bear came to my room last night." She would stop in triumph.

"A bear! What on earth did he want? Was he a friendly bear?"

"Oh, very friendly. He wanted me to help him."

"What did he want you to do?"

"He said he had a friend, his friend was a bear too, and his friend was stuck way up in the hedge, he climbed up there and couldn't get down, and he needed me to help him get down because he was scared when the daytime came people would see him up there and want to shoot him and he had to get down while it was still dark, and I had to help him." Another pause.

"So did you?"

"Oh yes, the bear that came to my room said it was very important, so he helped me climb out the window and he carried me down to the ground and then I took him to the garage and he helped me carry the ladder over to the hedge where his friend was. His friend was crying and crying.

"So," and she took a deep breath, "I climbed up the ladder because the bear was too scared, and I told him to stop crying and he did, so then I carried him down to the ground again, and he was really happy."

"What happened after that?"

"They helped me put the ladder back in the garage and then the first bear carried me up to my room and put me back in the window and I went to bed."

She stopped, considering, then decided the story wasn't finished. "They said thank you, though, and they said they'd come back sometime and do something for me, so I guess I'll see them again."

I was terribly pleased by her imagination; always she had more than Elliott, who was likely to tell the same story over and over when he found a particular favourite, and it was rarely his own, but one I had read to him.

I made all the beds and often carried laundry downstairs to the basement and the washer and dryer; Katie trailed after me everywhere, asking questions — why was I washing my nightgowns, how did nightgowns get dirty anyway when you only wore them to bed, what time was it, what time would Elliott be coming home from school, how long away from now was that, (I think she must have picked up my mania about time, for it seemed always to be on her mind) and what would we do with the rest of the day? I had to listen, answer all her questions, and I had to do it carefully, not flippantly, or she would be hurt.

We would read together, or take a walk if the weather were good, and late in the morning I would put an album of children's stories on the record player and she would sit, blessedly quiet, listening to them while I got lunch. And then Elliott would be home, full of what had happened in his morning, and I would listen and Katie would interrupt, trying to get back the attention she'd had all morning, but she would have to understand that this was Elliott's time. The three of us would eat lunch, clamorously, always an upheaval or a quarrel, and I would try to smile and be patient. Largely they seemed fond of each other, but lunchtimes were always bad because Katie was clinging while Elliott tried to retrieve me.

Elliott often went to play with friends in the afternoons, and sometimes I went with him, lugging Katie, to visit the mothers of his friends. We would pack the children off into recreation rooms while we sat and drank coffee and talked about the children obsessively, as if even in absence their presence overwhelmed us. Katie would play with the others for a while, but soon she would be back, leaning against me, touching me, tugging at me, talking to me — it was too hard to make her understand that this was not her time.

Later I would start making dinner, and sometimes, if Elliott and Katie were being good, I could do some ironing so that I would have more free time in the evening, when Stephen was home.

Usually he arrived at a quarter to six and played with the children until dinner at a quarter past, and then while I did the dishes he watched television with them until Katie went to bed, usually reluctantly unless we'd been for a long, tiring walk during the day. Then Stephen had time with Elliott alone, while I could work or read, and Elliott would repeat all the important things he had told me at lunch, and he would go to bed and Stephen and I would be there, alone, together, for the first time. He would tell me about his day and ask about mine, but I kept my stories short for fear of boring him. There was rarely anything new. We could read or Stephen might work, and sometimes there would be the Japanese monster late movies and making love on the couch and popcorn. And we would finally go to bed, regretting that we had to, because we had so little time together and it seemed a shame to waste it sleeping.

But late nights and early mornings exhausted me, and during the week I became more and more tired, less able to listen, less able even to do simple things like sort laundry with a clear mind. Thank God for Saturdays then, when Stephen would take the children and I would sleep, and sleep, and sleep, and occasionally wake up to remember it was Saturday and I was free, relatively. I would turn over believing that I could with great content spend several weeks, if not my whole life, in bed.

Sometime around noon Stephen and Elliott and Katie would come proudly in, carrying coffee, a breakfast tray and a flower. It was part of their Saturday morning ritual: they would go for a walk after their breakfast, stop somewhere to buy me a flower, and then come home and make my breakfast. I remember Katie always got to carry the flower.

They made different things — pancakes, eggs, once even

chocolate cake, and although my stomach always lurched at the thought of food as soon as I woke up, I didn't have the heart not to eat it all and tell them how good it was and how much I appreciated what they'd done. And I did; always their proud faces touched me, for it was done with love. And yet when I woke up on Saturdays, usually just before they came in, there was always a pinch of dread in my stomach, a gearing up for the performance.

Later, after I was dressed and had had another cup of coffee, listening all the while to Elliott and Katie talk about their morning with their father, arguing over details and interrupting each other, and yet at the same time happy that they had shared all this with Stephen, we would do something together, go skating or swimming, depending on the season, or for a drive around the city, and often we would stop somewhere and have dinner and then come home and the children would go to bed. Saturday was their favourite day because we were all together doing things. Stephen used to tell me he didn't know how I could look after them all week, when he was exhausted after just a day. He sounded as if he honestly admired what I did.

The memories of those years have a sameness, a furriness, as if nothing at all happened for days and months and years except for that routine. Could it really have been that way? Is it true that nothing happened?

What was I thinking about then, I wonder? What was I feeling? Where was the "I" in all of that? I was the lover, the giver, the doer, the mother, the wife, and that is where the "I" was. Which makes me sound martyred, only of course it wasn't like that. I didn't think of it that way; in fact I cannot remember that I thought, or felt, anything about myself, except that I loved these people and they depended on me. I don't remember assessments, times when one thinks, "well then, am I happy, or just what is going on, anyway?" I think I must have just assumed it, for I had everything it had ever occurred to me to ask for. All of it was as it was supposed to be, although sometimes I was so tired.

And yet, here I am now and the garden is done for today. Should I ask Katie to stay for dinner? I think not. It's been too long a day, I don't want to go any farther. I shall ask her to leave,

61

and then have my dinner, and later I may sit outside in the dusk.

I hope I will be able to sleep. I don't want to go through what I did last night, lying awake, remembering. I have remembered enough for today. It has gone far enough.

6

But once begun it is, of course, relentless.

The memories forage on into the next years, that began when Elliott was almost nine and Katie was six and in school all day. I remember the bad times. I must say now, at the beginning, that there were also the good times, the moments of pleasure, for they must, for truth, be acknowledged. It is just that I do not remember them as well.

Partly, I think, it is that my memory is clinging now to the bad, a defence, perhaps. But what went wrong did not come on me swiftly and inexorably, like an avalanche, but subtly and with periods of relief. Those periods were the good times. I might look at my children and my husband at dinner and see them surrounded, like a miracle, by an atmosphere of great love, the most important people I could ever see, and I was so happy that I could understand that, that I would have to leave the table for a moment to cry.

Or I might go to Katie's room in the morning and find her already awake, lying quietly in bed, and she would look up at me and smile and say, "Hi, Mommy," and I would melt and hold her and be terribly grateful.

Those moments, which were shiny, were not so very rare. They were like a window opening for an instant to show me what could be really there, what I really had if only I could see it all the time, without falling and failing into those lapses of inertia which were beginning to come, and against which I struggled.

And against which, finally, I ceased to struggle. But not yet. Not for a long time yet.

The children were changing. Elliott had already learned that there were unpleasant things, unpleasant people, teachers, other children, rules, an order to be obeyed that was not always the same as the order he was used to with us. We tried to help him, explained that other people might have different standards, and he should not think that they must share ours. We managed, I think, only to confuse him further. It wasn't that he was having a bad time; it was just that things weren't turning out the way he'd expected.

Now Katie was out in the same world, but she was a better survivor than Elliott. She learned to keep her impulses shut away, a secret, untouched, and on the outside did what she had to. She was scarcely unblemished, but she salvaged and balanced herself; she seemed to recognize instinctively the schizophrenia of her position as a child, and just as instinctively dealt with it, and if in the process she learned to deal in dishonesty, not outright dishonesty like stealing, but presenting a false face where she felt it necessary, in herself she did not change; she was a firmly rooted little girl, or so it seemed to us.

Stephen and I talked often about the children; we marvelled at their differences, astonished because we thought we had given the same of what we had, including love, to each. We liked to tell each other fantasies of what Elliott and Katie might become; we were determined, because they were both intelligent, to encourage them to go to school as long as they wanted. Education, then, was the answer to everything; I was beginning to think its lack in my own life must be the source of the rootling of unease that was already in me; I thought it was because I was essentially helpless.

"It really bothers you, doesn't it," Stephen said. And I grew inarticulate, unable to explain.

"It's just that it makes me so dependent," I told him. "There's nothing I can do."

For I did think, briefly, of getting a job as a means of filling the spaces of my life. I mentioned the idea to Stephen and immediately regretted it.

He did not take it personally, did not think I was rejecting him or that he had failed me in some way, or that I was failing him. He was, as always, cool and rational.

"What sort of thing would you be interested in?" he asked solemnly, respectfully, although he must have known how narrow the possibilities would be.

"I'm not sure," I said vaguely, "something maybe helping people, some kind of social work. Or maybe something in an art gallery or a library, something I could care about."

"Interesting," he said. He looked at me as if I had shown him a side of my personality he could admire. "Interesting. Why social work?"

"So I could help people. Get involved with them, I guess." I began to feel tongue-tied, ridiculous, putting into words these absurd formulas that I knew were just romanticizing, the picture of myself as the middle-class angel of mercy swooping down on the poor, giving to them my love and generosity, fighting for them, winning what they wanted, glowing from their gratitude, being a second mother to their children, so that they came to love me, and I could have them to my home, afternoon tea with me while their children played happily with my children, everyone learning that we're all the same, it's just a question of money and the breaks, and they would be so eternally grateful.

Bullshit. I knew it was bullshit, that these ghostly poor would be more likely to spit at my condescension, and their children would beat my children and break their toys, and later, in the middle of the night they would come back and steal away all the things I had that they didn't. And they would be right to do it, my fairy godmother fantasies deserved that.

"Well, maybe not social work after all," I said hesitantly. "I don't have any qualifications. And anyway, I'd get too involved, it would be like having dozens of families to worry about instead of just one. It wouldn't be a good idea, really." I sat there in defeat, wanting it to end.

But Stephen plunged on. "Well, an art gallery doesn't sound like a bad idea. You do have experience selling. You could just sell paintings instead of dresses." There was a small eruption in me, no-meaning words triggering rage. Why?

I saw myself in a gallery, hanging paintings, dusting sculptures, and the people drifting in, pointing at the paintings, touching the sculptures, talking about them with that awful art critic jargon, pretending they understood, me pretending that I understood. And the others, looking for something for over the fireplace to match the wallpaper, and do I think this artist's works would be a good investment, so that if they ever got the living room redone, they could sell them for more than they paid? Ringing up sales — do they use real cash registers in art galleries, or is everything done much more discreetly in a back room somewhere with no tell-tale ring to announce it?

Where, I wondered, had all this bitterness been, all this dislike, this contempt? It didn't seem to be like me, for I still thought of myself as essentially gentle and loving. It puzzled me, for this feeling was like — well, it felt like hate.

And that left, what, a library? Where I would reshelve books, my head spinning with cataloguing systems, no contact with the books, just their numbers? I pulled away from the anger, frightened by it.

"Actually," I said, almost in tears, "I don't really want a job. There's plenty for me to do here, and I'm not a bit unhappy; I just thought working might be a new interest."

But he was worried, not quite believing, wanting, with all his generosity, to help. "Have you thought of going back to school?" he asked. "It wouldn't be any big problem for the rest of us, we'd manage, and you could train for something you really are interested in."

But that wasn't it either. I wanted an answer, a completion, not a preparation.

Somewhere in me was some deep-buried worm that gnawed its way through the hidden places of all the parts of my life, so gently, so delicately, that I could not tell, until the hidden places had all been eaten away and there was nothing left to root me to what I had or what I was.

A church teaches that despair is the gravest sin. I was sliding into despair.

Time was huge, vast, a wasteland. After Katié and Elliott and Stephen left in the mornings, all of them excited or dreading the day but at least feeling some kind of anticipation for it, I would drink my coffee and smoke my cigarettes and wonder when I should stand up, and when I stood, what should I do, which direction should I turn, which room should I go to, and I would have another coffee and try to decide. Everything seemed very bright, and at the same time hazy. I was alert to sounds, smells, and everything was unreal, as if I were not a part of it; or as if I were only that, a part of it like a couch or a lamp.

Time. God, the times in the years before when I had said to Stephen, "I can't wait till they're in school, I'll be free then." Free for what? Faced with it, I was alone, really alone, for the first time in my life, and terrified. I thought perhaps that I was losing my mind; and then, worse, that I had no mind, and that the existence of these people had hidden that.

But no, I knew I was not stupid. In school so long ago, secluded and safe, I had done well. I had absorbed and understood and been praised; I had even, at times, been curious about certain things.

But what kind of mind did I need, and not have, for this?

I could have cried out with the frustration, for it seemed that in me was a fog that smothered me whenever I approached the door that might lead to freedom. I knew the door was there, I could almost feel it, heavy and wooden, far inside the tunnels of my skull. I could not *get* to it, and I struggled, but always when the door was still some twists away, the fog would melt around me and what energy I had would die in triviality. I could get hold of nothing.

"All right," I would think firmly. "I've got to get to the bottom of this. This can't go on." And I would make a coffee and light a cigarette and try to think. "The problem," I would say to myself, "is that I lack initiative. I can't seem to act on my own. Now, what is it that will give me the ability to *be* something on my own?" For the first premise had now to be that, for a large portion of my time I was, in fact, on my own.

And thinking of that, I would remember the children, and thinking of them, I would worry. I watched the clock, waiting for them to come home from school, afraid for them. My day, my own day, was over when I caught sight of them, everything geared to that moment when I'd see them coming up the street, turning up our walk, climbing the little rise to our house, submitting themselves to my hugs and my help, and then, more often now, going back out again to play with their friends, leaving me alone again, waiting for them to come back, worrying and counting then the moments until Stephen came.

I heard myself saying things I never had before. Dredging Stephen for details of his days at work, just as I did with the children. Piling onto him the details of my day, boring, I could hear myself talking, knowing I must be boring him, filling the spaces, trying to make him fill mine.

"And then what happened," I would demand, watching him eagerly, pushing him to tell the last detail of some office anecdote. Or, "I mowed the back lawns today and it took forever. I wonder if we need a new mower, there seems to be something wrong with the starter and when you do get it going the blades sound as if they're going really slowly, it just creeps along. It took almost three hours, and if it takes that long I don't have time to get a proper meal ready. I wanted to go out and pick up some mushrooms and bean sprouts so we could have Chinese food tonight, but I really just didn't get a chance, so we're going to be stuck with baked ham, I'm afraid. Did Elliott tell you what his teacher said today . . .?" And on and on, and he listened, patient, puzzled, wondering, he must have, what was happening to me, and I couldn't tell him because I didn't understand it myself.

At the same time, running alongside my curiosity, my need to fill myself with everything I could find out about the lives of these three people, a strange kind of indifference, a neglect that had never been there before, was developing, and that frightened me more than my own vacancy. I wanted them with me, and when they were, I was filled with irritation. I didn't cook good meals, and it was not because I didn't have time to shop. I spent less and less time on the house. By the time Katie was seven, in Grade Two, the only gift I had thought I had for them, my concern for giving them a loving home, had dwindled until I scarcely bothered with any of it. Katie's questions annoyed me. I began to tell her and Elliott to do things because I said to do them, skipping the explanations Stephen and I had decided they should always have. I thought I loved them. I began to cry during the day, until I lost the energy for that. I was thirty-two years old, almost thirty-three.

When they were not there, I was empty. I felt as if I did not exist. I had no power, no way to be known. There were months filled with that kind of emptiness, the motionlessness of a mannequin in a fairy tale who only comes alive when real people appear. I could laugh a little at the picture I presented, so I must still have been a little sane. "I am a metaphysical problem," I told myself and giggled. "Do I exist when there is no one here to see me existing?" But it was not funny, and I could not really laugh, because it seemed that the answer was no.

Stephen could glance at the business reports over breakfast. After they all left, I got into the habit of reading the whole paper, cover to cover, from the front page to the classified advertisements. I learned to stretch the reading out to a couple of hours, by which time it was noon, the lunch hour, and only a little while before I could start thinking about the children coming home and worrying about them. No time, between this moment and that moment, to try to grip the emptiness.

There was a secure, but at the same time disquieting, disorienting feeling about my reading of the paper. The security was in knowing that most of the events didn't touch me, that inside my house, inside my city, I was safe from the greater part of it. People were fighting? It was somewhere else. Children were starving? They were somewhere else, and all I had to worry about was that goddamn car coming down that hill and around the curve before my children could get home to the dinner I would so carelessly prepare for them. City council was building an expressway, or fighting an expressway? Either way it was all right with me: I wasn't going anywhere.

And yet the irrelevance was terrifying. Apart from this one, very small household, there was no reason for me to be alive; if they knew, it would make no difference to them. Perhaps it was enough, should be enough, to be important to three people. There must be some, I thought, who aren't even that important.

One day I found that I had gotten up and made breakfast for everyone, had my coffee, read the paper, and then gone to lie down again. When I woke up it was almost two o'clock. I roused myself, made a small stew for dinner, and left it to simmer; later, I thought, I would make salad and with bread it would be enough. And then I couldn't think of anything else to do, nothing for which I had the energy, and I found myself back in bed. The children woke me; I hadn't been waiting for them at the door, and they looked frightened that they had had to come to the bedroom to find me; they thought I must be sick, and didn't know what to do.

How do you tell children that you couldn't think of anything else to do, so you fell asleep? That sort of thing doesn't happen to a child, there are dozens of reasons why they don't want to sleep, and it must be incomprehensible to them that one would deliberately choose to do it; although it would be harder still to explain to them that a deliberate choice was not part of my life at that moment. I told them I'd had a headache but that it was better now, and I went to special lengths to entertain them until Stephen came home. I found myself thinking, "What if I'd killed myself, and they'd come home and found me?" I couldn't imagine why that thought would come to me. Why should it? Three people loved me, and I loved them back as best I could. We needed each other.

I could not let the children be frightened again. I had to do something. Something about it. What to do?

That night, while Stephen worked, I went through an old telephone book of my friends. It had been so long; the friends since high school had been Stephen's, and I had no idea how to find these people from my own past. I called my mother and asked her to call their mothers for addresses and phone numbers; suddenly it seemed necessary to find out what had happened to them.

My mother found three for me. Only one was in Toronto, so I pinned my hopes on reaching her. I would call tomorrow, she would be home, we would be glad to talk, would get together for lunch, at her home because I needed so badly to get out of mine.

Although we had never been really close. Sheila, her name was, Sheila Hayward, now Nelson, and we had moved generally in the same crowd in high school, but even in crowds some people are closer than others and she was always too hysterical, too loud, for me. A very tense person. But people change. I had, God knows. I think.

70

But when morning came I was frightened. I woke with the thought, "I'm going to call Sheila today," and then I got breakfast and saw everybody off and drank coffee and read the paper, all the time with Sheila, with the lifting of the telephone receiver, in my mind. Whatever did I have to say to her?

I couldn't back out. It was impossible, with the resolve, but when I finally dialled the number I was trembling, and felt it was my own failure when no one answered.

I called three times that day, each time with more difficulty, and then I decided to forget it, it was too hard, and by then it was time to watch for the children coming home.

I didn't try again. But my mother had re-established contact with her mother, and let me know that Sheila worked all day; if I called at night, she said, I would be likely to get her. I never did.

Sheila's mother, through my mother, brought me up to date on the old friends. Sheila apparently kept in touch with some of them, which, I thought resentfully, was just like her. Some married, some not, a couple still living in the home town, some gone out west, some successful, some counted not so successful, no one actually a disgrace. Sheila herself happily married to a dentist, working as a librarian, one child; her mother was very proud of her, my mother said, and they lived not all that far from us but in a different kind of neighbourhood, not as "good" as ours. My mother said I had accomplished so much more than some of them.

My mother phoned me on Sundays and I called her on Wednesdays, so that we were in constant touch. I felt close to her but not honest, which I thought was a possible relationship with her; I felt there were many things she must understand, for at times in my life she had been very wise — but still I could not tell her. I told myself it was because I did not want to worry her, thinking I was unhappy, but perhaps it was because she might be too wise, see too much. And so while the feeling of affection went out to her, the right words never did; instead I told her how well Stephen was doing at work, how well the children were doing at school, how pleased I was that they were happy and that now I had time to do the things I really wanted.

"What do you do with your time now then, dear?" she asked, and I said vaguely something like, "Oh I see friends and go to

71

the museum and the art gallery and the library, and I do quite a lot of reading about things I'm interested in. It's such a luxury to me now, to have so much free time." I tried to keep my voice light; I wonder if she knew.

We were almost out of things to say one Sunday when she remembered a piece of news.

"I heard a sad thing about one of your old friends from Mrs. Hayward yesterday, dear. One of the girls in your class, Selma Finnerty, the one that took the figure skating lessons, apparently she killed herself last week. Mrs. Hayward was saying she had a home in Calgary and was married to a man who has something to do with oil, three children I think. I gather she sent the children over to stay with a neighbour and when her husband came home he found her dead in the basement. She'd hanged herself, poor thing."

"My God."

"You remember her? Mrs. Hayward said she didn't know if you and Sheila would have known her well. I wonder why she'd do a thing like that? So cruel — I know something must have been very wrong, but it's a cruel thing to do to the people that are left behind. Think how her husband must have felt. And the children, at least she had the sense to fix it so it wasn't them that found her. You do remember her, then?"

Selma Finnerty. Yes, I remembered. I agreed with Mother, it was very sad, something must have been very wrong for her, yes, it was cruel. Thank you, I said, for letting me know.

I remembered Selma Finnerty. I remembered her a great deal over the next days.

She had been at the fringes of our group, a pretty girl, but painfully shy so that it was too difficult for people to get close. It was hard to talk with her, although she was intelligent; I remembered her blushing easily, blushing whenever anyone's attention turned to her; I remembered her stumbling over answers in class, even though she knew the work. The eyes on her, the judgements, overwhelmed her.

And yet, difficult as she was, we all said she would do well. She was so pretty, so gentle, kind almost to a fault, because she couldn't bear to hurt anyone; we all said that someday she would find someone who would take the trouble to get to know her, bring her out of herself, which was a phrase our mothers used in those days, and love her. She would be worth loving, we thought, and maybe underneath all our brash popularity, which was vital to us then, we envied her a little. She seemed — apart, wrapped in an immunity from the things that ruled us. She stood above us; she was simply good.

She and I used to talk a little sometimes, never directly about how we felt, but about books, things we were studying. She liked poetry and hated science because she didn't like pulling things apart. She said it didn't matter what the parts of a flower were, she wanted just to enjoy them. It had never occurred to me before that it might be a choice one could make; it was something we were told to do, and so I did it, and I learned their parts, but I hadn't thought about it.

She didn't think much about love, not the way we did at any rate. It didn't seem important to her that she wasn't in demand, and I thought it must be a fine thing to be so independent, to be able to go on, considering the flowers, simply being. I could have wished to be like that, but I wasn't.

I think under it all she must have had a very tough mind.

And she had hung herself? Had hidden whatever despair it was, had planned it, maybe even consciously gone out and bought a rope, had sent her children away, made sure she had plenty of time before she would be discovered, had gathered up the rope, walked down the stairs into her basement, found a chair and a suitable beam, knotted the rope, flung it over the beam, stood on the chair, placed the rope around her neck and kicked away the chair? Selma Finnerty had done all that, and it was impossible to know why, even her husband and her children did not know why, so how could I, who hadn't seen her, hadn't even thought of her, for almost fifteen years? Maybe even she didn't know; maybe it just seemed like the thing she had to do at that particular time.

I tried to tell Stephen about her, but I couldn't explain why I was thinking about it, why it was so important. Yes, he said, it was a terrible thing, but what more could he say, what was it I expected him to say? How could he know what to explain, however was he to know? She kept coming back; I even, one day, went into the garage and found a rope and carried it slowly into

73

the basement. Yes, there was an old chair down there, it would do, and over on the other side a solid-looking beam, and I would just need to drag the chair across the room, stand on it and do it.

I didn't, of course, I had no reason to, no desire to; all I wanted to know was how Selma might have felt, but I couldn't because I knew that what I was doing wasn't real, and she must have known that what she was doing was very real. Still, there was something frightening about it, and I hurried upstairs to put the rope back in the garage. I tried not to think about it after that, but sometimes in that half-here half-there moment before falling asleep I would see her, not dead, not yet, but in the process of becoming dead, climbing onto her chair, placing the loop around her neck and suddenly pushing with her feet and the chair falling. In my semi-dreams I always watched the chair falling; I never saw her face.

Selma's death had something to do with me, I felt it but I could not tell what it was. I tried to see, but it kept slipping away from me. The time slipped away too: the days and months and seasons went round and round, while I sat bewildered in the centre, unmoving, wanting vaguely to make it stop so that I could get a grip on it, but nothing would ever stop and I could not catch up, and meanwhile my life was leaving me behind and I was thirty-four years old and it was winter. Dear God, the time, the time was disappearing, and I was nothing, was always nothing.

I tried to understand why I could not catch up, why I could not get a grip. I sank further into the bog of my mind, trapped there now and desperate. The end was very near.

It must surely have been this — detachment — that was the flaw. There used to be, I have read, such a thing as a fatal flaw, but that was long ago when a mistake, a missing part, could bring death, when the world was small enough that such things counted. It was my flaw that I could not come to grips. I could reach nothing, could fasten onto nothing. I could get only so far before I found fog, and I could never get beyond that. I might even have been comforted if I had thought that the flaw could lead to death, that it was truly fatal. That would have finished it, no need to be concerned. But this would never be fatal; it might even preserve me, untouched and therefore unscarred and therefore alive, if that can be called alive.

74

I needed belief: that was what I concluded. I needed to know something for certain. But it had to be real, I would not accept anything that tried to fool me, that was just part of the fog. I bogged down, exploring beliefs, in simplicity, in detachment, and if one got further than that, it faltered eventually in the mist through which my mind could not go.

What, after all, was there to believe in?

I remembered once believing in God. He was as real to me when I was a child as a member of my family. My parents, I remember, took God for granted and used Him effortlessly.

"Thank God that's done," my father would say, coming in sweating from mowing the lawn, reaching into the fridge for a beer.

"Thank God she's better," my mother would say, hearing of a successful operation on some friend or relative.

But it went much further than that. Somehow, and my memory would not tell me how this happened, God became doing right. And doing right was simply a matter of not doing wrong. It was right not to steal, right not to lie. God was an ethic and a negative. It was not, "God is love," but "God is not wrong." It might amount in action to the same thing. If one loved, then one would hardly do wrong, for wrong equalled a hurt to someone. But I learned only not to do wrong; I did not learn, or I never saw, the other half of the equation.

When I grew up, I discarded God without thought. God could not exist, for if He did, where was He, and what could He be thinking of? Surely if He were paying attention, I would feel His intensity, (for surely a God's attention would be intense), and I felt nothing.

There was a God in the back of my mind, but He was stunted and retarded; He had gone no further than my childhood and my childhood conception, and He would not meet me where I was now. He did not help, and He did not exist.

Love? Surely one must believe in love. There were so many songs that said so. People had turned from God to love, and it was a rule that one must love.

And I would weep, because now *I did not know what love was.* I could not recognize it. Tenderness, passion, protectiveness — all those I had had and had felt. But love? What was that, and how could I believe in it if I did not know

what it was? Perhaps the tenderness and passion and protectiveness were love — I had called them that, but how could I *know*?

I considered a belief in detachment, for that was most surely
what I had. But that was believing in absence; something that
had neither positive nor negative aspects, a zero, could surely
not be believed in.

I wanted faith. Faith was not a job or going back to school or
living with a man or holding children. Faith was — what? I
needed it.

It did not occur to me to believe in what I did, to believe in a
moment, and finally to lose belief and have just the moment. It
did not occur to me that each one was eternity, that I was
infinity, that beside my life everything else was pale, and that
my life was pale beside everything else. It never occurred to me
that it was all the same.

And so I drifted through the void, wanting out. I was
paralyzed, could not reach out a finger, much less leap the gap
of belief. And the fog closed in, closed in, over weeks, months,
until I could barely see, could make out only shapes, of my
children, my husband, the cashier at the supermarket, the
people on the streets. I smiled and smiled and made words, but I
could not even see myself, through the fog.

Such a thing, despite the words and smiles, could not be
hidden. For a while, yes, a depression, a vagueness, this would
be tolerable. But not this, and the life became punctuated by
Stephen, reaching through the mist, trying, always trying. "Is
something wrong, Abra?" he would ask, again and again. He
would offer his help when I could not answer. "Do you want
this? Would you like that?" I could not tell him. The last thing I
could believe in was the power of another person to give me
faith. Faith had to be in me somewhere. I could not abdicate it to
someone else, however tender and kind and good willing. I did
not realize then that that stubbornness was in itself a sign of a
strength in me, a signal of the end.

It was my struggle. I could hardly say to Stephen, "I want
faith." Where would that get me? Into another kindly, logical
discussion of alternatives?

What were the things he could not speak of to me? Did he
have faith, or did he not look for it, did he not care? Was it

possible not to care? I would have vaguely liked to know; knowing might bring us closer, might put a dent in my detachment. But I did not want it enough to reveal my own despair, to be vulnerable to his reason if he did not share it.

"Nothing's wrong, why?" I would say, turning to him brightly, blankly.

"I just thought you didn't look too well."

"Don't I?" Vaguely. "I feel all right. It's just the winter. It always gets me down."

"Maybe we should get in some vitamins. They'd probably be good for all of us."

"Good idea." Knowing I would never go out to buy them.

With variations we replayed that conversation again and again, while he probed gently, too gently, into what was happening.

"Well, what did you do today?" he would ask, all hearty and trying, just in the door from work.

"Not much. The laundry, dinner, you know."

"Feel like a movie tonight?"

"Not really. I'm kind of tired, and it doesn't look good outside."

He kept trying, little pinpricks in my life, and it exploded with the dinner party, because the idea was terrifying now, I was lost in my own despair and I did not think I could manage such an event. I was afraid, I think, that I might collapse under it, that it would be the one thing that would finally weigh me under. I don't know why that particular event, so normal, signalled such disaster to me then.

"Look Abra," Stephen said, almost pleading, trying to understand. "We've got to. It's our turn. I don't see why it's such a problem for just one evening. The cleaning woman can come in that day, and that woman who always cooks and her daughter, and all you'll have to do is get your hair done and put on a dress. It's just one night. Anyway, there's no choice; it's our turn."

But I was almost crazy with fear. I would have done anything to avoid it, and in my anguish, I did a terrible, hurting thing to Stephen.

"Look," I said, and my voice was trembling with anger, "I

don't give a shit whose turn it is. They're your friends, not mine, you need them, I don't, and I don't want them in my house any more. They're just make-believe people, they make me sick, being with them makes me sick, you make me sick, you're one of them." I listened to what I had said and was stunned.

Stephen's face was white, so very white, and it was he who looked frightened now, bewildered, wondering how we had reached this point without his knowing. I also hadn't known we were at this point, and suddenly I was unbearably sad, looking at this unhappy, gentle man who had done everything he could. And only asked such a little thing of me, my end of the bargain, so to speak, and I had turned on him.

"I'm sorry," I whispered. "I'm sorry. I didn't mean any of that. I'm so stupid, I don't know what's happening to me, I'm sorry." I was beside him now, my arms around him, pulling him toward me, and he was limp, hostile but not resisting. I cried for a few moments, my head on his shoulder, for I really did not know what was happening.

"We have to talk about it," he said quietly, at last. "Something's wrong, obviously, something's been wrong for a long time, and I can't tell what it is. What's the matter? What is it, Abra? I can help, I want to help, but you never tell me what it is. Can't you trust me to try?"

I shook my head, my mind gone into the fog without words, no explanations, no reasonings, not even the surface ones; because they were not real. I could say it was boredom, but it wasn't that, it wasn't really all this time I had. What could it mean to Stephen to say there was something happening far down where I couldn't reach, hadn't reached yet, that was simply wrong? It was the bald statement of something out of joint, but I couldn't explain what it meant.

I kept on shaking my head. "I don't know, Stephen, I feel as if I've been falling apart, I've been so tired. I don't know what to do." I looked at him, tried to be reassuring and strong. "But it will be all right. It's getting better now, everything will work out." I wanted him to believe that; I couldn't bear his concern. It was too heavy a burden.

I was grateful when he just nodded and hugged me, and later we made popcorn and watched television and made love on the couch, except that something in me was away from it, watching, judging, hiding, covering it all up, trying to be somewhere that I wasn't. And yet I still "loved" Stephen. I wanted to protect him, I wanted to be what he thought I was.

He could have said, "do you want to get a job," or "why don't you try going back to school," but he had the grace not to say either of those things, perhaps because he knew by then there was no point.

The next day, and the days after that, I tried, I really did. I straightened up the house and made large, elaborate meals. I was a whirlwind, laundering, dusting, even polishing the silver that we rarely used and was so very tarnished. I told Stephen we could reasonably plan the dinner party for two weeks away, to give everyone plenty of notice, and my days were suddenly full again. And yet, and yet, I was doing it all for Stephen, I felt I was making something up to him, but there was nothing in it for me.

I began to see it in that light: I owe it to them, but there is nothing in this for me. Surely an ordinary enough thought, and yet for me it was utterly foreign. I had never before separated myself from them like that, and it struck me, over and over, crashing inside my skull each time like a surprise.

The dinner party went well. I looked good, I worked all day at looking good, and I was pleasant and nothing went wrong, and Stephen was pleased. "That wasn't so bad, was it?" he said afterwards, his arm around my shoulders, all the guests gone and us in the living room getting ready to clean up the remains of the party.

"No," I said brightly, "it was fine. Everything went well, I think. It was just fine."

And it had been. I hadn't felt any different, was still observing, smiling and being gracious, and it was all the same. But then why was I so tired the next day, so that I stayed in bed and let Stephen get breakfast for the children and himself, sleeping on and on until noon, and then getting up, tired, and drinking coffee, getting dressed just before the children came home, feeling so terribly weary, interminably weary, with the sense that this feeling had been with me for all the time that I could remember, although I knew very well that at some time things had been different for me. But no one must see it, the children and Stephen must never see it again, because they depended on me, and so the grinding effort of energy began again late in the afternoon when they came home, and stayed with me until the evening was finished, Stephen finally tired himself. More and more the rhythms were out of joint.

7

I don't know how long after that it was when I saw the advertisement — many weeks, I suppose, since winter was just over. If I hadn't been so thorough about reading the newspaper, I would never have known about it. (Or would it have happened some other way? I cannot conceive of it not having happened.)

"Winterized cabin on seventy acres, stream and bush, suitable for vacation or hunting lodge," the ad said under "Out of Town Properties." It gave a name and a telephone number.

I saw it and felt a yearning, not even a verbal thought, just a sensation as if a thin string were pulling me toward — what?

I shook my head and didn't think about it again that day. I read the rest of the classifieds, then the comics, and then I washed my coffee mug and went to lie down again. My eyes hurt and the day was like all the others. I had given up trying to puzzle out why; I had given up trying to understand how to act against it.

The next morning, though, I remembered the ad and I read the rest of the paper with the feeling that toward the end there was something waiting for me, something to look forward to. The advertisement was still there: "Winterized cabin on seventy acres, stream and bush, suitable for vacation or hunting lodge. Call Mr. Chapman, 771-4893, Toronto."

"What harm would it do?" I thought. "It sounds interesting, I'm just curious, it doesn't mean anything." I wasn't sure just what I wanted to know, but the desire was strong enough to overcome the apathy, and that was something important and a relief. With an ease that astonished me, I picked up the phone and called the man.

"I read your ad in the paper," I said awkwardly. "I wanted to know something about the place."

He was apparently a busy man. He told me the facts swiftly, as if he'd memorized them from a list, and I had difficulty taking it all in.

The property, he said, was about a hundred and thirty miles northwest of Toronto. He wanted forty-four thousand dollars, which he said was a good price. Nothing grew but weeds and trees. The one actual field had not been cultivated for some years. There were deer, which would make it a satisfactory hunting retreat, but it wasn't good for much else. There was a small town not far away, but the place itself was off an old country gravel road.

Was I a hunter, he asked, amused. No, I said, I just thought it might be an interesting — second home. Suddenly I thought, "Yes, that's it, if we could afford it, it would be good for the kids and I to have another place to go in the summer, and Stephen too on his holidays, he doesn't hunt but still. . . ."

And that's what I was thinking when I agreed to go with Mr. Chapman two days later to see it. Irv, he said, call me Irv.

The knowledge of the place gave me an energy that carried me swiftly, easily, through those two days. I had an adventure to look forward to. I shopped and cooked and cleaned and listened to Elliott and Katie and Stephen, and I loved them. "You look wonderful," Stephen said hopefully.

I tried to tell myself the property might be nothing, that we couldn't afford it, or that Stephen would think it was a stupid idea. But those doubts weren't real, and the advertisement and the draw it had on me were. Something was out there waiting for me, I saw it clearly, there was no hesitation, and my heart was ahead in the time when Mr. Chapman-call-me-Irv and I would travel to this place. There wasn't even a picture of it in my mind; just an idea. It felt like something solid.

(I find it odd now, remembering who I was then, that I did not question that feeling.)

The property, Mr. Chapman told me in the car, had been left to him by his father, who had liked to go there in the fall to hunt, or perhaps just to escape. His father had died just a few months before; Mr. Chapman didn't hunt, didn't like the outdoors, and wanted to use the money to invest back into his dry cleaning business. He didn't want to sell through a real estate agency because he didn't want to have to pay a commission; he figured that with a lot of people "flush", as he called it, and wanting to get away from the city periodically, there might be a market for it. He himself couldn't be less interested.

"I'd be bored stiff," he said. "My father used to take me up there sometimes, but I couldn't take it. Drove me stir crazy, nothing but trees and birds. I couldn't sleep. And there wasn't anything to do up there. My father killed things, that was his entertainment, but I don't want to do that. Why the hell he left it to me, when I couldn't have cared less and he knew it, I'll never understand. He must have known I'd want to sell, so I guess he didn't care any more."

He was thin, this Mr. Chapman, with graying hair, early fifties probably, I decided, sharp-featured and gentle-voiced. I could see that he was not a hunter, and his skin was the same kind of gray as my own, a city-dweller's skin. He had a pleasant, warm voice, but tired; he had little hope that this trip would produce anything for him, thought it was a day wasted from a life that had no time to waste. For as he pointed out, even if I liked the place I would have to talk to my husband about it, and we would have to take the trip again.

He warned me about it. "The thing is," he said, "you shouldn't expect too much. It was only my father who was ever interested in it, and he didn't keep it up all that well. It was just a place he went to to get away, and he didn't care much what it looked like. I haven't seen it myself for a while, but the last time I was up the inside needed a lot of work. Outside — well, really there's no point. It's not good farm land, it's all rocky, that area, and there's just the woods and a small pasture and a stream and the area around the cabin, which is mostly just bushes and weeds. Except there's a big willow by the cabin. As I said in the ad, it is winterized, there'd be no problems there, because my dad did like his comforts. There's a fridge and stove there already, they've always worked, and a big kitchen. The other rooms are a pretty good size, too, and the plumbing is all modern. I wouldn't want you to expect too much, though, it's an old place. And it's pretty far back from the road, and even the road is pretty far back from the main route that goes into town."

He started to laugh at himself, a kind of heaving that caught in his throat and turned into a cough.

"You're going to think I don't really want to sell it, the way I'm talking. Maybe I should have turned it over to a real estate type — it sure doesn't sound like I'm much of a salesman. Actually it's a great place if you like that sort of thing."

"It's all right," I said. I was watching out the car windows, seeing how the countryside changed as we went along, driving fast over the expressway past small cities that might be so much like the one where I had grown up, the kinds of cities I dislike from memory.

I smiled at him. "If you were a real salesman, I likely wouldn't believe what you said. We'll wait and see. Even if it isn't in really good shape, we might still be interested. It'd only be a retreat away from the city. Although the price . . ." I left that hanging, doubt in my tone, because I really didn't know if we could afford it. And I was wondering now if Stephen would agree that we should buy a place so far away, so expensive for a piece of useless land and a cabin that needed work, when we had specifically bought the city house to give us space and freedom enough.

"Well, maybe we could talk about the price again after you've seen it," Mr. Chapman said. "And after you see what your husband's got to say. I'll tell you the truth, it's a bargaining price, it's not a solid one. It'll take some discussing."

We curled off the expressway and onto a more rural highway. The towns here were smaller, but no more attractive to me than the little cities we had been passing. I knew these places, too, from far back in childhood.

We made more turns. I had lost track of where we were, would have to ask Mr. Chapman for directions if Stephen and I were to come up, until finally we turned onto a narrow gravel road with deep ditches at each side, flowing heavily with the water of early spring. It seemed instantly very quiet, as if the trees and bushes and water overpowered the sound of the car. It was a kind of tunnel, this road shrouded by the trees, and I was startled when we met another car a little distance along and Mr. Chapman had to ease far over to the right to let it edge by.

"Just a few farmers up this way," he said, "cattle pretty well, there's not much else to be done with land like this. It's poor country, nobody makes more than just enough to get by. They're all small farmers; it'll all be gone one of these days, not for development for a while yet, but most likely to people like yourselves, wanting to get away from the city. There's no point in most of these old guys hanging on, there's nobody to take over the farms from them, nobody wants to live like that any more.

"I tell you, if you think about it, farmers are bigger gamblers than anybody who goes off to Vegas. There's this guy my dad used to know up here, used to come over and visit now and then, and I tell you, he'd be buying spring stock and he'd graze them over the summer and hope the prices went up for when he sold them in the fall; had to sell them in the fall, couldn't afford to winter them because he couldn't grow enough feed on his place, and sometimes the prices would be 'way down and he'd lose thousands of dollars, no choice, just a gamble every spring on what would be happening with prices six or eight months ahead."

He shook his head. "Those guys, they never win. They don't have any chance at all. Just keep gambling and losing, gambling and winning, and when they win it's hardly enough to make up for the losses. Nobody up here knows what it's like to be out of debt, they must owe thousands most of the time, and they've gotta know there's no way they'll ever get out of it. It's a remarkable thing, what they do."

He had stopped the car and was looking at me. "But you won't have to worry about any of that," he said. "We're here. I'd rather walk up the lane if you don't mind, it's a little tricky driving, especially in the spring when the ditches tend to flood. It's not so far."

"Of course," I said. "That's fine."

I wasn't in a hurry now, was in fact grateful for the chance to walk, to see gradually this — whatever it was that had been pulling at me. I was also a little apprehensive, afraid almost, wishing I had left it as a dream.

Walking up the lane, it was as if I were being inhaled by it, the trees beside it were enclosing me, drawing me up, and if, like Lot's wife, I had looked back, I felt I might see them in a semi-circle behind me, closing off the way back, holding me there. There were birds and squirrels, I could hear them all, and yet it was the most silent place I could remember.

The sensation grew stronger as we walked on, but I could not identify what it was, not yet, until we reached the top of the lane and ahead of us was a space, a small piece of land, with just bushes and weeds, and beyond that an enormous willow hanging heavily over a gray stone cabin; it seemed to me, from that perspective, that the tree was protecting the cabin, and the cabin itself was small and solid-looking. Two of its windows were broken, and I felt as if I must be a different person, seeing this, feeling suddenly — what was it? I searched, looking for a name for it — wanted? New? Feeling that this was home.

This was the ending, here. Like driving head-on into a brick wall, knowing it was over, reduced to the core of person that does not think or know, no chance given for regret or sorrow or second thoughts, in the brilliant last moment. The landscape whirled and beckoned and I was whirling too, light-headed and out of myself, and Abra was dying then, although she did not know it.

Mr. Chapman's hand was on my elbow, guiding me into, through the cabin, and he was careful to show me all the points that would need repair, all the places where work would have to be done. But I barely heard him. When he suggested we walk around the property, I almost refused. I wanted just to be there, to sit down in what would be the living room, in front of the dead fireplace, just sit on the floor and never leave. There was nothing I had ever felt before to guide me. This was my home.

But Mr. Chapman's voice grew louder, more insistent, it penetrated and when I looked at him I saw his face was nervous, wondering. I must look strange to him, I thought, and some of the Abra who did not want to cause worry returned. I gave in and followed him outside, and we went for a walk, out to where the pasture meets the woods, so that I would see the fall of the

86

property and understand its boundaries and what it contained. The land, yes, it held me too, but it was the cabin that was truly my own, and when we returned to it I told Mr. Chapman that I wanted to go back in, to think about it for just a few minutes, and if he wanted to start back down the lane to the car, I would catch up shortly. My voice seemed to be coming from far away, saying what was necessary, but everything must have appeared all right to him because he gave me the key and asked me to lock up when I left.

I was inside. The counters, all in natural wood, I felt them, unfinished but without splinters, smooth, solid, the kitchen large and warm. Through the low, brief passage to the living room; the fireplace, bare peeling walls, work to be done, yes, and a breeze coming through the broken window panes; and into the bedroom, peeling also but plain and the window looking up into the willow, how good, I thought, to wake up and know the willow is keeping watch, everything shabby, and me wanting to just stay, to curl up in it until I absorbed it or it absorbed me, this odd peace that was not peaceful, no memories, no bars, just a holding. The house belonged to me, it was right, and nothing could matter beside that. And the smell of spring, of rushing water and greening things, I hadn't known about any of this before, and yet here it was, part of me, so that there was no confusion, and I wanted to lie down in front of the fireplace and just be left.

I stayed there for a long time before the old part emerged again, the practical one that reminded me that someone was waiting, that I had to make a decision, had to get home. Except that it wasn't home, and why did I have to go there? Because the children would be getting back from school, and Stephen would be coming from work, but it seemed like another lifetime, someone else's life that involved all those people, and why shouldn't I stay here when this was mine? But no, of course I couldn't, I had to go back; so I stood and walked again through the kitchen to the door, and opened it and held the padlock. I looked around and it was all still there. "I'm coming back," I whispered, a secret, and then shut the lock, turned away and walked strongly down the lane.

The confusion came on the way home. As we drove away

from it, the cabin and what had happened there became less real — less good? I felt unhappy now, torn, and worried too by the effect the place had had. It hadn't frightened me then but now it did, and I thought, "I mustn't ever go back." It was terrifying that it had been so vivid.

But returning to the city repulsed me. Suddenly I was hating, really violently hating, the idea of seeing Elliott and Katie, of greeting Stephen, of being what they wanted, of having to hug and comfort and listen to them; and then I was feeling faint, I couldn't make any of it fit together, something had happened and I couldn't put it in its place. Something radical had broken, and I could not get back to the old way.

I was chilled, shivering when that came. I could not get back to the old way, and what did that mean? It meant it was over; there had been no decision. We stopped in front of the house and I looked at it and could not bear it. "Well?" said Mr. Chapman. "What do you think?"

"Please," I said, turning to him, begging, "let me call you tomorrow. Please don't show it to anybody else. I just want a chance to sort things out, if I can call you tomorrow?"

"Sure," he said. "I'll be at work. You've got the number." He smiled. "Nobody's going to see it before tomorrow, that's for sure. That's a long drive, and I don't think I'm up to a return trip that quick. You just talk it over with your husband, see what he thinks, and give me a call. If he wants to look at it, I'll see you get a key so you can go up on your own. I hope you take it, I'd like to get it off my mind."

I was just taking off my sweater when the children got home. I wanted to cling to what was not strange, but it was not possible. I hugged them, asked about their days at school, but I wasn't listening; I looked at them.

Where had they come from? What did I have to do with them, or they with me? I felt a moment's rebellion against these people who had come to me, who took so much, who had taken something I didn't even know I had. And then the rebellion faded, and they faded too. It wasn't right to blame them; it was not them. They were like the dinner parties, where I had watched and nodded and smiled, but as if I were seeing it all through gauze, detached, slightly away from all of it. That was how they were to me, Elliott and Katie, excited, pink-faced, talking simultaneously, sharing their day with me, except that I wasn't there, I watched them but I wasn't there. I heard their sounds, I saw their faces, but they were remote, not objects of my caring. There was nothing. I knew that it was wrong, that something had happened to me that was making my vision of them wrong; and I hugged them both again, wanting touch to make them real, but it didn't work.

And it didn't work later, when Stephen came home and there was the same sense of displacement, and it stayed with me, while I watched them all, played with them and talked to them until, one at a time, they went to bed. I told Stephen I wasn't tired; I sat up very late in front of the fireplace that was so different, more ornate, less functional, than the one I had sat before earlier in the day, and tried to understand.

Was it escape I saw? I did not think so. Or if it was, it was not so much escape from this life, although I was dead in it, as an escape to something. Filled now with life, a sense of purity and, at last, belief, I could no longer quite recall the emptiness of yesterday. I was a different person. But still there were the ties of past life, the remembrance of duty, the words that said that whatever I might want, I was responsible to these people I had created, and that duty must rank above desire.

But desire was not the right word. Can duty rank above love? For surely, if anything was, this was love. And can it overcome compulsion and obsession? Surely duty has no strength against that.

The picture of the cabin as I had first seen it, at the end of that lane, with the willow leaning over it, was in me and the confusion disappeared and I was certain. And then I came back and saw this living room, this one I was in now, and I could see the children upstairs, asleep, Stephen upstairs also, sitting up in bed, his glasses hanging low on his nose, reading, waiting for me to get tired and come to bed, and I did not know any more. The pattern switched back and forth through an infinite night, long past the time when Stephen must have stopped waiting and gone to sleep: the flash of the cabin and knowing; the picture of this house and these people, and instantly the turmoil again, the guilt, the needs, the ties, the memory of loving. Back and forth it went, back and forth until I couldn't bear the upheaval, the comfort was with the cabin, that was where I was.

And then the choice was finished, there was no confusion, there had been no choice. There were things to be done, arrangements to be made, very practical things, but the image of the cabin stayed and it must be managed.

I felt very loving then, as if I were dying almost, and I went upstairs and stopped in the rooms where the children slept, making sure they were covered, and then I went to Stephen, who woke up when he felt my weight on the bed, and we made love and I was there, with him, but it was as if I were saying good-bye, a mournful kind of loving.

It was the last time; things moved very quickly after that.

8

There was no question, then, of saying anything to Stephen. My excuse for going to see the place, the idea that we might use it as a retreat, was gone. It was not to be shared. It was a private vision, and just the sound, the presence of these people, any people, might take it away; it could be frightened, would make itself a secret again, and I would not find it with them.

For my own sake, too, I could not talk of what I planned. In telling it, I would lose it. And in any case I would not find the words, Stephen would not let me get away. He would surround me, want to "help" and prevent my escape. He would have to do that because he was a good man, and he could not see with my eyes.

And I could not see, in truth, that I owed it to him to explain. I think that was because I no longer saw him; after all this time what I had assumed was real about my life had turned out to be a mask and a charade, a play in which I performed, admirably on rare occasions, but without truth. It was not his fault; it was no one's fault, not even my own, as far as I could see. I had been confused, too willing, without purpose, but now I was filled with strength. No, it was never Stephen's fault; it had nothing to do with him. Nothing had anything to do with him, although he would not be able to understand that, and so it was best not to explain.

I was impatient; I wanted to be gone, out of this baffling place where the children and Stephen were just shadows, demanding that I be one of them when I could not. The cabin and the land were in me now, the confusion gone. The vision was both pastel and vivid, a lingering impression, stark and comforting. The place seemed to me to have great strength, and I borrowed on that so that I was strong too, and very practical and efficient.

I called Mr. Chapman as soon as everyone had gone the next morning. I kissed them all and wished them to have a good day, the way I always did, and none of them seemed to notice. The newspaper lay on the table where Stephen had left it after breakfast, but I didn't need it any more; I put it in the garbage, cleared away the breakfast dishes and went to the telephone. It was not so difficult, I thought, using it. Or being devious in the cause of something needed. I was hard, because nothing must go wrong.

"It's Abra Phillips, Mr. Chapman," I said. I could hear a dim clatter of machinery in the background, and thought of him at his desk, gray and thin, working to show a profit in his dry cleaning business. "You showed me the cabin property yesterday. I'm interested, but I think we should talk about price." My voice was steady, brisk. I knew what I was doing now.

"You mean your husband's seen it already?" He was surprised.

"No, he hasn't, but he said he'd accept my judgement. He suggested I handle it and put it in my name." This was the weak area, where I had to lie because I was vulnerable. A woman trying to do business on her own would be doubted and checked; I wanted to imply that Stephen was involved, and then I hurried past the point.

"It's the price that's bothering us, and if we're going to buy, I'd like to get it settled as soon as possible. Holidays are coming up, and we'd like to get some use out of it."

"Well, we can talk about it. What sort of price did you have in mind?" He sounded amenable, easy to handle. Because I was strong.

"Frankly, I can't see that it's worth more than thirty-eight, especially considering the repairs that are going to have to be done. I'd offer you that, but I think I've got a better deal than that for you. If you'll come down to thirty-six we'll give you cash. Total payment immediately."

I was capable, almost cunning. I did not know where this instinct for dealing with money had come from, but I felt certain I was handling it well. The lure of cash in his position would be strong and I did not think he would turn me down.

"Let me think it over," he said. "I'll call you back later today."

I called the bank and asked for the manager.

Grandmother's money, the money I had inherited, the money set aside for our children, was in a separate account in my name, untouched over the years, gathering interest and dust. It must be worth now a good deal more than it had been thirteen years before when it became mine, I thought.

"Let's see," the manager said, "just give me a moment to look that up." He went away for a while and left me on hold. "It's not dead accurate," he said when he came back, "we can figure it out to the penny if you want, but roughly you've got sixty-seven thousand in there now. Were you thinking of investing it?" His voice was hopeful; he'd suggested many times that we invest it, it was going to waste sitting there gathering a normal interest rate, he always said.

"No, I wasn't. I'm withdrawing it, probably tomorrow, and I'd like the whole thing calculated."

He sounded concerned. "Was there something we did wrong? Were you going to deposit it somewhere else?"

"Not at all," I said firmly. "There's no problem. It's just that there's something we want to buy, and we want to do it with cash. I hope it isn't difficult to arrange the withdrawal, we'd like to get it done as soon as possible."

Again I deliberately said "we," knowing that if he assumed it was a decision Stephen and I had reached together, I might be able to deal with the situation without complications; if he thought I was doing it on my own, he might very well call Stephen, and then my plans would fall apart. Bank managers then, maybe now too, never really thought a woman could handle large sums of money, even if it were her own money. I didn't want any risks.

"I'll be down to pick it up tomorrow," I said. "Stephen's tied up, so I'll have to deal with it. Do you think that's time enough?''

"Certainly," he said, puzzled. "It'll be no problem tying off the account." He hesitated. "Is there anything I can help you with? Any financial advice or anything of that nature?''

"No," I said politely, "I think we've got everything worked out. I'll likely be in the bank about, oh, eleven-thirty tomorrow. Is that too early?''

"It'll be fine. We'll get everything prepared this afternoon; you'll just have to sign a few things. How would you like the money?''

"Cash. In hundreds, I guess." I wanted everything simple, straightforward, and I wanted to leave no traces, no cheques, no transfers of the account.

"Cash!" He was shocked. "You can't go walking around carrying sixty-seven thousand in cash. That's dangerous." There was a pause. "Why don't you leave the account open and pay for whatever it is with a certified cheque?''

"No, it's all right, I won't have it long. Please don't worry about it, we've figured everything out and a cheque won't do. I'll be by in the morning. Thank you for your trouble." I replaced the receiver gently and prayed that he wouldn't think it necessary to call Stephen and protest. Perhaps, and I giggled, he would think I was being blackmailed and would be discreet. Equally, he might be outraged and want to check. It was the largest chance I was taking; I waited tensely by the phone, but nothing happened, there were no calls from Stephen, so I guessed that for whatever reason, the manager had decided it was simpler to do what he was told.

I sat down to work out a budget. If I could get the place at thirty-six or thirty-eight, I would have about thirty thousand left. Assuming a very simple lifestyle, it should last me for a long time. But I knew it had to be for good.

There was no other money. I had no insurance policies that could be cashed in without Stephen's knowledge. I would have to accept what I had, take what I could, and simply hope that it worked out. I made lists of things I would need: pots and pans, food, fuses, paint, furniture, curtains, towels, toothpaste — everything I could think of. Much of it I would buy in the little

94

town near the place; basic things to get me started I would take from here.

I burned the budgets in the fireplace.

The memories are clear in me now. Everything that day was very sharp, and I was deadly calm. I knew exactly what I was doing; I knew I needed to be at that place I had seen, it was urgent and necessary, and I did what I had to.

The children came home from school; Mr. Chapman still hadn't called back, but I was not concerned. I knew nothing would go wrong, not now. It was something inevitable, there was not a question about it.

Katie and Elliott were not hazy now, as they had been earlier. But still I was far away, I could see them and they were sharp and distinct, but at a great distance. I watched them, assessed with absolute detachment what I was doing. I was their mother and I was deserting them. I was taking the money that would have been theirs. There were no justifications, no reasonings and no guilt; they failed to move me.

I carried on normally. I let them help me prepare dinner. I promised that later we would make cookies. When the telephone rang we were all in the kitchen, and I warned them to stay away from the stove while I was out of the room. I did not wonder who would warn them after I was gone.

"Mrs. Phillips?" The voice was Mr. Chapman's, and it sounded relieved, as if the decision had come clear for him also. "I've decided to go pretty well for your cash offer. Except that I don't want to drop quite that far. I'll take thirty-seven cash, but I can't go any lower."

The bargaining was over, and we were both satisfied. "Fine," I said briskly. "How soon can you draw up a sale agreement?"

"Actually," he said sheepishly, "I thought you'd probably go for it, so I talked to my lawyer today. I hope you don't mind. I can call him at home tonight so he can get it finished. I just wanted to be clear that you and your husband want it in your name, not joint."

"That's right. It's to be in my name only. Tax reasons. Can we get together to sign the papers and turn over the money tomorrow?"

"Good God, you folks work fast, don't you? I've never seen

people make up their minds like that. Sure, I guess so. I'll call the lawyer tonight and see, and then I'll let you know."

Stephen would soon be home, and I didn't want Mr. Chapman calling back. "I'm afraid we'll be out this evening. How be you find out tonight and set a time for tomorrow afternoon when we can get together. I'll call you in the morning and find out what you've arranged. Any time after noon is fine with me. I have a car so you can pick any place you want. I'll have the money for you by then, all of it. I'll give you a call about nine tomorrow."

And that was all it took. Stephen walked in a few minutes later and found Katie and Elliott and me in the kitchen. They were arguing about what to put in the salad I'd set them to making. Katie wanted cheese, Elliott said cheese was a dumb thing to put in a salad. They turned to Stephen for arbitration, and he voted with Katie. I watched him.

I saw him, tall, strong-featured, with traces now of graying hair, discussing the salad issue with mock seriousness, a forefinger on his chin. The children loved him for taking them seriously. "They make a nice family," I thought. I didn't see myself in it, not any more, and I wondered if I ever had, when I had watched them before. Maybe I'd always been standing off to one side, admiring the complete family that didn't include me.

But no, that wasn't true; once I had been among them, in my way, and that had changed.

Katie and Elliott went outside; Fletcher needed exercising, and I could hear them, arguing over whose turn it was to run with him today. Stephen leaned out the door and suggested they both take him, leave him off the leash for once and just let him go, only stay close to him; with both of them, he said, it should be all right. His talent for keeping them happy amazed me.

The two of us were left alone together in the kitchen. He sat down at the table, watching me peel the potatoes; it made me nervous, being watched.

"How was your day," I asked, to divert him. "Anything interesting?"

"Not really, it was fairly good, normal, I guess." I looked at him; I wondered if he ever got tired, or felt that maybe he belonged somewhere else. He must, I thought. Or maybe not;

maybe he was the way I had been once. Maybe he didn't know the difference. It wasn't fair, when he tried so hard, but still there was no regret.

"There's going to be another dinner," he said hesitantly. "Two weeks. Ray Johnston. It's okay to say we'll go?" He looked at me, wary still, afraid I might make another scene. But he didn't know it didn't matter, wouldn't even have mattered if I hadn't been leaving. I would have agreed.

"Sure," I said confidently. "No problem." He looked relieved.

I didn't want to spend the evening just with Stephen, not tonight with the strain of so many secrets. I wanted to suggest we go to a movie, anything to be away from conversation, but that would be cowardly. I had to be able to look directly at what I was doing. I would be stern with myself, and be certain. And, too, I think I wished almost to feel some kind of regret, or guilt, or something — anything. I wanted to have every opportunity for that. It was odd to be so cold.

The children were noisy at dinner, and I was grateful. They told Stephen about school, and he listened. After dinner the three of them went into the den to watch the news on television; it was another thing they shared, started early. Stephen wanted them to be interested in what was going on in the world, and they were proud that he thought them grown-up enough to understand. Sometimes, before, I had been afraid that they would understand too much, would see all the death, and that it wouldn't matter to them after a while. But Stephen talked with them about what they saw, how sad and painful it was, and how he wished we could make it better for other people, and I think they listened to him. He also told them that what they saw wasn't all there was, that there were kind and good things, too, that were not news. They seemed to know what he meant, and tried, like him, to be good.

I could hear them telling him we would be making cookies after I got the dinner dishes done. Alone in the kitchen, I watched the dishes as I washed them, blue patterned, figures of people and woods, tried to make myself feel sadness that I would not see these figures many more times — testing still — but there was no sadness. There was nothing. A vacuum where the past and the things I had loved, once, had been.

Soon, too soon, Katie and Elliott were in the kitchen asking about the cookies. Stephen would help too, they decided. The four of us must have had fun that evening, because there was much laughter, even from me. I felt grateful that it should be ending like this, with pleasure. I wondered if they would miss me; yes, of course they would, that was stupid. But they would still have Stephen, who was too solid to go away, even if he found the place to go, and that was important. I was the one who had always been there for them, always available; but I think they felt closer to him. They would come to me with a problem, hoping I would be able to solve it; but they could talk to Stephen about how the problem made them feel, which was a much deeper thing. It didn't matter.

Would Stephen miss me? Very likely more than the children. What damage would I do to him? He would be bewildered, wonder what he had done wrong, and I wished for a way to tell him that there was no wrong involved. But he would have to try to understand by himself; there was nothing I could explain.

I was laughing with them; we would have just one more evening together. The children went to bed early, and Stephen and I followed shortly after. It had been a good day, he said. It was good to come home to his family and see that it was all worthwhile. (I wondered if he thought he did it "all" for us.) I think when he said "family", he was thinking more of the children, for he had had to make such an effort with me, the last couple of years had been hard for him, too; he handled me with such delicacy now, realizing that there was unhappiness, some fragility between us. He could hardly know that all that was gone now, that we were two people together and I was seeing him, not as an equal, for that implies a relationship, but almost as a stranger, a person who was in my life and whose presence I couldn't properly explain. I knew there must have been closeness and caring, that there had been two of us, but now there was just one and that was me. We were too tired to make love, or whatever I would have called it then.

What happened in me was like a slow-forming concrete, growing gradually harder, so that by breakfast it seemed there was no feeling whatever left for the three people with whom I talked and laughed. They were old, in the past, like dead people brought back to memory, so that I could recall how I had behaved with them, but there was no presence in it, no sense of reality. As soon as they had gone, I called Mr. Chapman, who said we could meet at his lawyer's office at two-thirty.

I did the breakfast dishes and vacuumed the main rooms, out of some confused wish to leave things finished, both for them and for me. I called the cleaning lady, because I thought it was right, until Stephen made other arrangements, to have her come in twice a week after I was gone. She sounded pleased by the idea of extra money.

I showered, put on a dress and nylons, and wore my spring coat that was beige with threading of light blue. I locked the door behind me, leaving Fletcher tied up in the backyard. I felt impatient at something that was past due. Tomorrow, tomorrow first thing. . . .

At the bank, the manager wanted to talk to me, wouldn't let me get it over with quietly, still trying to persuade me to withdraw the money in some other way than cash. I was adamant and annoyed; so much was in the way, when everything was already settled, and I was full of restlessness.

I separated thirty-seven thousand dollars from the rest, shoved the money into two large brown envelopes the manager gave me. All but two hundred of the rest I put into another envelope, and I had the two hundred broken down into smaller bills and put that in my purse. The manager sent a messenger next door to buy me a small briefcase. When I left he was still worried.

I went back to the car, put the briefcase under a mat in the trunk and locked it. It was noon, lunchtime, but I wasn't hungry. I drove instead to a supermarket, not one I usually went to, and began to stock up. It was food mostly, canned goods and meats and bread. The air was cool enough, I thought, that none of it would spoil in the trunk of the car overnight. I also bought a pail, a mop, a broom and dustpan, some floor cleaner and wax, soap and toothpaste, and a new toothbrush for my new start. In all I spent more than eighty dollars and had enough food for a couple of weeks. I would spend more, tomorrow or the next day, in the little town near the cabin, where there would be paint and ladders and hopefully some old furniture. I felt desperately eager to be going, for it to be completed; I had to keep reminding myself that it would take time; I must learn to be patient, to make no mistakes, leave no gaps. To finish everything here.

It was time to find the lawyer's office. After that, the place, so vivid in my mind, would be mine and freedom would be so close. I tried to be calm, but I could feel my body trying to push ahead the time, the blood rushing, the muscles quick and tense; I forced myself to breathe slowly, to let the muscles relax, but then there would be a surprised surge of excitement and it would all begin again.

(I don't think I could feel that way now. I've learned, I hope, but I knew so little then.)

I parked the car and went around to the trunk. Under all the groceries and underneath the mat was the briefcase. I pulled out the two envelopes that held the thirty-seven thousand dollars, relocked the trunk and went into a low building that seemed a little shabby, a little failed. The lawyer's office was on the second floor, and I was surprised when I reached it, for I didn't know that lawyers still had such places; I pictured them all with brightness and modern furniture and strategically-placed plants and woven drapes. This was very old, dark and dusty with small windows and venetian blinds, ancient, chaotic-looking files sprawled on desks, and an old-fashioned wooden railing instead of a counter, with a swinging gate through which I was admitted.

The lawyer resembled Mr. Chapman. I wondered if they might be brothers, but the names were different, and it must just have been their grayness that made them seem similar. "Mrs. Phillips?" he asked.

"Yes, I'm here to see you and Mr. Chapman."

"Right this way, you're very punctual. Irv isn't here yet but he should be shortly. Meanwhile maybe you'd like to look over the papers I've drawn up? I understand you're paying cash?"

"That's right."

"Literally cash?" he asked, eyeing the envelopes.

"That's right."

A pause.

"Oh. I assume you'll want your own lawyer to go over the documents before we finalize everything?"

I hadn't thought of that; I looked for a way out that would not make him suspicious, cause delays.

"Our lawyer is out of town at the moment, and we want to get this finished up as quickly as possible. We did locate him by telephone, and he told me what to look for. Maybe if I could take a look at the papers now. . . ."

"Certainly, please come this way." He led me into a small, even darker office with a heavy desk, a wooden swivel chair for him, a straight-backed chair for me, and rows of undusted law texts on undusted shelves behind him. He handed me a file, and I started to read.

It couldn't have been simpler. It was just a transfer of ownership, including the deed, no mortgage, no interest rates, the boundaries of the property all outlined and guaranteed in a surveyor's report, and a short list of what went with the place, including the fridge and stove.

"It seems clear enough," I was saying when Mr. Chapman appeared at the gate in the outer office. "He's here now," I told the lawyer.

He was fifteen minutes late. I kept checking my watch, concerned that I should be back before the children got home from school. If I could no longer offer them love, I could at least be punctual, I thought.

"I've had a look at the papers," I said. "Everything seems to be in order. I've got the money here," and I indicated the brown envelopes, "so let's just sign these things and get everything wrapped up."

Both of them seemed stunned when I handed over the money. They counted it out in piles of ten hundreds each, and I think neither of them could have seen so much cash in one place before. They stared at it. I hadn't seen anything like it before either, but it didn't matter to me; it was nothing but a means.

I didn't get away until almost four o'clock, by which time I was irrationally furious with them for the delay. It meant the children were already home by the time I got there. I hugged them and listened to them, gave them all my attention, and when Stephen came home I was exhausted. I had to be so careful to give no sign that tomorrow would be different.

I told them I planned to go shopping the next afternoon; I would telephone the woman next door to see if it was all right for them to stay with her until I got home. "It's nice to see you getting out," Stephen said quietly, and the sadness, the hope of that came the closest of anything that night to making me cry.

I slept badly. I made an effort not to think about the cabin and the future. It was the last night, and it had a kind of symbolism, a hangover from old ways. I felt I must try to remember it all, feel it all, so that everything would be heightened and excited. It was as if I should cling to the mattress, make it special after all these years of sleeping on it and making love on it, and that it should be the same for every thing that was in the house. Except the people. I had already made my farewells to them.

(It seems to me now that there was a great deal of false sentiment in that night; false because I was trying to make myself feel what I thought I ought to, what I thought was normal, instead of accepting that I could not feel any sadness for it at all.)

The next morning was the last time. I kissed each of them as they left and wished them a good day.

When they were gone, I washed the breakfast dishes and made all the beds. It still seemed important to leave everything the way it ought to be; I wanted them to find themselves starting fresh, and I wanted myself to leave nothing behind, uncompleted.

I prepared a dinner and put it in the refrigerator, so that it would only have to be heated. Then I began to pack.

I sorted carefully through my clothes, kept only those that would be serviceable and practical, bunched the rest, all my long dresses and fancy shoes, into garbage bags, loaded them into the car and dropped them off in a Salvation Army box near the house. I felt, when I pushed them through the slot, that I was finally making some progress, becoming unburdened at last.

I took exactly half the pots and pans, three settings of old dishes and silverware we never used, and three mugs. Everything was wrapped in the four sheets and six towels I was taking, and I found boxes in the garage for them. I drove my car into the garage and loaded it there.

I thought of a clock, the little travelling alarm that Stephen had, and was discouraged by the idea. How tired I was of time, schedules, I thought. How much freedom there could be in leaving time behind. And the mirror, I could have taken the one from the hall outside the bathroom, but that was like the dresses and the shoes, a burden of appearances and past use. So quickly, so instinctively, I made the choice, not knowing what it meant.

I went back into the house and took a final look around; everything seemed to be in order, nothing out of place. It was all very tidy, very clean, gleaming, right — and empty. There was only the note left; it was the last act.

"Dear Stephen," I wrote. "I know you will be shocked, and I'm sorry I can't help that. I hope you won't be too hurt, and most of all I hope that you won't take this as your fault. I am leaving and I won't be back. There is no other man or anything like that; I just want to be on my own. I have bought a place for myself with the money from Grandmother's trust fund. Please don't try to find me; I want to be left alone. The children are next door, waiting for one of us to pick them up. It will have to be you. Dinner is in the refrigerator. Please try to explain to them that it's not their fault, and that it has nothing to do with them or with you; no one could have been more understanding or more gentle. I wish I could explain it to you, but I can't. Abra."

It was clumsy, I thought. But each sentence had been an effort, and I could not bear to try again; the note said all that there was to be said, and it was pathetically little. I folded it over, wrote Stephen's name on the outside and propped it against the salt and pepper shakers on the kitchen table, facing the doorway. He would see it as soon as he came in.

I thought a moment of Fletcher, of taking him with me; but I couldn't do that, it was not right to take a companion. I wondered if I would be lonely, if I should be afraid, but I couldn't make myself feel fear, any more than sadness. I tied Fletcher in the back yard.

It was over. Everything was done. All that was left was to leave.

I looked around once more, turned away and walked out the side door. I locked it behind me, then took my house key and pushed it back under the door. Now I had just my car keys and the key to the padlock on the cabin. I opened the garage door, started the car and backed out the driveway into the street. I had to get out again to close the garage, then I went back to the car and looked once more.

Already the house seemed vacant. But still it was a safe place, familiar, and for the second time I felt a little like crying. I wanted, for a moment, to run back to it; the cabin was not real, but this house was, it was so close, and I opened the car door but I couldn't move. It was over, it was only safety, not belonging.

I drove away then. I didn't look back, not even a glance through the rear-view mirror. I drove an extra block to avoid going past the school where the children were waiting for the time when they could go home, except that today they wouldn't be going home but next door, expecting me to arrive to pick them up, but instead, later, Stephen would come for them and he would be pale and upset. He would take them home and they would ask where I was and he would have to explain to them somehow, something that he couldn't possibly understand himself. I felt — sorry, I supposed.

I turned onto the expressway and was on my way.

Stephen would find another woman, a good woman I hoped. There was no pain in thinking that. Katie and Elliott would grow up, they were half-way there already; I had done what I could, and that, too, must have scarred them. I was not trying to make it sound right; there was no need to justify what I was doing.

The miles ticked on and as I took myself physically farther away, the past became more and more remote, the people more and more ghost-like. It was still early afternoon. I wondered whether I should drive directly to the cabin, or stop in town and pick up the rest of the things I would need. It would be best, I thought, to stop. That way the next day would be without chores, and it would be the real beginning.

It was four o'clock when I got to the town. I saw the time on the town hall clock, and wondered how I would ever manage, not knowing from now on.

The children would be leaving school, but I wasn't thinking of that; the distance had moved me too far. I found a hardware store and bought a step-ladder and fuses. I went down the street to a furniture store and bought a mattress, which I had them tie onto the top of my car. It would do for a bed, until I was settled properly. I also bought a small freezer and ordered it delivered to the cabin; it would be necessary to store food in bulk, I knew, and I had no intention of doing it the hard way, in the ground. I paid in cash and they promised to bring it to me the next day. I told them to be careful on the lane.

It was late, almost six, when I had bought enough to get me started. I set out for the cabin then, tired from the day and the duties. The cabin was pulling at me, I wanted to be in it, but something else had kept me back, wanting everything to be ready. The country roads enclosed me.

I drove very cautiously up the lane. The car was badly overloaded, and I didn't know what I would do if it slipped into one of the ditches, now almost overflowing with spring run-off. And then suddenly the cabin was in front of me, the sunset making its windows reflect gold as if it had lit itself up for me; and I was home.

I was startled for a moment when I realized that I had never doubted in these past few difficult days, that this would still be my home.

I pulled the car up in front, as close to the door as I could manage, and got out to unlock it. The cabin drew me inside, and I walked slowly through the rooms, feeling welcomed, and then I did cry, but it was for joy, not regret. There was no past here. The cabin held me.

I sat again, as I had just those few days before, a life ago, in front of the empty fireplace. It came to me that it was mine now, that I could light it, that I could do whatever I wanted, and so I went outside and found some kindling, and then I thought I needed paper so I unloaded the groceries and put them away and crumpled up some of the paper bags to put in the fireplace, the kindling on top of them. I would need larger wood as well. I went back outside and found some logs, piled haphazardly at the back of the cabin, a legacy, I supposed, from Mr. Chapman's father, and carried them in.

While the fire got going, I dragged the mattress through the cabin and into the bedroom. The place was small, but still its emptiness echoed, and it was pleasant in the living room with the snapping of the fire bouncing off the walls, and its reflection too, so that the whole room was centred on the fireplace. I watched the flames for a long time, and maybe I fell asleep on the floor for a while, I don't know, but when I realized again where I was, from being lost in the fire, it was dark outside and the only light was from the moon.

I walked outside and there were new sounds, a breeze moving through the branches of the willow, and the branches scratching softly on the roof of the cabin; there were frogs by the stream, I could hear them clearly, very loud, and mingled with them the sounds of crickets. It was not silent, and yet it was peaceful. There had been nothing like it before.

I had forgotten a flashlight, and when I started to walk, quietly, trying not to add any human sound, I tripped on something and fell. Abruptly there was silence, everything listening to me. The frogs and crickets, undisturbed all this time, knew there was something now that did not belong, and they were watchful, wary. I lay sprawled on the ground, shocked by the fall and the sudden silence, and then I began to laugh out loud; tomorrow and all the next days the animals and insects and plants and I would grow used to each other, and they wouldn't be silent when they heard me, and I laughed because it was perfect.

I pulled myself up off the ground. I wanted to shout at the frogs, tell them it was all right, they could start their scratching songs again, but that would be pointless; they would start when they felt safe. I groped my way back into the cabin and turned on the lights. The kitchen was very bright. I realized I hadn't eaten, and decided I was hungry. Something hot, I thought. Soup.

While it heated I put away the pots and pans, set detergent beside the sink, put out dishtowels, and when I was finished the kitchen looked almost occupied. I would hang the pots on hooks, I decided. They were copper; they would add something.

I ate in front of the fireplace, then went back to the kitchen to wash my dishes. I kept feeling spasms of joy, instants of realizing, and it happened when I saw the bowl and the

106

saucepan to be washed, all there was of my meal, just my own, from now on.

I walked through the other rooms, thinking of what I might do with them, and I could see them as I wanted them to be when I was finished. I knew they would be slightly shabby, and I knew they would not be perfect, that some things would be crooked and others wouldn't fit right, but it was my place and I could have crooked things.

I was very tired, exhausted suddenly from the effort to be here, so that now that it was completed and I was here, I could let go.

I unpacked my clothes and hung them up. I put sheets and blankets on the mattress, and changed into a nightgown.

The mattress was directly beneath the window. I lay there for a while, looking up at what I could see of the moon through the branches of the willow. Everything in the world was right, because this window and the willow and the moon were the world.

When I woke up, the sun was shining on my body, and it was warm.

9

Oddly, there were not the feelings of letdown, of doubt or panic, that should have been expected. Although they might come later. Would they come later?

It was morning, the sun was on my body, and there was no looking back. I felt no emptiness or lostness in abrupt change. I did not wake up that first morning and think, "I'm free, there is no one wanting breakfast or a kiss good-bye." I thought simply, "I'm free."

I lay in bed for a long time, looking up out of the window. It did not feel strange to be there. Birds, starlings I think, were singing ferociously in the willow, sounding as if their energy was too great for their small bodies. In the distance there were crows calling back and forth to each other, and I imagined them on the edge of the pasture, in the border trees of the woods, coming together to make some kind of plan for the day, and the sounds were familiar, as if I had always heard them.

I could hear also, very faintly, the stream pelting over stones, bursting hard against its banks, almost too large to be contained, like the force of the starlings. There was a very little breeze, moving only the smallest of the willow branches.

I felt some curiosity about the place, an eagerness to begin, and so, finally, it was time to get up.

In daylight, the cabin looked barren. The broken window panes and peeling walls were forlorn.

I made coffee and, holding my mug, wandered again

through the rooms. After a while I went to my purse and got out a pencil and paper, sat down on the floor of the living room to make plans, listed the furniture I would need, and the supplies that would carry me through some time here alone. Material for curtains, second-hand furniture, the freezer which should be delivered today, a kitchen table, a proper bed, a desk. There was pleasure in planning the place I wanted.

I washed the coffee cup and walked outside, wondering what might be done with the land. It occurred to me, an indication of how little I had considered the facts of coming here, that I must have a garden, or else too much of my precious, dwindling money would disappear. There was a spot not far from the cabin, down a small slope in the yard, that looked as if someday, probably years back, it had been a garden. It was marked somehow, perhaps the growth of weeds was different, but in any case it held an outline, a rectangle. It would not, I thought, be so difficult to turn the soil over and pull away the weeds and plant something for this year. The idea did not attract me particularly then, but I was beginning to understand there would be many things I would have to do to survive that I might not enjoy.

The plot was about fifty feet by twenty-five, and I had no idea how much food could be grown in such an area. It seemed to me that a garden should be bigger, but tackling more was a tiring thought. I would have money for extras if it fell short, and meanwhile I would learn.

I drew plans for the garden: tomatoes, lettuce, green peppers, squash, beans, onions, broccoli and brussels sprouts, and half a row of cabbage, laid it all out in rows on paper and felt that I had made large steps already. I wondered what time it was, felt for the first time the frustration of not knowing, thought perhaps I had been foolish, tried to go too far.

(Despite that, I wonder now at how swiftly I changed. It seems odd to me, unlikely, that I did not think at all that day, "Well, the children must be at school now, and Stephen at work. I wonder who got breakfast and what they had? I wonder how they miss me?" None of that. How could that have been?)

The men arrived to deliver the freezer, teetering in their truck up the lane. I saw them and was startled by the intrusion, remembered then who they must be, remained resentful.

"You planning on being here all summer?" asked the one who was broad and dark-haired as they put the freezer down in the kitchen.

"I plan," I said firmly, "on being here permanently." There was an irritation in me, a new wish not to be bothered — and a new knowledge that I didn't have to be. I suppose it was normal for them to be curious, or perhaps it was only polite conversation, and I should have understood.

"Got a family then?" the man asked.

What I told him was not, to me, a lie. "No, I'll be here on my own."

"You're going to try and manage here all by yourself?" He was startled. "What're you going to try to do with the place? D'you have any idea what it's like here in winter?"

"Not yet I don't, but I will." His doubt made me stubborn and more sure. "I don't plan to do anything with it but grow a garden to feed myself. I just plan to live here, that's all."

He looked at me intently. "You're from the city, aren't you." It was an accusation. "You don't know what you're getting in for. What kind of a damn fool idea is that, anyway, a woman on her own coming out here to live in the middle of nowhere? It's lonely out here, even for people with families." He shook his head. "You'll never make it."

I was angry; he had overstepped. "I'll be fine. It's what I want, so it's no business of yours. Is the freezer hooked up then?" I was still surprising myself with this new certainty and confidence. I did not need this man to like me; and perhaps there was some calculation, too: the image of a crazy bitch-lady living nowhere by herself was not a bad one, if the purpose was to be left alone. I could see how the story would spread.

"It's ready," he answered curtly. They left and no one said good-bye. I watched them drive down the lane, to be sure that they were gone.

It was unusual for me, this wanting just to be rid of everyone. Or was it? How long had it been there? Perhaps it was just the ability that was new, and it had come with the place, this place. It was pleasing to feel strong.

I was hungry again. I had had nothing since I got here but a bowl of soup and a cup of coffee. I got out an egg and scrambled

110

ʻit, and put it between two slices of bread. I also heated up what was left of last night's soup. It was pleasant — more than that, it was luxury — to be able to eat what I wanted when I was hungry.

There was the question of wood, and I went out to get ready for another evening fire. There were twigs everywhere, old ones blown off trees and bushes in years of storms and never gathered. But it would not be long before the small pile of logs behind the cabin, left over from the tenure of Mr. Chapman's father, was gone, and I would have to replenish it. For tonight, I gathered in some of what was already there; but already I was planning how I must get more, would have to get it by myself, me who had never had anything to do with surviving.

It astonished me, how little I knew. I wondered how I could have lived for so long — thirty-four years old and unable to look after myself. I could look after other people, I thought sardonically, but not myself.

The lists, the preparations, were done and the fire was lit; the first day of this different way was finished, had gone into small occasions, and I was pleased and tired. The freezer and the refrigerator made humming sounds, and now and then when the fire touched a vulnerable part of the wood, it would spit and a spark might fly onto the floor and I would have to jump to my feet and kick it back into the fireplace. I pulled the mattress from the bedroom and lay on it in front of the fire, watching the flames sideways. There was so much to be done, so much to learn, I thought I should be frightened, but I was not.

I did not consider, not then, whether I was lonely. There weren't labels; I was learning something already, that labels came from outside, when one stood away and said "yes, that looks like what people call loneliness." But there were no people here, no reasons to stand back and look.

I was inside myself. I could feel everything, and it was very tender. Raw.

The heat from the fire touched the side of my body, and it was hotter and clearer than any fire I had felt before. The mattress was firm, its hardness solid under me. My body was relaxed, tired and rested, no muscles pulling. There was a kind of bewilderment in my mind, a confusion of freedom, for now

111

there were so many things I wanted to do and I was filled with an energy of peace. I smiled, for I thought this was how happiness felt.

The next day I went back into town. At the Salvation Army I bought furniture and asked them to deliver it. There would be food needed soon, and I stocked up for the freezer. I spent a long time in the hardware store, picking over garden tools and selecting seeds. I bought pencils and notebooks and did not start conversations. I opened a bank account. When I found materials that blended blues and greens I was happy; I bought thread and needles, for it would all be done slowly, by hand, and sandpaper and oils for the new furniture. Again, when I went back, I drove the car tentatively up the lane and knew it would be the last time for a while, that I would drive it back down and leave it in the shanty-garage there, and I would be settled.

I arranged the furniture when it came, and considered what to do with it. A new and sharp and shiny axe stood inside the kitchen door; I would have to learn to chop and split wood, and the garden must be dealt with right away. There was so much to do, so many things at once, but the prospect was not tiring; I wanted to start immediately, eager, but I made myself slow down, try to relax. I was still fighting time — but at least I was fighting.

I had meat for dinner and potatoes and a salad, the first proper meal; and in the evening, with the fire going again and the woodpile dangerously low, I measured the bedroom curtains and began to hem. The work went quickly, if unevenly; when I went to bed that night, they were hanging at the sides of the window, leaving the window itself bare to frame the willow, and already the cabin was changing, becoming more mine.

There was real work to be started the next morning, and so I had a real breakfast, bacon and eggs and toast, before I took the hoe, new, and a shovel that I found on the grounds, and went out to turn the first garden. It was a much harder job than I'd thought, sweating, stinking back-breaking work, digging down to the roots of the long-grown weeds, pulling them out, shaking the soil off them and flinging them away. Sharp spikes from the weeds went through my heavy gloves, my legs pained with squatting, and my back ached from bending. The sun poured down and I was flushed, becoming burned; but still there was progress being made, I could move to the side and see that there were new spots cleared and a rising pile of weeds, and in the earth I could see worms jolted to the surface and the moist rich soil from underneath, so that it was no wonder the weeds had been so tough and healthy. By the time the sun was high, I was exhausted, and I returned slowly to the cabin, dragging the hoe, leaving the shovel lying where it was, and made a coffee and tried to sponge away the sweat with a towel.

It was partly the hair, I thought, the hair was down my back, clinging, damp and curling from the sweat, and I couldn't make it stay out of the way, pinned up it just fell down again, and it was sticky, itchy on my skin. That was when I picked up the scissors and cut it away, the first time, with the same lack of nostalgia with which I'd thrown out all the long dresses. I hacked at it, almost angry, and it came away in great chunks. I could feel that it was uneven, and I tried, at the bottom at least, to clip it so that no ends hung lower than the others, but God knows what the overall effect was. It didn't matter.

It was pleasant, sitting outside in the afternoon, muscles slowly, grindingly, returning to normal, with my old-new kitchen table, the sandpaper scrubbing at it, wearing off the paint and underneath the smell of wood, clean and breathing, as if it had been smothered for a long time and was now released. Later in the afternoon I would take the axe and try my hand at chopping wood, but for now I sat under the willow, where the sun did not beat down on me as it had in the garden, changing the rhythms of the sanding to suit my energy, looking out over the weeds and bushes, down into the empty lane where no one was expected, listening, and from here I could see a little patch of cleared garden. More would be done later, but it was an accomplishment already.

The axe was difficult, heavy and unwieldy, too long for me, for when I swung it down it got out of my control and I did not know what part of the wood it would strike. I shortened my grip, and the muscles in my legs and back, already stretched from the garden, protested; but I did not want to put it off, the preparations had to start now, for although soon the time for the fireplace in the evening would end with the summer heat, still the winter would come and it would be necessary to be ready; everyone seemed to warn about it.

And in the evening, body exhausted, I sat thoughtless in front of the fire, my own wood this time (no more from the dwindled pile in the back, it was to be added to, not withdrawn from) mind empty, tired too, and satisfied. Early sleep, in the bedroom with rain coming down outside, the first rain here, striking the baby leaves of the willow, spring leaves and on the roof too, gentle rain but overriding all the other sounds, no stream or frogs or crickets, do they sing when there is rain? And the next morning sunshine again and the garden weeds waiting, and that was the first thing because later it got too warm and the muscles protested but were forced, they felt paralyzed but they could be dragged into action, and more progress was made.

The wallpaper was standing in rolls in the living room. It was pre-pasted; all I had to do, the instructions said, was measure, moisten and put it up. It was delicate, feathery, old-fashioned, and I struggled heavily with it, trying to smooth the wrinkles and failing, using scissors to hack away the parts that overlapped on windows and doors, and in some places the edges of the strips did not meet, tilted off-handedly to one side and there was a barren patch, just a spot of the dull green paint underneath, but by then it had dried, instantly it seemed to dry, and there was nothing to be done about it. At first, when it was finished, I was disappointed, but in the darkness of the evening, with the lights turned out and just the fire blazing, it was very lovely. I had a shower, thank God for hot water and things that are not primitive, and when the fire went down, I went to bed and slept, hard, exhausted, deep.

And again the sun shone in the morning.

What time is sunrise in late spring? Whatever, it was when I rose and started my day. How long had it been since I had seen a sunrise? I could barely remember one, and now it was each day.

Everything was fresh to me. Hours were long and exhausting; when I slept, it was complete, and when I was awake, it was complete. The days grew warmer and I wore fewer clothes. I could see my hands and arms growing brown, and as I learned to use the axe with more dexterity and pull the weeds

114

without having to dig at their roots, I saw the muscles hardening in my arms and legs, could see them stretch and flex under the skin, and I delighted in all of it.

It took many days of work, no thoughts, just the labour, the effort of making things happen; perhaps that was why there were no memories or regrets, no pains or remorse. When finally the smallest, most hidden weeds were taken from the garden, I used the hoe to dig the earth down deep and turn it over, and the earthworms rolled into the sunshine and burrowed away from it, and then I drew the shallow furrows with the hoe and brought out the packets of seeds and the tiny tomato and green pepper plants, no flowers but only food, and waited to see what would come.

I still was sanding furniture, gently in the afternoons, outside, and as I finished the kitchen table I took a soft cloth and the oil and rubbed it into the wood, and as if it had been dying of thirst, as it had been dying for breath, the wood soaked it up, until finally it could hold no more, and it sat there in the sunshine and gleamed. It was the first perfect thing that I had done.

Late afternoons I would go in search of wood, now foraging farther, into the outskirts of the woods, which was a long walk with the axe, and I could not easily carry back what dead wood I found to cut. There were always dead trees, and always new living ones sprouting up, growing taller, so that the woods, by itself, stayed almost the same. I found I could manage, doing a little at a time, first cutting down a tree, then stripping off the branches for kindling, then cutting the trunk into sections for logs, and finally making the long, painful trips back to the cabin, loaded down with the wood. I realized, finally, that there must be an easier way, and devised and built a kind of sledge with a rope in front, like a toboggan, so that I could pile wood onto the sledge and pull the whole thing along by the rope. I was proud of that. It was hard work too, though, and often wood rolled off the sledge and I would have to stop and replace it, and the ground was rough and difficult to pull a heavy load over, but still it was easier than carrying it. I had two piles of wood behind the cabin now, one of kindling and one of logs, and both of them were growing.

There was still much of the inside of the cabin to be done,

and I painted and scraped and fixed the window panes and put up hooks for the pots, and finally it was what I had seen that I wanted.

Outside, the garden was planted and small green things were appearing. I could not tell, then, which were plants and which were weeds, and so I left it all alone for a while, not wanting to destroy something I had put there. It was remarkable to me that food was emerging from the earth simply because I had planted it; I watched the plants carefully, wondering how they evolved from the seeds; I thought they were miraculous.

It was well into the summer before the basic beginnings of life in the cabin were in order; the inside done, the garden planted, my primitive logging operations underway. I was achieving a rhythm.

It was possible then to have moments that were not spent in work. It had taken a long time, for there had been so many things that I did not know, so many simpler ways there must have been to make curtains, refinish furniture, cut wood, but I didn't know any of them, and so I learned alone, by trial. There were times when I was annoyed, impatient with my ignorance, but still there was pleasure in doing things slowly, even if I was clumsy, and knowing when they were finished, satisfied, that however they had turned out, they were mine.

And there were other ways in which my ignorance rather pleased me. I could watch the birds and animals and insects that lived here and know nothing of their habits or how they grew and lived. I was accepting, uninquisitive, like the dead friend who had not wanted to take flowers to pieces, not finding it necessary in order to see. In a way, I was surprised that I was not frightened, for there must have been larger animals about, perhaps a stag now and then, although I never saw one, and other things, like snakes, of which I might have had a horror, and yet I had no fear. There was a sense of impenetrability about me here; that I belonged, and nothing would hurt me as long as I belonged.

I went exploring, walking around and through my land, discovering what it held, although I could put names to very few of the things I saw. Everywhere were flowers, weeds I suppose, although I do not wholly understand what it is that makes some plants flowers that one cultivates and others weeds that one destroys. I have never tried to grow flowers; what was here was here, and I knew simple ones like daisies and Queen Anne's lace, which is also wild carrot without the romance. Why would Queen Anne's lace, gray and delicate and sturdy, be a weed? It made no sense.

Once I took some left-over garden seeds into the woods and sprinkled them near me, and then sat down to see what would happen. I sat very still for a long time and slowly, very gradually and tentatively, two squirrels approached, shying, chasing each other away, but almost imperceptibly coming closer each time, and I sat rock-still until finally they nibbled at the seeds, and I wanted to reach down and stroke them, incredible flurried tails they had, wide and gray and proud, and fat bellies too, stuffing themselves, greedy animals, but it is dangerous to try to touch a squirrel, they are nervous and sensitive and will attack; and besides I did not want to affect or change the life here; I wanted just to be part of it, have it accept me. It was necessary to put away fancy human urges to capture or control, or just to make some kind of difference, to be noticed; it was necessary to be an animal. I did not know that right away, and made mistakes, but as time, years, went on I became, I think, part of the wildness, inseparable from it and acutely aware of my very minimal place in it. And I have found it comforting, that I am not so important.

(I became an animal, which is a fine thing, and now after so many years I am going back, pulled back by Katie and words and time and memories, into a person, a thinking, rationalizing, remembering person, and it is not comfortable. I have lost both my worlds, the old one that she knew, that I am unfitted for now, although once I may have suited it; and this more recent one that has become mine.)

There was time, that first summer, to notice many things, slowly, at my own rate, not thoughtfully but wholly, so that they rolled under and over and through me until they became myself.

Still, I could be surprised by a self separated from the experiencing, so that, startled, I would find myself watching myself and know that something new was happening. It was like a visit from the old Abra, those moments. (And that is what I feel is happening now. Eventually the visits stopped, but in the beginning it was the way it is now, a watching, an assessing.)

I might sit by the stream, and although it was so very cold, for a while I could hold my feet in it, and I would sit on a rock beside it, or on the bank directly, and my feet would be a kind of dam, but insignificant, not holding, and I would feel, watch, the water striking against them, then drawing back as if confused and flowing out around them, finding new routes, new outlets, not held back long by the obstacles. I could watch as that happened, continuously with all the rush of water and yet singly, also, as if I could see each drop of water coming up against this barrier, pulling away to consider, and then, recognizing that it could not push through in its usual route, adapting immediately and finding another way, a way around, and on the other side coming together again and going on, as if almost nothing had happened, perhaps with just a faint, unclear memory of something back there that had made a small, temporary difference.

And then suddenly, and I could not tell why this happened, I would be seeing myself, as if I were standing away a few feet, watching this person who was also myself, ridiculously cropped hair although I had never seen it, jeans rolled up, bare feet in the water, staring down intently, God knows for how long, and the moment would be gone, I would be aware of myself again and realize that my feet were cold, that it was time to move on. Eventually that part that interrupted and judged, I thought, died a natural death; I see now that it was simply dormant.

Water insects fascinated me, especially the striders that lived in the calm side-pools of the stream, occasionally moving out and downstream, going about their odd, flicking business. I suppose it must have been that they were eating, getting some kind of nourishment from the stream surface, but it appeared aimless and also effortless, their incredibly swift movements, just dartings across the surface. They seemed to be totally relaxed — and then suddenly frenetic — and then instantly relaxed again, floating.

118

Occasionally, but only very occasionally, I saw a frog. They were there, all right, from the sounds they made at night there must have been multitudes, but in the daylight they were hard to spot, green and brown morsels lying still as leaves and twigs; sometimes I might hear a plop as one dove into the stream, but I would rarely see it.

Sometimes in the woods, especially in the early summer and again in autumn, there have been deer here, and while I have never tried to touch them, I have held out food and watched them come close, cautious, sniffing, slow, until they are near enough to gently extend their necks and reach forward, noses velvet-looking and twitching, wary of a trap, and then quickly, carefully, taking the food and backing away, still close but out of reach. I have often left food out for animals, but they do not depend on me; they seem to know, and accept what I have when I have it, and do not expect more.

In the pasture, poppies miraculously appeared, red-orange and tall, maybe planted there sometime long ago, but more likely sprung up from blowing seeds — I don't know how these things happen — but they were beautiful, standing above everything else although the pasture was deep in growth. After a while they shrivelled and disappeared again, but for a time, while they were full, I walked out to see them every day.

When the weed-flowers were in full bloom and common, I picked them sometimes and made bouquets. Funny bouquets in coffee jars, dandelions and violets and Queen Anne's lace, in the kitchen and on the mantel of the fireplace. I glued remnants of wallpaper over the coffee jars and they became vases. There were feathery flowers in the fields that looked as if they would be attractive dried for the winter, if I knew how to dry them. I didn't, of course, I didn't know any of those things, but I picked some anyway and tied them together and hung them upside down inside the kitchen door, and some of them wilted and dropped and others survived, so I had learned something. I let them hang there for weeks, until I was sure which were right, and then I cut them down and put them in two jars and set them by the fireplace, out of range of sparks, and they softened the room.

I took some of the paper I had bought, and a pencil, and sat outside trying to draw what I saw. A bird, a flower, a squirrel, I tried the water striders but they would not be still and I rarely got what I wanted onto the paper. I have never been good at drawing, I can see what I want in my mind, but I can't make my hands transfer it onto paper. But that wasn't the point anyway. I looked closely and really saw; once I wondered if things would have been different, before, if I had been able to see this way. But it didn't matter, was irrelevant; a multitude of things might have been different, but they hadn't been, and it had ended here and that was fine.

I had no regrets, and memories were rare. I recalled lethargy, inertia and unease, but could not grasp them. They belonged to someone else. Here was energy, sensation, the beginning, perhaps, of understanding. The beginning, perhaps, of faith? Of belief?

I saw how I was surviving, and it was good. I sometimes remembered the other people, wondered what they were doing, and felt only relief that I was not there with them. I knew already that they would survive. Not in my way, unless they were very lucky, not with this sense of joyful discovery every day and labour that made me happy, if happiness was a word that meant anything to me by then; but in their own more difficult way that forced them to go on in the face of their lives. It seemed to me that when I had been with them, in that other life, that I had lived against myself, and perhaps they had to also. Now I lived with myself. I had done something to them, but I could not feel guilt.

Once, I thought, it would have hurt to know that they would get along without me.

10

It was autumn of that first year. I had been alone — what — seven months, more or less. I had seen only a few people — the men delivering furniture, and the farmer down the road, who appeared one day in the summer, rolling up the lane on his tractor; that was all.

The farmer introduced himself as something Brocker — his first name eludes me, although he is still on the next farm — and said he'd heard someone was living at the old McAllister place year-round now, and he was surprised he hadn't seen me out. He asked me if I needed anything, any help, and he seemed to mean kindly and so I refused gently. He told me his wife kept chickens, and he sometimes delivered eggs to neighbours, and asked if I would like to be put on his route. Eggs seemed very precious to me by then; they were something that could not be provided here, and they were too perishable to store, and so I agreed. But, I said, there was no point in him struggling up the lane; he could drop them off, a couple of dozen every two weeks, in the car-shanty at the bottom of the lane, and I would pick them up. I would leave money for them there. He agreed, although he seemed puzzled that I didn't want him coming to the cabin.

"Anything else you need," he said, "just let me know. It's going to be tough for you, I'd think, being here on your own. Especially in the winter." He drove off down the lane again, and although there have been several times when I have needed his help, we have never talked much, and I don't think he knows any more about me now than he did after that first visit nine years ago. The very pleasant thing about him is that he has never asked.

The garden was good, although there was no credit to me, because I didn't know, that first year, what I was doing. I froze many of the vegetables for winter; I knew that much about getting through the season that everyone I had spoken to warned me about. I was feeling some urgency to be safe, and the fall was a season of hurry. Cutting the last of the wood, adding it to the enormous, satisfying piles behind the cabin; freezing, preserving vegetables, working hard all day, sweat pouring in the evenings from the boiling water for blanching, sometimes seeing myself stranded here in mid-winter with a freezer-full of spoiled food, cold, hemmed in by snow, deadly alone, and the vision added fuel to my urgency.

Almost everything that could be done was finished before the first snow. There was nothing left to can or freeze, no space left, in fact, in the freezer. There was a little wood still waiting to be dealt with, a few squash still in the garden, but almost all over. I was exhausted, and worried, too, about the enemy coming up, for that year I thought of winter as an enemy, and I rested and cleaned and made lists for a couple of days before I made, as I had to, the trip to town.

I was reluctant to go, frightened, for I did not want to disrupt my balance here, didn't want to face people; I had achieved a sense of well-being, but it was still a delicate thing, and I had no wish to dislodge it.

The trip, of course, was necessary. There were dozens of things I would need for the winter that I could not supply myself: fuses, an electric heater for the bedroom, food stocks like milk power; I had gone without meat after the supplies I brought with me ran out, and it seemed that I didn't miss it. There was only one luxury that I pined for, that I wanted to indulge; I had a picture in my mind of the winter, and I wanted some coal oil lamps, perhaps three, because I thought they would add a softness, tranquillity, to the time. I wanted to be able to spend the winter in dimly-lit rooms, reading or sewing, or sketching or writing by the flicking light. A romantic picture.

I hardened my mind, ready for town. I settled on a day, made no room for changes, and when the morning came I even combed my hair, although I could not see the result, before I walked down the lane to the car. I wore jeans and a pullover sweater, loose and practical. I was clean but hardly, I guessed, attractive.

The car felt strange. It started after a few tries, and I sat for a moment, the motor running, looking it over, feeling the steering wheel, touching the gear shift, disoriented, but I could not put it off for there was much to be done. I backed out onto the road; it was awkward, but not impossible, and enough of it came back to me.

The gravel road I'd driven on so many months before, lined with heavy dark trees, was now all colour, a set of flames running along each side, like driving through a forest fire, and it seemed to crackle with brilliance. On the main road into town it became more barren; there were fields here and wire fences, and fewer trees; it was cultivated, used — a civilization here. Already I felt far away from the cabin. There were other cars here too, with people in them that I could just glimpse, and then I reached the town and the cabin no longer existed.

There were people on the sidewalks, multitudes it seemed to me, although it was a small town and there could not really have been so many, and through the windows of the car, driving slowly, watching, I could see their mouths in conversation, their bodies moving in progress, and I was remote and unrelated. They had nothing to do with me. What was my body like? Was it similar to theirs? When their mouths moved, what happened? What came out? Could I make myself understood to them? Could I speak to them?

I tried, sitting enclosed in the car, making the sounds, practising, and the voice was strange, hoarse, and as if it came from somewhere else. But I was remembering and I knew the words. I read the lists I'd made aloud and was able to make them out, and that was all I needed. But I could not, right away, get out of the car.

I watched. It was like seeing a new species of animal, being hesitant to move and startle them, except that there was something senseless about these and, too, something sinister. I think I was frightened because they were like me and yet not my

123

own kind any more. They moved innocently, walking and talking and stopping to look into store windows, there was no danger to me except that I wasn't part of them, couldn't remember them.

There was a woman coming toward my car. She was holding tightly to the left wrist of a little girl with blonde hair, the same colour as her own. She was walking quickly and the little girl was crying, pulled occasionally off her feet and stumbling with the pressure of keeping up with the woman. The little girl's face was red and blotched with tears, and her eyes were squeezed almost shut, her mouth open crying protest; the woman's face was pale, determined, closed, compressed. They were beside the car, and I could hear the weeping of the little girl, almost hysterical with the pain of failing to make the woman hear. The woman was refusing to pay attention, although it was paining her, too, one could see that.

They were past before I recognized them: they were Katie and I, just once, I only let it happen once. It was several years ago, before Katie started school, and we had gone downtown to shop, a rare occasion, and both of us had gotten tired, of the walking and the stores and all the things and people, and also of each other, too long together under strain. Katie had begun to cry, softly, like a whimper, simply exhausted, and the sound had maddened me, snapped something so that I grabbed at her arm and began dragging her, forcing both of us to plunge into more stores, Katie crying progressively louder, my face, I could feel it, getting tighter, wanting, really wanting, to hurt her, blind, not thinking. The rage died when we got home and I was hopelessly ashamed, trying to make it up to her. But she pulled away from me, ran upstairs, too exhausted then for tears, and it was several days before we were normal again. Afterwards I was just a little frightened, of her and for her. Of her, I guess, because now she knew this thing about me, and for her because I'd seen it too.

That woman and the little girl were Katie and I, and suddenly I was out of the car, striding easily into the stores, for I had recognized something of myself and I could be among them. I was human too — I remembered now.

In the hardware store, an old dark wooden place filled

incongruously with shiny things like toasters and frying pans and bright bits of metal, an old man served me; stooped and shrunken and thin, he looked disjointed and vague, as if he did not really belong there. A younger man, plumpish and dark-haired, watched him, frowning.

It was the younger man that I asked for the coal oil lamps, and he seemed displeased. I could almost see what he saw, an untidy, browned, tough-skinned woman with garish hair; he shrugged and told me to wait, then went over to the old man, who straightened, looked less vague and came toward me. The younger one went back behind the counter; he continued to watch us.

"You're asking for coal lamps?" the old man asked.

"Yes, do you keep them in stock?"

"I doubt they're stocked any more, but there's stuff from years back in the basement, and I can go take a look if you don't mind waiting."

He disappeared into the basement and I wandered around the store, followed by the eyes of the younger man behind the counter, keeping a tally of the items I picked up: light bulbs, fuses, the electric heater. I looked wistfully at a chainsaw, but that was ridiculous. A scythe, perhaps, I thought, to cut an area for sitting outside the cabin for next summer, but that wasn't needed yet. I put my purchases on the counter and waited for the old man to reappear.

He came back eventually, carrying three ancient boxes, crumpled at the corners. They were very dirty, but the old man laid them on the counter and began to open one, setting dust flying, dirtying the counter and a pad of receipts, and the younger man started to speak but then held back. The old man was absorbed; I don't think he noticed.

The lamp he pulled out was not dusty, protected for years by the box. They decided to sell me the three of them for six dollars, because if I didn't buy them, it was unlikely that anyone ever would. "Will that be all?" the younger man asked. He spoke abruptly, as if he wanted me gone.

"Yes, thank you." I turned deliberately to the old man. "Thank you for going to so much trouble. I'm sorry you had such a search."

"That's all right ma'am," he said, grinning a little. "We don't get any call for them any more. I've — we've — got things down there nobody's ever going to want, now. It's probably time to clear it all out, but it's a hard thing to do. So many of the old things. . . ." His voice trailed away.

"I'll need coal oil, too," I remembered and the younger man stopped making up the bill and sighed.

"It's all right, Frank," the old man said, holding up his hand against the younger man's irritation. "I know just where it is. Won't take a minute." And he hurried off again, down into the basement, leaving the two of us wordless, hostile, at the counter, waiting for him to come back and break between us again. I wondered what it had been that, without words or incident, had made us enemies, and why I cared.

When he returned, the old man had an idea and a question. "Say," he said, handing the coal oil containers over absent-mindedly to the young man, "you wouldn't by any chance be the lady living up at the old McAllister place?"

"I've heard it called that," I told him, remembering the farmer. "But I didn't buy it from any McAllisters. It was a man whose father had it for a kind of retreat or hunting lodge."

"Oh no," he said, "it wouldn't be the McAllisters. They haven't been there for years, it's just they were the last people who were there full-time, and that's how it's known. I guess you'll have heard the story?"

"I haven't heard anything about it, except that the father of the man I bought it from used it. I never asked what happened before that." I wasn't really encouraging, but something perverse in me wanted to stay in the store, talking to him and annoying Frank.

"Well," said the old man, "it's quite a story. Goes 'way back twenty years, and maybe you don't want to know about it, if it's you living there now. You're on your own, I hear?"

"That's right. But please tell me. If whatever it is happened twenty years ago, it won't bother me."

"Dad," the younger man began, warningly.

"It's all right," I said, waving my hand in Frank's direction but keeping my eyes on the old man. "I'm interested." And oddly, I was.

"Well, all right then, if you're sure," he said doubtfully. He

126

took a deep breath and his eyes hazed into the memory.

"It's a good twenty-five years ago that the McAllisters first turned up around here. A young couple they were, from down East I think, not from around here, anyway, and they had some savings. He'd been working in the city and they were looking to buy a place around here for some modest farming. Which," and he grinned, "is the only kind of farming goes on around here.

"Well that seventy acres you're on now was for sale at the time, and I guess it seemed like a lot to them, although all of us knew it was nothing, wasn't worth anything, wouldn't grow anything. We warned them not to buy it, but they were young, I don't think he could have been more than twenty-six or seven and she was maybe twenty-five, I don't know, and they wouldn't listen. They'd worked hard and now they were ready to own some land, and the price up here was right. The lad said he'd start with the seventy acres and buy up more as time went on; he just wanted a start, he said, that was all.

"They were right on the line after they bought the place, so the first thing they had to do was get a loan from the bank. They didn't have much trouble with that; everybody around here borrows, there's nothing unusual about it, it's expected. I don't think old John Forrest, he was manager of the bank over there at the time, thought they'd make it, but he gave them the money anyway. They were a real nice young couple, and people hoped they'd make out, but nobody figured they would.

"Anyway, young McAllister bought forty head of cattle, which was stretching it hard for the amount of grazing land he had there. He wanted to get clear as soon as he could, though, and I guess by then he'd heard so many people saying they wouldn't make it out there he got stubborn, wanted to prove he could. That was back in the days when people believed you could do anything if you worked hard enough. I suppose people know better now; anyhow it's different.

"Say, are you sure you want to hear this? It's not that nice a story." I nodded.

"Well then let's get comfortable. There's lawn chairs over there that beat leaning on a counter." I nodded again, and we moved off to a corner and settled into two plastic chairs, while Frank glowered behind us.

"Okay then. McAllister built a stretch of chicken coops and

handed them over to his wife. She was supposed to keep the chickens and sell the eggs. Everything counted, he said, especially the pennies. I thought at the time she didn't look as happy about it all as he did, but then nobody could have been as happy and hopeful as him.

"They put in a huge garden, must have been almost a couple of acres, figuring to sell what they didn't eat. Poor kids didn't know what they were getting into, didn't have a clue how much work was involved in something that size. And I don't know who they thought they'd sell the stuff to; nobody was about to drive way out there for produce we were all growing in our own backyards. They didn't even have proper equipment, just hand tools anybody with a little garden plot would have, not what you need to work a patch that size.

"They were lucky that year. The weather was good, just the right rain at just the right times, so the grazing land kept up well enough with the cattle's appetites, and the garden was real good. They lost a few hens with some disease, but still things went a lot better for them than anybody'd figured.

"Of course they found out the hard way that there wasn't much trade around here in garden produce, although some of us went out specially to buy stuff, just to help them out. They caught on quick, though, and hired a truck to haul it all the way into the city and peddled it to a few small grocery stores. I don't think they got the prices they wanted, but it was something, anyway, and he figured that the next year he'd rent some land by the main road and set up a produce stall. Catch a lot of people out for Sunday drives, tourists, he figured, and we all thought it was a pretty good idea.

"The best thing that happened to them that year, though, was the cattle prices. Can't depend on them at all, but he was lucky; a lot of people were that year. By fall they were trading for a good bit more than they'd been in the spring, and his had fattened up, so he made enough to cover the bank loan and have some left over to support them and buy seeds in the spring. He was downright crowing that fall, for he'd made it when everybody'd said he wouldn't, and it wasn't much but he was pretty proud. They'd worked their fingers to the bone that year, both of them were rail-thin and stringy by fall, and brown as

Indians, and she was looking pretty tired, but I think she was proud of what they'd done, too.

"We didn't see much of them over the winter, just a couple of times they came into town, but it's pretty hard when you're way back in on those roads, and sometimes if there's a storm the township don't get round to plowing them out for a few days. But they were back in first thing in the spring.

"Everybody noticed they'd changed. We figured the winter had done it, just the two of them back there in that cabin together, nobody else and not much to be done except fix the place up, and they couldn't do much of that with the money they had. He was quieter, didn't have the energy he'd had when they'd first turned up, or even what he'd had in the fall, when he was excited about selling the cattle.

"It wasn't showing that early in the spring, but it turned out she was pregnant, due in September. But she was thin, terribly thin, they both were, skinnier even than they'd been in the fall, you'd have thought they'd have fattened themselves up over winter. Her hair wasn't the way it was before, I don't think she was bothering much to wash it, it was kind of coarse and stringy, and when we first saw her the year before she was all round and pink, and her hair and eyes were shiny things; the women saw her now and shook their heads. Those women knew the lives they had, and they knew hers must be that much tougher; they said she wasn't going to make it, and they blamed him. They said he was killing her, keeping her back there on that poor farm with no company, nothing but him and work. They couldn't understand why he didn't see it and do something, but they should have known; their own husbands didn't seem to notice what happened to them over the years."

The old man sighed, looked disgusted.

"I grew up on a farm myself, watched my parents work from sunrise till after sundown, saw the lines in my mother's face get deeper every year; she died when she was only fifty-six, and I think she was just worn out, nothing but just worn out. My dad spent so much time working outside that his face got all squinty-eyed and his skin was a red colour all the year round, but still he must have stayed healthier than her because he lived to be seventy-two. But he never noticed what was happening to

129

her, and then she died. I got out just as soon as I could. Came into town, borrowed from the bank and started up this store. The old farm was sold after my dad died, and I've never been sorry it's gone. It's a devil of a life." He sighed again.

"But anyway. The women thought it was killing young Belle McAllister, and when they heard she was going to have a baby, they were really furious; she looked so frail then. Of course they blamed him; they couldn't blame their own husbands for what happened to them, so they blamed McAllister. At least that's what I figured.

"He went straight to the bank that spring and got another loan; he had good credit by then, no problems the first year. He wanted to buy more cattle that year, maybe fifty head, but for once he listened to us, maybe he was tired of thinking it all out for himself, and we told him forty was too many for that land, so much of it was bush and the rest pretty well scrub, never mind fifty, so he bought forty again. But the loan was bigger than the year before anyway, because cattle prices were up that spring.

"They set out to do it all over again, but things were different that year. It was a blazing summer, that one, I think it set records, and everybody was having troubles. Not enough rain, August was just one long, hot dry spell, and everything turned brown and there wasn't a thing anybody could do but watch it happen. Belle was still raising her chickens, and she brought the eggs into town to sell. God she looked terrible that summer, looked as if the child she was carrying was eating her alive, she didn't seem to have anything for herself, and there she was, working like the devil. She was real listless, just brought the eggs in and sold them and went home again, didn't want to talk to anybody. He came in with her sometimes, and he was dead worried, getting the squinty pinched look my dad had. Mostly he stayed out on the farm, though, because she couldn't work much in the garden and he had to do almost the whole of it.

"He'd set up some kind of hose connection with a pump from the creek out there to the garden, so as long as there was water in the creek, he could keep the garden alive, at least. He said he wasn't going to bother renting a spot for a roadside stand, though; he didn't have time to sit by the road selling vegetables, and Belle wasn't able to. He said the baby was coming at just the wrong time.

"Nobody wanted to ask about the cattle; we could guess. All the fields around here were stunted and dry, and there was no way his few acres would support the forty head that year. He didn't mention it the few times he came to town.

"Finally, early in September, I guess he figured he couldn't hang onto them any longer, so he had them trucked out for slaughter. He broke even on the price per pound, but they'd lost weight. Goddamn bad luck for them that year; nothing went right, and by the end of it they were well in the hole.

"The only good thing happened was the baby. By God she was a pretty little thing. They couldn't afford her, of course, couldn't have even if they'd had a decent year, but when Belle and her were back from the hospital they started bringing her into town with them, and you could see it didn't matter to them that they didn't have the money. They were so damn proud, he'd come around the stores holding her, trying to make her laugh so everybody could see how pretty she was, and Belle looked better, too, more rosy again. He kept saying, 'Things'll be better next year.'

"Belle never came into town all that winter, and neither did the baby. It was just him, and that not often, just to pick up supplies. Back then, I don't know what you've got now, but back then there was just a space heater in the living room and a wood stove in the kitchen, nothing in the bedroom, and I think the plumbing must have been pretty old-fashioned. One time McAllister was in town he said the baby had a cold.

"You have to understand how hard it must have been for them, especially Belle. She'd have to heat up water on the stove to do a washing or have a bath, and that would mean hauling wood. That winter it was as cold and blizzardy as the summer had been hot and dry, and they must have sat around, cooped up in that cabin, for weeks on end, all wrapped up in clothes and blankets trying to keep warm. In the spring, when Belle and the little girl turned up in town one day, you could see she'd made an effort, they were both clean and tidy. But the baby didn't look right, not healthy, it was the way Belle had turned after a year, the shine was gone, the prettiness was worn out.

"It was Belle, though, that scared us. Her eyes were crazy-like, they wouldn't keep still, wandered all over the place, and she couldn't talk very well, couldn't get sentences out, it seemed.

131

It made people edgy, the way she looked, and maybe they kept away from her a bit.

"That first time into town that year turned out to be the last time she tried to spruce them up. After a couple of months she and the baby were both real thin, and just plain filthy dirty. Nobody knew what to do. It was real bad.

"Some of the women tried, they got together and took turns visiting her, trying to help out, taking up food or cast-off clothes. It wasn't easy for any of them, because they had their own work to do, but they kept on trying all that summer. They said Belle always let them into the cabin and she always thanked them for what they brought, but she seemed vague and limp somehow, the cabin was filthy and so were she and the baby, and now young McAllister was getting that way too, and thinner, because Belle didn't seem to be able to look after any of them. She wasn't doing anything, the women said, and he looked more and more hopeless every time we saw him. He brought the eggs into town that year, and he did most of the sitting at the roadside stand they had, although sometimes he would drop Belle and the baby off instead; even people who knew them, though, and felt sorry for them, didn't like buying food from them. It was the dirt, and the way her eyes were.

"He broke even and a bit more that year, with it all, and paid off a little of his bank loan. He said he'd taken to hunting, and wanted to bag enough rabbits and such to keep them from having to buy meat that winter. He looked exhausted with trying to do everything and no help from Belle. He talked all the time about the farm, how he planned to keep it going, how he'd figured it would be tough the first while, but things were sure to get better and he was no quitter. He was real tight and determined. He didn't say a word about Belle.

"Late in the fall, the three of them came into town for the big winter shopping. We figured they must have game stored away that he'd shot, for they didn't buy much food, no meat or vegetables, just things like flour for baking bread. All three of them were pinched-looking, even the child. Belle just looked blank. We figured no matter what he'd said, they couldn't stick it. There was an air about them that day that just spoke right out and said 'it's over.' We figured come spring, they'd have to sell out and go into town, settle down there, pay off the bank loan and pull themselves together.

"It was a while before we noticed they weren't around at all. Must have been January or so before somebody said, 'say, McAllisters haven't been in at all this year, have they? Winter hasn't been so bad, you'd have thought they'd have been in by now. Anybody seen them?' Nobody had, and we chewed that over for a few days, until it came to us there might actually be something wrong, we hadn't thought of that, but once somebody mentioned it, it was in everybody's mind. So somebody rang up the fellow on the farm next to theirs and asked him to take a wander over, see if things were all right. He said he'd get to it as soon as his chores were done.

"Well I guess it was about eight o'clock when the call came in, the fellow was all out of breath and the police couldn't make head nor tail of what he was saying for a while. When they finally got it straightened out, they took off like sixty for the McAllister place. Although Lord alone knows why, because there wasn't anything rushing was going to help.

"What happened was, they found McAllister himself in the kitchen, sitting on a chair right inside the door, sort of tilted over and his shotgun at his feet. The place stank so bad, they said, one of them had to go right back outside and throw up. Real bad, they said. Back in the living room they found Belle, or what was left of her. Most of her head was gone, they said — just shot away. Of course they knew what was going on by then, they knew the little girl wouldn't be alive, and they went back outside again. For fresh air. Figured he'd shot Belle and the child, then killed himself. People do that, I know, but it's never been somebody around here, and it just didn't seem possible. I don't think those fellows had ever seen anything like it before. They radioed back into town and then sat around the police car for a while. They were both dead sick, they said.

"Next time they went in, they kept going and found the little girl in the second bedroom, all curled up like she was asleep, even had a pile of blankets on her, they said. Just for a minute, I think maybe they thought they'd been wrong and she was all right, but then they pulled the blankets away and they were all stuck to her with blood. I guess he hadn't wanted to make her

133

look ugly like Belle by shooting her in the head, so he shot her in the stomach instead, ripped a hole right through her.

"There wasn't any note or anything, he'd just done it. The coroner said they'd been dead about a month, and there was some rush to get them buried. We all went to the funeral, closed casket of course, and nobody had much to say about it afterwards. I guess we all felt bad we hadn't tried to do more. But how could we have known?"

He stopped then, and we were silent. The picture of what had happened more than twenty years before was too vivid, more alive in my mind than the present, and I guess it was the same for the old man. He came to first, glanced at me apologetically, then at Frank, and his movement brought me back. I looked too, and saw that Frank was furious, lips tight with rage. The old man began to look frightened.

"I'm sorry," he said. "I shouldn't have told you all that. I guess I kind of got carried away. I hope you're not upset."

"Not at all. It's a very sad story. I'm grateful, really, that you told me."

"Well I'm sorry I went on so long. I've kept you here a long time."

"You haven't kept me from anything." We were looking at each other, understanding — something. "Thank you."

I left then. On the way home, back to the cabin that was my home, where people had died, I began to grow uneasy. I wanted to know, was afraid to find out, if the cabin would be changed for me, if the story gave it a past I didn't share, that would make it different.

But it didn't. There was a little light left in the sky, just enough to see the outline of the cabin when I reached the top of the lane. I wished I'd left a light on inside, to welcome me back.

But I was home. The place was still mine, nothing had changed. I wanted to be sure, went into the kitchen and tried to feel the McAllisters, tried to see him, thin and rotting, sitting on a chair inside the door, slumped over with his shotgun at his feet, were his eyes open or closed? and I could raise the picture, but he didn't belong there, not in my kitchen.

I went on into the living room, seeing the young woman, tired into age, her head shot away, and she was there too, but only like a photograph, unreal. In what had been a bedroom, my small escape room, there would have been a little bed with a child in it. I could see her, blonde and fragile, and I could pull down the blankets and feel them stick, clinging to her wound, and she too was long gone.

How had he felt about this place? Is that why he did it, to hold it for them in just a single moment?

It didn't matter any more. They had had their time. Now it was mine, and someday it would be for someone else. The place stored passion. I went back outside, unloaded the car, packed my supplies away and lit, for the first time, the coal oil lamps. Their light flickered on the walls, competing with the fire.

I went to bed early and slept. I dreamed of the old man in the hardware store, and woke up content.

11

I should not have been afraid of winter; I should have understood that not even its toughness could hurt me here. But I was afraid for a long time, of many things.

Food. It seemed to me there was plenty — the freezer was full, I had shelves of preserved fruits and jams, and bags of baking supplies, and every few weeks the farmer down the road would leave off eggs; but would it be enough?

And I was afraid too because of the great difference between a home and a prison. In the rest of the year there had been at least a choice, and I could have sought company or help if I had wanted; for much of the winter here that choice would barely exist. The weather would bury me and I did not want to chafe against isolation because it was forced and not voluntary.

The wood was another question. The piles looked to me enormous, but what did I know about what might be used in a cold winter? Still, if it ran out, it wasn't as if I actually needed it for warmth; the fires were more a prop than a physical necessity.

I looked ahead and saw — something that did not fit the fear, a place where fear had no part: the snow falling, driving or gentle, piling up around my windows, touching them, myself inside, wrapped in a quilt in front of the fire, reading or watching, and the picture was — serene.

And then, seeing that, I relaxed. I understood the fear came from somewhere else, from other people, and that it wasn't part of me or of this place. When I saw that, I could let it go. I wondered, "How many fears have there been that I've learned to make mine? What am I, just myself, afraid of and what have I been taught to fear?" Maybe in the other life there had been something; here, now, considering it, I could think of nothing.

There were still the questions, and the winter still seemed to me to be the main test of whether or not I would survive here. I had a sense of trial ahead, of hurdles before the end, but I was not afraid, not any more. I thought, "Perhaps it's courage I'm discovering, maybe that's the name of it."

As the weather of late fall became increasingly cold, I moved more and more inside the cabin. There was nothing that had to be done outside, and for a time it was pleasant just to stand at a window and watch the season turn silent, fold me into itself; especially the cloudy days, they seemed softer than the others; when the sun shone it was like a challenge to be sharp and clear like the day, but the clouded ones just fell around me and asked nothing, and I was full of content and safety. I felt alone, very much alone.

I watched the land for days as it changed, turned bleak and tough for the winter ahead, leaves gone, grass shrivelling under frost, no flowers now. The changes came swiftly, so that I could almost see the dying. There were only a few days when the cold released and there was rest from change.

And then there was a bitter day, with knifing winds that cut through the brittle willow branches so that they scraped and hammered at the cabin. I watched and listened and then I turned back to the inside for warmth and comfort, thinking how these two, the cold outside and the heat within made a world that was complete. And when I turned, seeking the softness of the cabin, it was gone, only harshness here, too, and I recoiled from what was there.

I don't know where she came from, the old Abra, but she was standing by the kitchen table, leaning on it with one hand, the other on her hip, accusing, looking at me with reproach and sorrow and yes, some pity, and I saw her so clearly that I wanted to run, to see myself in a mirror so that I could know who I was. I knew we were divided now, but not like this, not as if she still existed.

When I looked again, she was gone, and I thought, "but is

she, really, or is she only hiding, waiting to come back," and I thought, "I must be mad. I must have gone mad, must still be mad, for what am I doing here?"

It was the season, I can see that now, that brought the sudden forced drive into myself that followed. There had been some questioning before, to be sure, even some objectivity, that unfortunate habit of standing back to put words to what I was doing. But it had not come like this, not so sharply before.

But in that first winter, the pressures of physical survival gone, faced simply with this life and that life, given so much time, there was a space, inevitable I can see now, where it all had to be gone over. It is easy to be calm about it now, to see that there had to be a time when a balance sheet would be drawn up. It was terrifying then, a loss and a confusion, a feeling of weightlessness and not existing. I was overwhelmed by the old Abra, became her for a while, full of cold and logic (although that had not been how she was, had it?). I condemned what I saw: a young woman with two children and a loving husband, who had inexplicably disappeared, abandoned them, vulnerable, hurting, who had gone off selfishly to something else — something much easier, no doubt, Abra said. And what right does this woman have to selfish pleasure? None, she made her life, she must live with the consequences, she created these other people and their need for her, and now she must fulfill them. And that is normal.

It is not normal, it goes against all instincts, it is — well, it is mad — to turn away from that. It is a breakdown, something that requires help, a renewed vision of reality, for of course, Abra said, things never go just as they should, but isn't that part of growing up, all of growing up, learning that and learning to live with it, deal with it, make the best of it. Face it, Abra said, for this is life and reality. The tragedy of it, or even just the unhappiness, the discontent, is a measuring stick: if we can deal with that, then we are survivors; if we try to run away, we are broken down; we have had a breakdown. We are mad.

I lived inside that monologue for, I think, many days before it cracked a little, became two pieces so that a little light could enter and there was a space where I could burrow into it. The space strengthened me, and I tried to see where that truth and my truth diverged and how it had happened that now, by the light of what Abra said, I was mad. It came to me that her argument was sound; she had not been satisfied, things had not been as right as they had appeared, and she hadn't faced that reality, hadn't known what part of the mechanism that was Abra was not functioning smoothly; had not, in that way, grown up at all. That life contained the dreamer, wishing vaguely, uneasily, for something different; and at the same time it contained, for a very long time, the practical woman, coping and comforting. The two had co-existed and not, it had seemed at the time, with the kind of trauma that required this result. For some, perhaps, that co-existence, the two lines running along in the same person, separated from each other like lines on a railroad without ties, are not parallel, but come together at some point, and when they do there is this cataclysm called a breakdown.

And yet that was not, it seemed to me, what had happened.

The crack was widening; there was more space now for me to move around inside the discussion, and I was stronger.

The two lines had never met, they had remained parallel; but instead of continuing into infinity, or coming together with an explosion, they had simply vanished, at some indefinable, unanalyzable point had just ceased to exist. They had broken down.

I became able, after a time, to understand that there had been what might be called a breakdown. The theory, the logic, were acceptable.

The struggle could not end there; it was not possible to stop, although with the understanding, the old Abra had disappeared, and I was in charge of the questioning, no one else. I never, in all the restless burrowing, considered going back, never once felt an impulse to return to face their standards, to become a "grown-up." That was not, in any recess of my mind, a possibility. Still I went on, into "breakdown."

Accepting the word, it became simpler. If "breakdown" meant some terrible anguish, I had missed that part of it until now, questioning it. There had been strain, unhappiness, even fear, but nothing that could properly be called anguish. I moved to the next step: where had the breakdown come? And it came to me that all the components of the old life had, in fact, broken down: the home, the children, the marriage, whatever had made up life then. Everything else, everything outside of me, had broken down. I saw that I had not broken down. I had been put together.

And as soon as I understood that, as soon as that reasoning, achieved with such effort, had reached down into me and struck something that said, "That is truth," the driving days of questioning finished. I was whole again, but now with more assurance; it was astonishing how much the knowledge freed me, when I had already thought I was free. It was the beginning, the foundation, for all the things I learned here later. It was how I began to lose my name, my memory, the labels I'd used, and so my sense of all words. It happened over a long time, all the time here, but it began then.

I came out again, looked with surprise around me at the winter that had fallen while I had not noticed, and I began, again, to watch. I watched understanding that this was what existed, that at every moment what I saw and heard and touched and smelled was everything.

Some days I would see tracks, little paw prints in the snow, and a couple of times I caught glimpses of rabbits plunging through the yard, but mostly even the animals had hidden away like me and were also watching. It used to seem to me that the animals must long for the winter to be over, so that they could be free again; but now I imagine that like me, they simply see it, not with any longing for it to be finished, but just as part of what goes on.

I could stand at my windows and watch the snow come down, falling from some unknowable space out there, coming to rest on the ground, and then on the snow that had already fallen, piling itself higher and higher, and it insulated me, became a womb around my world. I became an infant and a child, unborn and born, sometimes going out into it to catch the flakes joyfully on my tongue, child-like delight, or throwing myself into it, making angels. The cold and the wet bit into my body. There was no sense of the ridiculous here because there was no one, not even the observing part of myself, who watched and judged. There was laughter; it was my own laughter, not at myself but coming from the joy. The first time I heard it I was startled because it did not seem it was a sound I had ever made before. It came bubbling out, no holding back, no forcing, just pure laughter. Where had it been before?

Sometimes the joy came up into my throat so that it seemed that everything inside was surging out, happiness that makes tears come. But more often there was calm, a sureness, and I might spend a day in bed, curled under blankets, reading or drawing or simply staring out the window. Time wasn't the way it had been before. It was nò escaping, no fighting. It was rhythm. It could be whatever I wanted.

I had never known before the deadening qualities of snow. It seemed to kill all sound, although there had been so little before, certainly none that was man-made; but now, with the snow, it seemed that sound could not even exist, would be soaked up by the whiteness and held, so that when the snow melted in the spring it would be released in a deafening bellow, a cacophony of storage. There were no rustlings of leaves, no stream gurgling, for ice had formed over its surface, and while the water continued to flow beneath, the ice hid it from sight and sound — all the things I'd become accustomed to hearing had disappeared, vanished, as if none of them had existed.

And that, it seemed, magnified my ability to hear, so that sounds I had not noticed before became clear. The call of a cardinal rang out piercing, bell-like, alone. A squirrel pattering near the cabin was somehow audible, although surely its running footsteps must have been muffled by the snow; yet something could be heard, perhaps just its breathing.

I put out food for the winter birds and the squirrels, and whatever else that happened by hungry, and I could watch them from the windows as they sorted out their feeding among themselves. Two squirrels might sit, eager and impatient on the ground, judging the power of two brilliant cardinals, perched on the feeder eating together amicably but jealously, watchfully, and suddenly there would be some sign, not one that I could see, and at what seemed the identical moment the birds would wing off and the squirrels would leap and take their turn at the seeds. The squirrels were fat and thick and shiny-furred, healthy but greedy, eating more, almost, than they could hold, looking bursting, bullies in some ways and sounding angry, chattering ferociously at each other, nibbling swiftly, glaring at each other; occasionally one would sit back, probably needing the moment to digest but angry still, nagging at its partner as if it were unfair for one to continue eating while the other had to rest. Incredible agility those squirrels had, in all seasons, swinging and leaping to ever-decreasing branches, always stopping short of one that would not hold their weight, somehow knowing instantly which ones would support them and which would not.

Inside the cabin, noises became apparent by contrast to the silence, and were comforting. It seemed always that there was something humming: the freezer, the refrigerator, turning themselves on and off, the electric heaters. The clicks and hums were like friends; they were familiar, indicating life and warmth, giving me assurance of reality. I felt my sense of hearing keenly.

With no jobs that had to be done, I ate, slept, read, thought, cooked and baked and washed, whenever I felt like it. It was absolute, total selfishness, and never before had anything been so perfect.

It was not that I had quite forgotten, not yet. Sometimes I deliberately remembered the other life, for in order to feel the gleam of the selfishness, I wanted to have a comparison, something against which the selfishness, the goodness of it, balanced. It was early, still, in my learning.

The remembering was quite detached and calm. There was no link now that might trigger fear or pain.

I remembered Stephen, who could not live like this, who was responsible still for what I had left behind; who had to be on time and do the things he was supposed to, and although he might feel he wanted it that way, he really, as it was, had no choice.

There were pictures in magazines, scenes on television that I remembered that were to do with death: a man being shot, a pistol at his head, brains spilling, surprise more than pain on his face; mothers Abra had cried for at one stage, carrying dead children, anguish so terrible it seemed all the hearts must burst.

It had seemed to her, for a while then, that something should be done; that someone should stop these things; and yes, that she should do something, that just seeing put some burden onto her. But what could she do? She might have joined a political party, or sent money and clothes, adopted an overseas orphan, gone back to school and become a social worker, she could have done all those things and helped, and she'd been through all the arguments. All that was long ago.

Instead I was here, out of sight and sound, an example to no one, away from all of it. There was pain everywhere out there, just, it seemed, because people existed and created it, just as Abra had dragged screaming Katie through the streets, manufacturing pain out of nothing. Did I have a right to be out of all that? Having, I assumed, inflicted much hurt did I have the right to avoid retribution?

I was invulnerable to the arguments. I remembered, but the memories were pictures and sound, movies of what was not real.

I had to go back into town twice that winter, when I ran out of dried milk powder, flour, sugar and coal oil. I had to make the trip down the road to the Brocker farm first, for the car had been neglected and wouldn't start, but I spent no time with Mr. Brocker or in the town, just drove in and back and no one tried to talk to me. They must have known by then who I was, but they didn't care, or didn't want to care, or had been put off by the eccentricity of what it appeared I was doing. I wasn't like young McAllister, who had to be warned before he attempted too much — he was someone they thought they could understand. I was something else, from another world, doing something utterly foreign to them, and so they let me be, watched me perhaps for signs that showed me to be different, looking for something — as if I should be branded by my madness? I don't know.

I bought more drawing paper while I was there, and notebooks, and also some burlap and some embroidery thread, for it had occurred to me that some of my drawings might be translated onto cloth and hung on the walls. There were many hours in the winter days and nights, and this seemed to me a pleasant way to spend them, although I had never tried such things before.

I did not buy much, however, because it was impossible to

get the car up the lane, and I had to carry what I got up that half-mile of deep snow. Mr. Brocker had offered to plow it out for me, but there seemed to be no point. I felt more protected this way.

I chose the drawing of a crow for the first embroidery. I was eager to get started on it, and when I put away the few supplies, I got out the drawing and began to trace it, with a piece of charred wood from the fireplace, onto the material. The burlap was a light blue; the crow, of course, would be black and filled in. I could feel my face pinch with the effort of concentration. And it was like the day of the drawing, when the crow had flown into the willow above my bedroom window. I had lain watching it while it shuffled its feathers and occasionally called to its fellows. I had crept cautiously out of bed, not wanting it to glimpse my movement and fly away, and gotten the drawing pad. As if it knew it was a model, it had become still, dignified, looking out over the acres like a general, and I had sketched it painfully, trying to follow its lines, and an extraordinary thing had begun to happen.

I started to lose myself, became even almost unaware of the drawing or the act of it. I saw the bird and the lines, the bird and the lines, began to fall into the bird, becoming it, feeling its existence, tracing that existence onto the paper, so that it was as if the pencil, the crow, the paper and myself were all parts of one thing. The crow sat very still, and it went on and on until there was no more to draw. And then I relaxed suddenly, realized I was exhausted.

Now I started with the needle and the black thread on the blue burlap, and I slowly stitched the outline, seeing the shape of the great black bird, moving carefully around it, knowing the curves and the points, and the thread, the material, myself and the needle also were part of one thing. And when the outline was done, I moved inside to the body of it, disregarding the details of eyes and feathers and shading, filling it in dead black, small, slow, painstaking stitches, seeing only the blackness, turning into it, becoming it, and I was the blackness and the blackness was everywhere and everything, nothing existed outside of it. Until finally, when it had stretched to the limits of the outline and I saw it was finished, the blackness diminished,

144

dwindled until it filled merely the outline of the crow on the blue burlap, and I realized the strain that was in my eyes, the pain in my fingers, cramped for so long. I had to sleep, and it was so late I was seeing the dawn as I lay down, memory of the blackness still in my mind as I went to sleep, without dreams, a deep, heavy, black sleep.

The next day I hemmed the edges under and made a frame with pieces of kindling, tying the corners with string, and tacked the burlap to the frame. I hung it in the bedroom, beside the window where the stitching crow could be seen beside the willow, as the original had been in it.

Now there are many of these works on my walls. Some are drawings, some are needlework, and each one, when I look closely, calls up that same mysterious intensity of concentration, the same sense of being what I see. There are flowers and insects and birds, some of them detailed with shadings, unlike the pure black crow, for now it is possible to feel the unity with subtleties of colour. I see each of them; I am each of them. What is on these walls is my experience here; they are what has happened to me. I know that anyone coming in would not see that, but they were not done for the outside.

I had thought, before it came, that in winter I would grow plump, insulated within my body as well as within the cabin. It did not happen.

When I was absorbed in the drawings, whole days went past, and I think I must often have forgotten to eat. And, too, there is something in that kind of concentration, that loss of self, that burns huge amounts of energy; the soul that is responsible uses energy without considering, without exhaustion, until it is done, and then it collapses. And so I grew thinner, and the heat of my energy kept me warm.

Occasionally I realized that I must eat, and at those times I went to the freezer and retrieved some kind of food, making a conscious effort to have a proper meal. Afterwards my stomach would feel stretched and painful, and the lethargy would come and I would retreat to bed, sleeping until my body was stoked up again, ready to go on.

I do not remember thinking about what was happening. The time then had such — not unreality, which is what I was going

145

to say. But considering it now, I see that what it had was a total reality, a complete sense of being where I was, doing what I was doing, with nothing between myself and the experience, no thoughtful mediator saying, "now I shall do this," and "that looks all right, now let's go on to this," or even, "this is very pleasant." There was none of that, and I only noticed in the absence of the mediator that it had ever been present. And even that didn't come until later, until after the winter was over.

The immediacy of living in that winter began the sharpening of my instincts, my perception of what was to be done. I did not think. I sensed and then I acted. So that when my body began to make itself known, after weeks of inactivity, showed itself tightening and restless, needing occupation, I let it tell me what to do.

There was no system of exercises, nothing that I knew of, and I let my body itself move, releasing it, with an understanding that it would know what should be done. I stood and it began to touch my toes, slowly up and down, or it wanted swift movement and urged me to run until I was sweating, around and around the cabin. I could let it have its time, choosing when it wanted to move and how, and it did not seem as if its demands were excessive.

The winter days had achieved a rhythm of their own, different from the other seasons. It was purely instinctive, not based on anything outside my own mind and body, every action a response to some impulse. Sometimes the urge was for exercise, other times for sleeping or sewing or eating. The instincts never failed me, even if they suggested only that I stay in bed or make a cup of tea. They required only that I be aware of them, and respond.

It was another leap, taking perhaps years, before the idea of separation I had within myself ended and I was a unit, body, mind and the other part that may be what is called "soul", just as the crow and the pencil and the paper and I had been the same thing. I am not certain when that knowledge came, or how, although I know it was gradual and not some sudden realization.

At some point that winter, I began to keep a journal. It seemed in the beginning there was something important about the writing of things, something that might hold onto the reality of events. I guess I thought a journal would give a kind of coherence there hadn't been before, so that when I read back over it, what it contained might come together in a pattern that I would see and could experience again. I wrote about the drawings and my body and what I saw; I wrote about breakdowns and becoming sane, and the mysterious awesome moment of knowing; and I wrote about the squirrels and the cardinals and the unbroken snow in the mornings. I wrote that when an act was right, it was preceded by a sense of rightness. The instincts, I wrote, could not be wrong.

I learned: that words were not adequate for describing what I was understanding that winter; and that it was useless to go back in search of a pattern. I would write what was happening, clearly, I thought, and later when I read it again I would find the words flat, for they could never keep up with the changes.

Still, understanding that at last, I wrote for the pleasure of it, randomly, no longer trying to keep pace, immersed in the words that would not say what I wanted them to say, and that I would never read again. There was so much that was new during a time that I had thought might be simple or peaceful or dangerous. I tried to put something of that into the journal, tried to explain the joy. I was consumed, so that I saw vividly everything there was, and at the same time noticed nothing around me.

Until one day I realized that the day was longer than others had been, that I was writing more without lighting the coal oil lamps, and for the first time in — how long? — I looked outside. Then I walked outside. There was a difference in the air, a knowledge that winter was coming to an end, and it was almost spring.

12

The new season drew me more and more away from the winter place, taking me to see what was happening outside. But the learning of the winter stayed with me, changing the way I saw things, changing what I saw.

A crocus. I moved into its bulging protected whiteness, felt its ripeness, was it growing. The stream flowed and I flowed in it, sitting by it, seeing it swell with the melted snow, and it moved on and stayed also where it was. The grass, left naked after the snow, was battered, green but dull, not fresh and sharp as it would be later, and I could feel it straightening after the winter burden, gathering up strength and colour. The spring came on me slowly, slowly.

I worked, too, but more deliberately now, consciously, without the panic or strain of preparation. There was, again, the garden. It was time to clear the space, but the task of clearing was itself the reality, not a job to be gotten through so that the planting could be done. I bent, pulled, dug, tossed to one side the plants of the last year, the aging weeds, building a pile of them, getting them ready to be the next season's compost, and I felt the earth as I dug into it, felt it cool and moist around my fingers, felt how it was for the roots of the plants, protective and nourishing and comfortable.

I returned to cutting wood, a little each day, seeing how it was not only for the next winter, but for this time, too. The muscles in my upper arms and chest pulled as I swung back with the axe, and my back and legs and arms went into the forward swing, and there was a rhythm, not just of the movement but of everything that went into the movement, all the parts of myself, and I could feel them shifting, straining, relaxing, pulling, again and again, and I was wholly the sensation.

I was eating again, regularly and fully, and sleeping deeply; there was a kind of glaze around what I was doing, and I was alone with the action, so that everything outside it was out of focus, not quite real. In turn, I came to everything, and it seemed that nothing was unknown to me.

A bird flew into my vision and I watched it, seeing it moving, cleaning, restless or resting on a branch, until it flew on, and I watched it as long as it was in view, seeing it dip and swerve on the unseen currents of air, following some hidden path of its own, and I followed it, was it, felt the currents, flying myself, for just those moments.

An earthworm, dislodged by my rootings in the garden, coiled on the surface, gleaming, moving disjointedly and slowly, comprehending the air and the light, its head occasionally moving, snake-like, upwards, turning slowly, tasting the atmosphere, deciding somewhere in its instincts that it was not right, not home, and turning again to descend back into the earth, calmly, without panic, moving away down into the cool moisture where it belonged, and all the time I watched, feeling the soil and the slime, knowing the compartments of the body and the movements, feeling the foreignness of the air, wanting the chill dampness of the earth and going back into it, not without a sense of danger from the exposure, but accepting it, not grateful that there had been no injury, just as there would have been no resentment if there had been.

It was a drifting, dream-like and very conscious time. When I saw the man, he was like a bird, catching my attention with his movement, holding it as my mind moved into him.

I saw him as he reached the top of the lane. I was in the garden, slowly pulling out plants, when I caught the movement and my eyes pursued it. He saw me almost immediately and stopped, then began walking again, toward me now, moving ponderously, steadily, and I watched him and felt the heaviness of the steps, the weight behind them. He was not like the earthworm on the surface; the atmosphere was alien to him, too, but he was frightened by it.

I watched him.

He was close now and I knew the face; it was odd that I had not recognized the body, the movements, the fear, but the face I knew and I, too, felt a foreignness and wanted to back away. I was threatened; and then, aware of that, I stopped, considered where the threat was. It came from myself, of course, nothing from this man who I knew would not hurt me. It was my own fear of having what I knew disrupted, perhaps destroyed, for it was only beginning really, it was not solid yet, it needed time and growth and I was afraid it might be trampled, as I could have crushed the earthworm.

I must be strong, I thought.

The man was in front of me now, standing over me, for I remained crouched in the garden, my hands still in the soil, and I could see myself through his eyes, like an animal looking up at him. I was both of us at once, myself seeing him towering above me, shocked and unhappy and brave, and myself huddled, it seemed, and watchful. I could not feel. I had not understood before how it would be to see a person so familiar and so far away, and not to feel.

The man's voice was very quiet. "Abra," he said.

I stood slowly, my eyes still on him. "Yes, Stephen."

It was all, I thought, that needed to be said, but of course he did not know that; how could he have? For I remembered that other world and what is not learned there, including when words are futile, and a watching is enough to know.

"Can we talk?" he asked.

"If you want." My voice was not unpleasant, not without cordiality. I felt strength returned, and so it was possible to be kind.

I began to walk toward the cabin and he followed, staying a little behind me; we were no longer equals, no longer a couple, and it did not seem right that we should walk together. In the cabin I sat down at the table in the kitchen and after a moment he sat in the chair opposite, looking around the room, not ready yet to look at me, while I waited calmly, my hands folded on the table. Finally he had to begin, and he glanced at me, then down at his hands, and he kept his gaze there while he spoke. There was a strain of rehearsal in his speech; he had prepared what to say, how to react, but I think it likely he prepared it with a fantasy that was much different from what was here. For an instant I felt protective, wanted to put my arms around him to tell him it was all right, but I knew he would misinterpret the gesture. If I held him it would not be directed at Stephen the husband, the man, but simply at a suffering person, and he would not understand that. I sat quietly.

"I came here," he began slowly, "to ask you what happened. In case you're wondering, I found you by accident. I looked for months, but nobody knew anything. Then the man who owned this place, the one you bought it from I guess, called one night not long ago to see how we liked the place. He told me where you were."

The prepared speech, like the prepared tone of voice, fell apart, he gave it up and looked at me, pleading and angry, demanding.

"What happened? Why did you leave like that? Didn't you know what you were doing to us? Didn't you care about the children, or your parents? Or me?" The last had the shrill tone of the wounded, the one who feels most injured, who has come to the real point. He tried to continue, could not find the words. I understood, because there were no words for how he felt. He didn't know that I could feel his pain and frustration and humiliation in myself because I was watching him and was him. And yet his pain and frustration and humiliation did not dislodge my knowledge of what was true, so that however far my understanding went, it would make no difference in the end.

I could see the whole scene, knew how it would develop and how he would hope and then not hope, would hate and love and rage and feel pity for himself. I could see it all and understand it, and beneath it, or beside it, would be myself, watching, understanding, surviving. And afterwards something would be changed for him, but not for me.

It was like a play, Stephen and I sitting at the table, his eyes shifting, groping for his lines, me knowing both his lines and mine, waiting simply for the end, when I would go back to the life I really had. There was acceptance of this gap in reality, this time to be gotten through, like an actress who knows that she has a performance to give before she can take off her make-up and meet her lover or go home to sleep.

"Aren't you going to answer me?" he demanded. "Don't you think you at least owe me that, an answer?" He expected me to be touched, but I was not. I was not holding back compassion; it was that this had nothing to do with me.

"I can try to tell you," I said softly, "but I don't know if you can understand." It brought the anger, his face contorted and he was shouting, his eyes furious. Something in his forehead throbbed.

"Why don't you think I can understand? Can you remember one moment, one moment in our marriage when I didn't try to understand? You know better than that. You could say any asshole thing you wanted, and you know I always tried to understand." He heard what he had said and stopped, confused and embarrassed. When he spoke again it was more softly. "You know what I mean. I knew you weren't happy, I know you wanted to be doing something more, we talked about all that, but it's not my fault. You can't say it was my fault, because I always encouraged you to do what you could, go back to school or whatever, but you never did. So you can't say I didn't try, it was you that didn't try."

Of course he was right. I remembered it well, and started to laugh, for just a moment, until his face darkened again, he thought I was laughing at him and I put my hand on his arm, quietening, and tried to explain. "I'm sorry, I wasn't laughing at you. It was me. You're right, of course, I had asshole ideas. I was so stupid. It all seems so far away."

"It is far away. You're like a different person." He was puzzled now, my hand was back on the table, folded again, and I was calm. "You know you look awful? Totally different?"

"I don't know how I look. There aren't any mirrors here. I must look different, though, because I feel so different. Can't you see that? I am someone else, it's not just the way I look."

"But your hair. It's all gone, and it was so beautiful." Wistful, remembering the old Abra. "What happened?"

I tried to remember a sequence so that I could tell him

something he might understand, that would not go too far, that would protect both of us as we were now. I sighed; it was an effort.

"I loved all of you. I worried. I wanted to protect you all from everything. I was so tired. I used to read the papers every day, cover to cover, and I waited for all of you to come home. One day I saw an advertisement in the paper. The next day it was there again. It meant something to me, I didn't know what, then. It was an impulse. I called the number in the advertisement, and then a man brought me up here and showed me this place. I can't explain what happened, except that I knew I had to be here. I went back to the city and got the money Grandmother left, and bought it. I didn't want to talk about it then. I just came here, and everything has changed. I know you want to know what happened, but I can't tell you. I don't have any idea. I remember being with you, but it's as if that was a different person. I don't want to hurt you. The other Abra didn't want to hurt you then, but something happened." I shrugged.

"I don't know what it was. That person died. I can't explain it any more, but she's gone as surely as if you'd buried her."

The fantasy he'd come with, whatever it had been, was gone. He looked horrified and frightened, and for a few moments there were signs of struggle on his face. Then he became quiet again, gentle.

"Oh Abra, Abra." He was shaking his head, sad. "I didn't know. You're right, I didn't understand. But I might have, if you'd trusted me. We could have done something, we could have gotten help." He was watching me closely, choosing his words cautiously. "Why don't you come back with me now? Just pack a few things you need and we'll drive back together, see the children. They'd like to see you. Stay a few days, see how you feel. Without the pressures. There's a housekeeper now, you wouldn't have to do anything. And maybe after you get rested a little, we could work together, you'd have all the time in the world and all the best help, you could put it together again, I know you could, and we'd help you this time, you wouldn't have to be alone."

He was so kind, he had always been so kind. But with his kindness he was humouring me, or the person he thought I was;

he didn't see it at all, but then how could he, it was not to be expected, I knew that, and I could not be angry.

"No Stephen," I said softly, firmly. "Give it up. I know you think I'm crazy and a little work with a psychiatrist will make everything all right again. But it's not like that."

I thought for a moment, how to ease it. "I know," I went on, "that you always cared enough to want what was best for me. You were very kind and generous and always fair. I know that what's happened doesn't seem right to you. I have been unfair and unkind and ungenerous, and I accept that that's true.

"But you must understand that I belong here. To you it's some kind of delusion, but the life I had before would be madness to me now. I couldn't go back to it ever, not after what I've seen here, not with any psychiatrist in the world. Why can't we leave it at that?" I leaned forward, making him look at me.

"Stephen you were my husband. I want you to live the best way you know. You have to go on with it, you must not imagine that I can come back. You have to make what you can, not live with something that isn't real. That's all we have."

He was looking at me, without understanding, but also without hope, and that was the moment when it was clear that he knew he would leave alone.

"Tell me now," I said briskly, assuming by a new tone that the subject was closed, "what's been happening with the children and you?"

"Do you care?" He was sullen now.

"I'd be interested to know, if you feel like telling me." I felt almost like a mother again, cajoling a child. And yet of course I knew he had to range from anger to sadness to childishness; what struck me was my own strength, that I could sit, quite calmly and in control, seeing this normal person and saying to myself, "Yes, so now he's angry, soon he'll be childish and then we'll go back to self-pity." It was not that he was being analyzed, coldly, like a laboratory experiment; it was just that I could see it.

"All right then. Here's what's been happening. Just since you left, of course. Most of it because you left.

"I've hired a housekeeper, full-time and live-in. In fact, I've hired several and fired them, and I'd like to fire the one we have now. It's a tough job, and I can't seem to find anyone who's up to it; the kids need special understanding, and no one seems to have enough to give to children who aren't their own. I've been trying to figure out whether it's better to keep on firing them until I find a good one, or to keep on the one we have, even though she's not really what they need, because whenever one goes they get more insecure.

"They cling. They stick around the house, and they follow me around all the time when I'm home. It drives me crazy, one of them is always behind me or ahead of me, or else I see them at the windows, watching me." He paused, waiting for me to say something. It was expected, a penance.

"Yes, well that'll be because I left. Of course it would have made them insecure." I was at a distance, nodding, and all of it was quite obvious, the situation there, and yet I was unrelated to it. He could see that, and the resentment was there, the feeling that I had caused it all and then cared nothing about it; and the self-pity, for he had been stuck with looking after it and picking up the pieces.

"Well," he mocked, a tone I had never heard from him before, "that'll be because I left." Then came anger again: "And you don't care, do you. You just think, 'well of course they're insecure, they'd have to be, and yes it's my fault,' but you don't care, you don't care what your own children have suffered. It's incredible," he was shaking his head. "I can't believe the person you must be, to just be able to sit there and not care. Who did I live with all those years, who did I think I knew? It's grotesque, it makes me sick." He was white and furious.

"I'm sorry," I said, "but it's done and there's no changing it. What can I say about it? It's my fault and I'm sorry they're unhappy." I spread my hands open and lifted my shoulders, questioning him. "What else can I say?"

"Oh no," he said bitterly, "of course you're right, there's nothing more you could say. Nothing else you could have done, either, I suppose, no way you could have thought more of them than you did of yourself, no way you might have considered them before you took off. Of course there wasn't anything else you could have done."

He caught himself, pulled back, stared at me. He was mining

hatred, but it couldn't touch me, had nothing to do with me.

"All right," he said coldly. "I don't think you'll likely feel too badly if I tell you the rest. I thought maybe I should go easy, but now you can hear the whole thing.

"Elliott's so screwed-up he screams when I leave the house, screams when the housekeeper goes out, screams when Katie isn't home when he wants her to be. He screams, but he won't ever talk about it. He's just closed right up.

"I don't think he has any friends at all now. Partly he's embarrassed, doesn't want to have other kids in because he doesn't have a mother there, and he can't even say his is dead, the way a couple of them can; but I think mostly it's because he doesn't want to take his eyes off me and Katie and the house-keeper, although he can't stand the housekeeper. Katie can't either. She's about fifty, pleasant enough but strict, and of course she's really too old to have the energy for kids that age, they need more attention than most, and after all she's only paid to do it. I don't know really what I expect from her, it's not fair to expect so much. In any case, the kids loathe her, but I'm scared of what might happen if I let her go, because they didn't like the others either but it was a hell of a mess when they left.

"It looks as if Katie's in better shape than Elliott, but I'm not so sure. She's quieter now. She doesn't dance any more, and we never hear her singing. She just kind of pads around the house, and she watches us. Just after you left I heard her and a couple of friends talking, and one of them was asking where you were. They were in the kitchen, at the table, and I was walking down the hall past the door. I saw Katie shrug, just the way you did a minute ago, and she just said, "Oh, she's gone." That's all. You wouldn't have known from her voice, but I saw her face just then, when she was saying it, and it was terrible, she was smiling but still it was so bleak, so lost, I wanted to go in and hug her and tell her to go ahead and cry. But of course she wouldn't have wanted that, with her friends there. I don't know how to help her."

Yes the picture, this one, touched me, and I felt for a moment as if I couldn't breathe, the need to reach out to the children was so strong in me.

And then I saw the way it was there now in that house, and

the way the children were, and it stretched ahead and I could see them growing up, growing older. I could see how they would be, insecure and unsure. But they would become strong against it, testing the unsureness until they found it was untrue, and I saw that finally they might be terribly powerful, in their own ways. "They'll be all right, you know," I said, and he looked as if he might hit me, there was that kind of tension in his body, but he didn't say anything.

"And what about you, Stephen, what's happened to you?"

"Oh well," he said ironically, "I suppose you could say I've been surviving. Nothing very interesting. Nothing like making myself a whole new life, just struggling along with the old one, trying to dó my best, you know the way it is."

"Yes," I said.

There was a long silence. He had come with hope and forgiveness, would leave with hate. And I? I would go on here, I was just an observer now in these things, and I watched him.

Finally he cleared his throat and very quietly now and gently, began. "Abra, there's one other thing. I didn't know whether I should tell you or not, but I think I have to." A deep breath. "Your folks died six months ago in a car accident. It wasn't their fault, it was some kid in the other car who didn't even have a licence yet. Stole his dad's car. I couldn't find you to let you know. I'm sorry." He put out his hand to cover mine. I was startled to see that mine had begun to tremble, that he still had the tenderness to try to help. Not hate. I could not speak.

I was still a child. I felt abandoned, hollow inside, nothing there but a huge gasp of air. I had not given them a thought here, but for them to be gone, out of reach . . . they took that first life with them and I had no past at all. There was no life remaining, only this one, and for the moment it did not seem enough.

So much alone. I could say nothing to Stephen. I was too hollow for words. There was so much silence.

After a while he said, "Well then," and stood abruptly, pushing the chair back from the table so that it fell onto the floor. He looked startled, turned to pick it up and there was a pause. "Well then, I guess there's nothing more. Is there anything you need I could send you up from the city?" He was leaving politely, like a guest instead of a husband. He thought I didn't care, and I had no strength to tell him.

"No thank you, that's very kind but I have everything here."

"So it appears."

We walked slowly, almost reluctantly, to the door and then on into the clean spring air. For some reason we both stopped and breathed it deeply, as if the air inside had gone stale and foul.

"Well Abra," he said, turning, and he was smiling, the same kind of smile I imagine Katie had when she was explaining to her friends that her mother was "gone," so that I felt sad for him and for me and again wanted to put my arms around him for comfort, but knew better. "I guess that's it, then."

We went on. I thought I would see him to the top of the lane, so that I could watch him leave, know that he was gone. Suddenly he stopped once more and turned to me, insistent again, desperate with the last chance.

"Abra please, can't you tell me? It must have been something, it really must have been, or else you couldn't have left like that. Was it something I did? I've tried to think, it's like something must have happened and I didn't even notice it, and it was so big that you left." He ran a hand through his hair, an old gesture. "Look, I know you're not coming back. It's just, I want to know, it would be something you could do for me, if you could just tell me." He wanted so badly for it to be something specific, so that he could point to it and say, "there, that was the thing," so that it could be classified and put away. I wished to be able to do that for him, but I couldn't.

I said wearily, "Stephen, if there had been something, I would tell you, I promise you. It was nothing to do with you, or with Elliott and Katie. It was just me, and believe me I accept that what's happened to them, and to you, has been because of what I did. But I can't change it, and I can't explain it to you."

We were at the top of the lane and I stopped. Stephen looked down where he would be walking, and then back at me, not wanting, even yet, to let go. I put out my hand to shake his.

"Good-bye then, Stephen. I hope that only the best happens for you."

He was angry again — I felt so vague, and what I said

sounded formal and polite, I suppose — and pulled his hand away, turned and began to walk, almost march, determined and defiant. I watched him and he didn't look back, not until he was far away, and then I saw him turn, but he saw I was still watching and so he turned away again, abruptly, and kept on walking and he didn't look back again and then he was gone.

And still I stood there. I felt scattered, as if I had radiated out over the fields, strands of me like spiders' webs of hollowness reaching everywhere, and I stood still until I felt all the strands winding back, returning to me, so that finally, slowly, I was no longer scattered but here again, and not until all the strands were secured inside did I move, walking slowly back to the garden. I knelt again, remembering where I had been when the man had first come, and my hands went back into the earth, and I felt more roots and pulled them out.

Later I sat on the couch, wrapped in a blanket before the fire — although it was not cold I seemed to need these things to make me warm again — and watched the flames. I moved into them, became a flame, became fuel, also, for the fire, and was consumed and consuming, all brilliant colours and leaping heat.

Later in my bedroom I watched the moon through the branches of the willow. The fire had been hot, the moon was cool. I cried softly, gently and with love. I said good-bye to my mother and my father.

After a while I slept and had no dreams. In the morning the sun was shining, a clear and perfect day. I lay quietly and felt the sun and listened to the birds; every day, it seemed, more arrived from the south, so that every day there was some new sound.

I got up and made tea, and then I went outside, taking the axe, for there was wood to chop, and my muscles stretched and pulled in the sunlight and were all in their rhythm again.

* *

One day a postman came with a registered letter. I signed the separation agreement it contained. Later, Stephen divorced me.

13

I recall that the first time I came down sick, the weather was warm but the garden had only just been planted. It must have been late spring, not yet summer.

With the garden in, bigger that year with corn for the first time, I took a day for a walk around the land. It was very green and plush by then, flowers and weeds growing taller, ready for blooming, the little early spring flowers like the crocuses gone now, bigger, brasher plants taking over for the summer. I walked slowly through the woods, seeing with one eye the fresh growth, and with the other the dead trees that I would cut in the next months for firewood. In the pasture I saw a rabbit, gray-coloured, standing very still, alert, and I stood still in the same way, watching, and it did not move, not a twitch, until after a long time I began to walk again, and then it bolted instantly, flying off in great leaps toward the woods. There were holes here, too, that groundhogs had dug, and I imagined the underground caverns where they lived with great dark-attuned black eyes, emerging occasionally to blink against the sunlight until the pupils narrowed to let in less blinding light. I found their entrances and exits, guessed at their underground trails from above, but did not see the animals themselves, hidden beneath or perhaps gone foraging.

The stream was still swollen, although becoming calmer than in the first early spring rush of water and melting snow. I squatted by it, watching it strike the stones and bounce away, rushing, not like the easy flow that would come later, and I saw that already there were some water-striders, just a few, stroking around the quieter eddies at the sides of the stream, not yet venturing out to the middle where the water was too strong and would carry them off against their flick-flick strength. The water was very cold; I kicked off my sneakers and rolled off my socks, hitched my jeans around my knees and waded into the stream. For a few moments the water whirling around my ankles was cold and good, then suddenly it was nothing and frightening. My feet were numb; I could not feel them attached to me. I pulled them out of the stream, put back the socks and sneakers, and hurried back to the cabin where I made tea and sat at the kitchen table, feeling the prickles of sensation returning like tiny electric shocks. I rubbed my feet with a rough towel, and later built a fire and put them up so that they got too hot then, and they seemed to be all right.

I was very tired, from the walking I thought, and went to bed early, shortly after dusk. But when I woke up it was very late the next day, the sun was high, another clear bright day without rain clouds, and I felt hot and weak and still tired. I lay there for a long time before I made myself get up to get tea, which I had in the dark comfort of the living room, not wanting to sit up straight in the kitchen and yet not wanting to give in entirely to going back to bed.

I made a second, stronger cup of tea, but then when I got up to wash out the cup I found that my legs would not move the way I ordered them, they were trembling and threatened to go out from under me.

I had to hold onto the cupboard with one hand while I washed out the cup with the other. I knew it was necessary to get to the bed, but it was a long trip through the living room, having to sit down once suddenly on a chair, resting, then hauling myself back up, pulling my way into the bedroom, falling onto the bed and, after a while, cold, clutching a blanket and pulling it around me, finally falling into a dizzying sleep full of twitchings and forgotten nightmares, a surface sleep of heat and cold.

I woke up in late afternoon, frightened, sweating and feverish, teeth chattering. I could get neither warm enough nor

161

cold enough, my body switching temperatures too fast, and I tried to sit up, to swing my legs over the side of the bed so that I could stand, maybe walk back to the kitchen, for still I thought that surely all I needed was another cup of tea and something solid to eat. But when I tried to put my weight on my legs they let me down and I was back on the bed, too hot and then chilled, and it was too hard. I crawled back under the sheets, damp now from sweat, pulled up the blankets and the quilt slowly, fingers trembling, and I thought hazily that I could sweat it out, no matter how hot I got I would keep the blankets until all the sickness went away in the heat; but then the fever came back, my body was stifling, and I forgot and tossed the covers aside, pulled them back again a few moments later when the sweat felt as if it were freezing on my body, sending cold damp chills all through me, shivering so that it seemed I would never be warm.

For a while again I slept, but it was worse. Nightmares closed in and they were on the surface too, like the heat and cold, so that I saw them clearly and could not tell whether or not they were real, thought sometimes that I was surrounded by these creatures of the dreams, knowing other times, when I was better, that I was asleep and that they were from my sleep.

It was very dark, sometime in the middle of the night, when I woke again, this time to a solid heat that would not go away, and I wished for nothing more than the coldness to come back to chill me. I was thirsty, baked dry, and I had to be strong enough to go for water. I tried my legs again and found that by putting some of my weight on my arms I could support myself, leaning on furniture. I started out that way, not knowing what I would do when there was no furniture to hang onto. At the doorway, clinging to the frame, I could no longer stay upright, there was nothing to hold my weight, and I fell damply to the floor. I think I lay there a long time.

I had to crawl then, moving across the floor of the living room, forgetting why, no longer aware of the thirst but only of the crawling, the need to move just another few inches, not even aiming at the kitchen now but simply pulling myself forward with my fingers, sometimes able to rise up onto my knees, no further, and it seemed as if there were long gaps, times when I might have passed out or fallen asleep, because it seemed that hours went by between one movement and the next.

I did not know, did not care, where I was, just pulled on vaguely in the direction I had started; and with one movement I found myself bumping over a rise and then a dip in the floor like a threshold, and then I was in the kitchen and everything was high above me, so that I might never reach any of it. I lay there, panting, sweating, hopeless, believing I was going to die, that this was death and a relief.

And then I looked up and above me stood the McAllisters, three of them, Belle and her husband and her child, watching me, and he was holding a gun. Belle and the child were smiling; he stood there, silent, the shotgun pointed at an angle to the floor, holding it loosely, looking at me, assessing me, his eyes squinting slightly. I tried to speak to them but no sounds would come out, and I didn't know whether I wanted to say "yes, please" or ask to be allowed to survive, surely I would make it. We were like four statues, none of us able to shift, frozen into shared time, staring, and it went on and on.

But then gradually light came into the room and the three shapes began to disappear into it; the sun was coming up, absorbing them slowly until they were gone, and I was lying on the floor, still wearing my clothes, cold now, terribly cold, and yet still sweating, and I looked high up and saw the cupboard where the sink was. I rolled toward it, hearing some faraway animal sound that must have come from myself, and slowly, gripping handles and the edge of the sink, pulled upright, reached for the tap and turned it, leaned further and put my head down into the water, the weight now on my stomach at the edge of the sink, feet no longer touching the floor. I let the water run into my mouth, over my face, careful not to choke, and then my stomach hurt, too full of too cold water, and I could not believe I had been thirsty, did not think I would ever be thirsty again. I started to fall and caught myself, aware in some dim practical place that I must not leave the water running, reached out and turned the tap, and let myself drop. I could not move then, and I fell asleep.

It was long bright daylight when I woke, and I was cold and clear, knew there were things I had to do to keep the sickness from getting worse. I pulled myself up to the sink again and filled a big glass with water, setting it when it was full on the counter beside the sink and sliding back to the floor for rest.

When I was able, I reached for the glass, got it safely down beside me; I should take some kind of food as well, I thought, but it wasn't possible, the water was as much as I could manage.

Pushing the glass very carefully ahead of me, I started back. At the same rise, which seemed to me now so huge, between the kitchen and the little hallway into the living room, I had to lift the glass and spilled a little water, just a few drops. Slowly, painfully, I continued, crawling, halting, until finally I was in a doorway. I could see my bed, enormous and white, far away as through the wrong end of a telescope. I pushed harder, keeping my eyes on the bed, the goal, and then I was beside it, left the glass of water on the floor and pulled myself up, the greatest effort so far, until my head and chest were on the bed and then one leg, and then I rolled, an enormous heave, and all my body was on it, and I didn't remember any more.

It could have been that I lost days then; it could have been also that I simply blacked out for a few moments. When I did wake up I was terribly thirsty, terribly weak, and it was some minutes before I remembered the water beside the bed, and was grateful that I had thought to bring it back. I held myself to only a few mouthfuls, remembering the hard journey, wanting to conserve what I had to avoid another.

I felt stronger. I was able to pull back the covers and slide under them; for a long time I was awake, looking up at the ceiling. And then I lost track again.

The cracks in the ceiling turned into patterns, the patterns turned into shapes of people and animals, and after a time the people and animals began to move, having nothing to do with me for I was just a spectator, but moving among themselves, flowing toward each other and then away, making silent transactions just with each other. It seemed to me that there were animals from everywhere, although I couldn't distinguish if it was the same with the people. There was a groundhog, I remember, and a smaller shape that looked like a skunk, with the flung-up tail, a misshapen giraffe with a cock-eyed neck, and what might have been a hippopotamus or an enormous odd bull, and among them all the people, who seemed to melt and float with the animals, not as if they were in charge but as if they were part of the whole collection.

I watched them for a long time, and then I went to sleep again and it seemed as if the sleep was the same as the being awake, for the same forms were in the dreams, with the same flowing, floating movements, doing the same dream-like things, without discernible purpose. It went on and on like that, waking, sleeping, the same figures, and after a while I was no longer a spectator but one of them, moving in and out of them, all of them flat, one-dimension, outlines only and I was that way, too, without substance; and in the same way that their shapes were without dimension, so were their spirits, so that they moved without time or space or joy or sadness or any emotion. I was in it too, only it was not an "I" that was there, just a form, no personality or feeling, just the floating outline, and it was neither pleasant nor unpleasant, for there was no such thing here, there was just the business of floating, touching, moving apart, floating, touching and moving apart. Like gentle bump 'em cars we moved, and I was on the ceiling too except that it wasn't the ceiling any more, it was everywhere, and sometimes I was asleep and sometimes I was awake and neither was different from the other.

And then I was falling, falling, drifting back, away, and I could no longer touch the forms and they could no longer reach me, and as I fell my outline and form changed, grew full until I was a body, filled in; and I could feel again, felt a sadness at falling away, so that the emotions were coming back, filling up again like the body, and finally I was back in the bed, looking up at the figures from a distance, and it seemed to me that they were slowing down, were not touching any more, and I watched and watched until I could see that they were patterns in the ceiling; and then they were no longer patterns, simply cracks, and then my eyes were closed and I was asleep.

It was almost the end of the sickness when I woke up. Thirsty again, I finished what was in the glass of water beside the bed. I lay still for a long time, my mind almost clear, but not yet willing to test my body, feeling it still weak beneath the covers. I wondered how I had been so sick, for my body had never collapsed on me before, I had been sick but never like this, and I was frightened that such a thing could happen, that I might be helpless. I thought about dying, remembered being in the kitchen with the McAllisters standing over me.

It seemed that it would have been a very simple thing to die, not painful or difficult, no clinging to life because I had been in no condition to cling to anything, and gradually my fright became calm. I thought, "yes, I might have died"; and then "yes, I might yet die here, alone, with no one to help or be with me, no one to know for days or weeks or even months." And I went back with my clear mind into crossing that infinite floor, and saw that it could not have been so dreadful if I had simply put my head down and given in. Sometime, when I was older and the body was weaker, I would not have the strength to keep going; when that time came, surely I would recognize it, know it was all right, and submit.

It was good. It seemed to me I could look directly at death now and say, "I'm not afraid, it will be simple to slip away, nothing can hurt at the point of death, there is no pain." I did not wish for death, being surrounded by life. But I wasn't afraid of it, would not be again, and that was the greatest freedom. There was nothing left I could not dare.

I slept again, and finally, when I woke, it was time to move, the body was very weak but it had to be fed, had to move to feed itself, and having faced death, I wanted to live.

I moved cautiously from the bed and stood, weak but solid, on the floor. A step at a time, slowly, making sure like a mountain climber that each step was firm before trying the next, and then I was in the living room, and across it to the threshold of the kitchen, and there was the kettle. I boiled water for tea and sat at the table, drinking it, feeling the heat of the liquid down my throat, into my body, feeling every drop of it and warming inside. After a while I stood again, still careful, and made toast. My stomach was already filled, for it had shrunk with the illness. I sat very still until the hunger came again and then I boiled an egg, almost the last of this supply, what day was it, I couldn't tell, there might be eggs going bad, waiting at the bottom of the lane. I made another slice of toast and poured the egg onto it, had another cup of tea and washed the dishes. I was tired and went into the living room to the couch, to lie down. I was weary of the bedroom, it had too much of the smell of sickness about it. After a while I fell asleep again.

In a few days I was almost well, much thinner I could see, hipbones jutting from the flesh, but almost strong again. I made myself eat and did very little. I sat in the sunshine outside the cabin and watched the birds and the plants; from my chair I could see the weeds growing up, still small but growing, in the garden, and I longed to go and pull them out.

I got the book I used for sketching and began to draw again. The lines seemed fainter, and I guessed I did not have the strength in my fingers yet that I had had.

These drawings were different, horrible in a way, but they did not frighten me as they might have before. In them, living things became dead as I watched, each of them freezing into death, and yet it was not disturbing, did not seem cruel. A flower translated onto paper would suddenly wilt, wither, turn brown in front of me and in the drawing, and I could leave it and think, "well, that's dead, that's done with, I wonder what will turn up in its place?" Or a bird, flying high, would suddenly plummet in the sketch, smash into the ground, and I would stare at it and then look up again, to see that in its place another bird was circling, and it would plummet and hit the earth, and above yet another one would be flying, and always when one went there was another in its place, and that seemed right and not at all sad.

As soon as I felt completely healthy, I attacked the garden, uprooting the intruder weeds and placing them aside on the compost pile. I felt and gave them a certain reverence, because they would die now. But it was not sad; they would be replaced, and I would uproot the replacements, unendingly, through seasons of living and dying, and they would break down and feed new growth.

I returned more slowly to cutting wood and dragging it back on the home-made sledge to the pile behind the cabin. My muscles were small again and loose, unaccustomed, and I let them build back up in an easy time. Again the piles of wood were growing, the season was good, the plants were healthy, the sun was hot and occasionally it rained, just enough.

The earth drank the moisture, took it down to the roots of the plants, and the plants became greener and fuller, while their time for death approached.

Everything I touched that year was touched with the

167

knowledge of death, and each time I tested it, told myself, "this thing will die, how does it feel, how do I feel?" And each time it was all right, I knew the time would come.

I was more grateful for my body. I protected it and strengthened it, and I watched what it did, thinking, "how simple this is, how lucky I am, it could just as easily be the other way."

It may seem odd that every year since then, each spring, I have become ill. Perhaps it's the release into the new season from the draining, sunken concentration of the winter that brings that fearful clarity of fever, so that all the colours are too bright, hurting my eyes, and I have to hold my hands over them because the brightness must be blinding. And the sounds, too loud, the frogs and crickets at night, the birds in the day shrieking, discordant choruses in a language I do not understand; moving too painful, the sheets rough as sandpaper, skin tender, even breathing painful, the air rubbing nostrils raw, going in and out, unstoppable, each breath a small agony. Until finally the pain eases, the light grows dimmer, the sounds recede and I am well again. I can stand, make my way to the kitchen for food and drink, and then outside where it is bright and noisy and not extraordinary, where the sunshine heals.

Each year the sickness comes; perhaps I even make it happen. Because for all the pain and discomfort, it is important at times to see things too clearly, to hear things too strongly, to feel things too harshly. Surely that must be why.

It never happens before the garden is planted and there is a small space in my life with room for it. Afterwards, the summer and especially the fall, are too busy, no time for illness. And it never comes in the winter, nothing comes except for that incredible sinking into the event, the action, the object, the calm, the cold, the flame.

I have been alone. My days and seasons and years have spun gently, unbroken, no time, only rhythm. I am rooted in a moment, and in a pattern of moments. I have been alone, and it is good.

Once I found a squirrel dying in the woods. A leg was broken, and it lay helpless under a tree, unable to move and starving. I carried it carefully back to the cabin, put clumsy

168

splints on the leg, fed it, hovered over it willing life into it so hard that it seemed there was almost an electricity, a current running from my body to his, my mind running into his life, like the electric jolt sometimes given to a failed human heart.

Slowly, he recovered. Once he bit me, in the fleshy part of the hand between thumb and forefinger. He began to follow me around the cabin, out into the garden, and he learned to be touched and to take food from my hand. I was not trying to tame him, I thought, only to make it safe for me to have him there, without fear of being bitten again.

But gradually and almost imperceptibly, he became a responsibility. Not onerous or consuming, but a presence nonetheless. He required some attention. His bright eyes watched me move around the cabin, and I was conscious of his watching. I was lulled by his company, comforted by it, felt a seductive pleasure in caring for him; I recognized the danger of the false comfort.

I turned him out. I cut away the splints, watched him walk until I was sure he was all right, and led him outside to the bird-feeder, where I showed him where I scattered nuts and sunflower seeds beneath for the squirrels. He began to eat. And then I turned while he was eating and ran, without looking back, to the cabin, slammed the door behind me. I think I may have been crying a little at the time.

Later I went to the living room window and looked out. There was a squirrel on the front lawn, standing crouched, one leg a little straighter, stiffer than the other, watching the door, his head cocking now and then from side to side. He took a few steps forward, stopped again, watched; and then it was almost as if he shrugged inside himself, said "what the hell", and turned away, back to the feeding place.

Now and then, since, I have remembered to keep an eye out for a squirrel with one hind leg just a little stiffer and straighter than the other, but I've never been able to pick him out. Maybe he went away. Of course he's probably dead by now, of old age if nothing else. I don't know how long squirrels can expect to live.

There is still a scar on my hand, between the thumb and the forefinger, and sometimes it still hurts a little.

I've never since had an animal in my home, and that is for the

169

best. It was not right, twisting the nature of something, making it less free. In a way, it's not right to do anything; or it's right to do nothing. It is necessary to let things be.

Still, I felt it necessary to try to save the squirrel's life; I could not have left it on the ground to starve. But I know that if something can survive on its own, then I have no right. Then it is necessary to let it be.

I've been alone since then. No one, nothing and no one, has been here. Until Katie.

Not until Katie.

14

I don't understand why she wants me to go back to the city with her, but she does. She's been pressing me for several days now, at first subtly, testing me out, now quite straightforwardly asking me. I would stay, she says, with her in an apartment; there is no question of going back to the other house, where her father lives.

He has married again, she tells me at last. (Did she think it would hurt me?) A tall woman who is thirty-five years old and who has deep red hair cut long and a low, calm voice. Elliott, she says, is not fond of her, apparently finding it strange to have a "mother" who is a mere fifteen years older than him; although surely he must realize that the distance between twenty and thirty-five is very great, not just any fifteen years. That cannot really be the reason.

Katie herself says she doesn't care particularly, but is not close. She worries because she thinks that sometimes she is deliberately cruel to Stephen and his wife, and cannot stop herself until it is too late. She told them, for instance, that she wanted to find me, wanted to talk to me. She did not say it accusingly, as if they were somehow failing her and she needed someone better, but she knew that that must be how they would understand it. They are, I gather, quiet people; it seems that Stephen has not changed and his wife is much like him. Katie says they were silent for a few moments after she told them she wanted to find me; and then Stephen said, quite calmly, "I don't

think she wants to be found, but I expect it's your right to look."
She could see that they were both hurt and trying not to show it,
and she was ashamed of herself. She wants to be very good.

Later Stephen went to her alone and explained why he could
not help her look for me. He talked about his visit here, said
with great fairness that he had to respect what I wanted as well
as what she wanted. She would have to figure it out for herself,
he said. It took a long time, several false starts; she is ashamed
because in the end she went through her father's desk at home
and found my address on some legal documents related to the
divorce. It was a terrible thing to do, she says, but she was
desperate. She cannot work out the conflict between his rights
and her desperation. She also cannot work out the conflict
between her wild resentment of me and what she says might be a
feeling of love.

It has taken us a long time to reach this stage. She has been
coming here long enough so that now I watch for her arrival,
accept that she is coming. She has entered my life. I don't use the
same words she does, and so I cannot say that I love her; but I do
look for her.

I think it is this place that frightens her and brings out her
resentment and her fury. She does not understand it — how
could she? — but she knows that it is my life. Because she can't
bring herself to blame me completely for what happened, she
blames the land, knowing that if I love anything, if I have any
use for the word at all, it is in relation to this place. I am in the
garden and I see her, watching me and frowning, and it is like
having myself of the early days back, the subject watching the
object, assessing, analyzing, and it disorients me; it makes me
aware of myself, clumsy and out-of-touch in the most literal
way.

She has tried to see what it is that holds me. In the first days
she came to me in the garden and watched, very quietly, what I
was doing and then knelt in a row across from me and began to
help. She didn't talk, just worked on in silence, so that she
became part of the atmosphere and did not intrude. She is very
wise, this Katie, in her way.

I failed to understand that she did not mean what she was
doing, that she hated the garden and working in it, was doing it

172

so that I would accept her. I did not realize because I assumed for some reason that she was like me, doing what she wanted.

She must have been crying for a long time, quietly and to herself, working her way along a row of beans, picking those that were ready to be eaten or frozen, casting aside the tiny shoots of weeds that would not give up growing. Then suddenly she was ripping out the beans, crying and incoherent, and of course I had to stop her, she was killing my food. I shouted at her, but still I was remote, not angry, did not feel shocked that this was happening.

She did not stop, out of control, and in the end I had to fight her, pull her away and hold her until finally, exhausted, dishevelled and dirty, she became quiet. I almost carried her to the cabin, put her on the couch in the living room and covered her with a blanket. She may or may not have been asleep when I went back outside, I couldn't wait to be sure; I had to replace the plants, see how much damage had been done. It was considerable, there would be fewer beans this year, but I replanted what I could and kept a careful eye on them after that, giving them special care. Then I finished what I had been doing, and went off to cut the day's quota of wood. I was not angry with Katie, or deliberately avoiding her, or being cruel by pretending to be angry; I was simply going on with the things that were to be done. She found that hard to understand, for where she comes from, where I came from, there are motives and angers everywhere. I can remember that. She doesn't know anything about blankness.

She thought I must be furious, and was humble and embarrassed when I went back to the cabin to cook dinner. She was awake by then, red-eyed and puffy, and said she had slept all afternoon. She had tried to comb her hair, but it was still tangled around her face.

"God, Mother," she said, "I'm so sorry. I don't know what got into me, it was like something just burst. I'm sorry, you must hate me."

I went on making dinner, puzzled. Why would I feel hate? "No Katie, I'm not angry." She must have thought that because I didn't continue, I didn't mean it, for she was still unhappy. She doesn't know, even now, how little there is to be said.

She was sad through dinner, and quiet, but it didn't occur to me that we hadn't finished with it; it no longer concerned me, and I didn't see that it would still concern her. But when she was leaving after dinner to go back to the hotel, she asked if she could come back again. "I know you probably don't want me, but I'd like to make it up to you. I'm sorry I came unstrung."

"Of course you can come back. I was expecting you to. Why would you think you couldn't?"

She looked at me, surprised. "But I've behaved so badly and you must be so angry. I can imagine what the garden means, it's your food. It was terrible of me to try to destroy it, it was unforgiveable."

What could I have said? Words were inadequate, wouldn't explain, and yet words were what she wanted, what she was accustomed to.

"Look Katie," I said firmly. "I'm not angry. I'm truly not. There's no reason for you to feel badly. Something just happened, it's finished now and it doesn't make any difference. I know how you must feel about this place, and I don't see that you have to pretend; you'll never get what you came for if you pretend. Now go on back to town and get a good night's rest."

"What do you mean, what I came for? I'm not pretending."

"Oh yes you are, Katie." I wanted to make it very clear, so that we didn't waste understanding again.

"You said you came here to get to know me. Well you never will if you're humouring me. I assumed that because you were in the garden, you wanted to be there, and that wasn't true at all. I can't know anything about you if you're doing something that's a lie, and I can't be myself if I have to keep worrying about whether or not you're happy. It doesn't matter to me if you want to garden or not; it doesn't make me happier that you're there, or unhappier that you're not. I do what I do, that's all. If you're reading in the living room, I don't join you if I don't feel like it. Just be yourself, Katie. If we like each other, we'll like each other. If we don't, we won't."

I don't think she understood. Not then. Maybe by now it's coming to her.

I thought after she left that perhaps I had expected too much. What had I known about honesty, back when I lived where she does? What did I still know about honesty, alone, telling truth only to myself? I would know for certain if I went back to that world and saw if it were very different, or if I was. Would I lose what I learned here? Was this strong enough to hold me? Was I really changed, or just protected?

That is why I have been considering her proposal that I go back with her. Back into the city and the people, where I would see if it is true. A test, surely? Another self-examination? Have I already passed, or would I fail again? With Katie comes another world, I look at myself with the eyes of that world, she brings it back to me and I have to think about it.

There is no hurry to decide. Katie has three weeks left of her vacation before she goes back to begin university. (You notice how I am aware, now, of three weeks. As a time span, I recognize it; I can't really say how long it is, it seems as if it must be a long time, but perhaps it's actually quite short. Katie said this morning, "I have to go back in three weeks," and it meant something to me. Perhaps I'm already slipping back; perhaps it's all just been a joke, by me, on me.)

Katie also says she has been here now for five weeks; that means, I calculate, that our time together is more than half over, which is extraordinary. Five weeks, what is that? It seems like a moment ago that I first saw her, shy and frightened, approaching the cabin as I watched, hidden, in the garden. It is pointless, of course, to wonder if I should have stayed hidden.

And, too, it seems as if Katie has existed here forever, in one of her forms, for we have gone through so much in the time. Her rage, her resentment, her pity and her self-pity, her love, all have been in this time. And also in this time I have felt the sucking, felt myself being drawn back, away from what I am. I have become sometimes unsettled, scattered, thinking about Katie and myself, and I have felt more and more that it is getting out of my control, that I am being drawn into — what? I am not as content as I was.

She is learning. She is learning, more and more, to let me be.

Our days, now that we are somewhat accustomed to each other, are simple. I have my work, the work I have always done here; she reads, lies in the sun, sometimes does some sketching, having seen mine. She is no better, no worse, than I. It amuses both of us to see what bad artists we are, and how much pleasure there is in it. Katie says she always thought there was a correlation of some kind between ability and pleasure, but now she's considering that there may not be.

At meals and for a little while in the evening, until it starts to get dark and Katie leaves because she doesn't see well at night to drive, we are together. Sometimes we talk; often we don't. Usually it is Katie who begins a conversation.

She wants me to tell her how I feel, and doesn't understand what that means. It is adolescent, to be sure, her probing, but she says it helps her. She doesn't imagine that it is possible to have a relationship (and she says the word as if it were capitalized,) without analyzing it. An instance: Katie and I are at the lunch table. We are drinking coffee which she has brought from town, and soon I will be going outside again to chop wood.

She is looking at me, wanting to talk. She says, "I've been watching you. You have a very interesting body language. Do you know your limbs are always open? Unless you're carrying something your arms are always down at your sides, your legs, look at the way you sit, your legs apart, you don't have any defensiveness about you. I bet you can sleep on your back. It's only people who aren't afraid who can sleep on their backs. You always look open, you always just sit there, kind of exposed. I think that's very interesting."

Perhaps she is right. What do I have to be afraid of? But she says that and instantly my arms want to wrap themselves around my body, my legs want to pull themselves up; I do not sleep on my back, but on my stomach, whatever that means, but I do not tell her that. I have, inside, reacted to what she has said: my body has wanted to protect itself from her watching, her analyzing; my mind acts swiftly, tells the body "no, don't show it." So suddenly I'm playing a role, consciously holding myself "open" although I have closed up against her. What is all this about? What sort of corners am I being backed into? It is all quite bewildering. I do not like being watched. I wish she would stop.

And then I am collected again, almost instantly, and I see that it's her way, not mine, and I go on with my work.

But you see how she is chipping at me?

I remember.

Stephen. I have said he was loving, fair, kind, gentle. I have said that people from his office told me he was efficient, demanding, intolerant of mistakes. Their view of him was different from mine. Still, thinking about him, I feel the tenderness toward him, such a good person. And yet, and yet. I saw what I wanted to see? He wasn't like that? It was a role? It was a role he played at work? He had depths I did not know about, and surfaces as well? He was a different person from the one I knew? Did I make him up?

Yes, of course I made him up; that is not so difficult to see, or to admit. I deliberately made him into nothing. I made everyone up. No one was what I saw; perhaps they responded to what I saw, but no one really was that. Each of them, Stephen, Katie, Elliott, my mother, the business people at the dinner parties, their wives, each of them was something entirely different. I made them up, gave them characters from within my own tiny view, assessed them, made them into people I knew. I simplified them. And then I reacted to what I had made up, behaved as if what I had invented was real. And of course they did the same to me. Absurd. It must always be like looking into a mirror, seeing what is recognizable through a particular set of eyes, not seeing the rest because it is shapeless without the eye's ability to form it. Of course. It was very clear. One could accept everything, knowing that. Yes, this is the person before me, this is the person I lived with, or who is my friend, or my child, this is the person I see, this is what he's like, except you have to understand I just made that up, he's not like that at all, this isn't what he sees, or how other people see him, this is all just my idea.

And so now I can see Katie and listen to her, understanding or not what she is saying, and say, "this is what she is offering to me, this is the face she is presenting, diluted and changed by my own face, this is what we have. I can accept that as long as I know it." She looks at me, she sees — God knows what — and she understands that small part and thinks it is the whole, or the essential root at least. Within those limits of misperception, we are together and that is all right.

I am glad Katie came, just so that I could understand that; it makes many things more clear. But, and it is an indication of my present confusion, I see that if Katie hadn't come, there would have been no need to realize it, and nothing would have been lost.

Katie has been reading her textbooks for next year, "getting a head start," she says. She seems quite practical. She says she will never make much money as an archeologist, but doesn't think that matters. She will like to be working outdoors, working carefully, a fraction of an inch at a time, being very thorough, a small-sized discovery painstakingly made can be a very important thing, she says. She says she likes the kind of thoroughness and patience it requires. I thought at first it was an odd choice of profession, digging up the past; now I look at it again and see perhaps what she means. It is like my garden, slow, delicate, careful work, protective work, and in the end something may come of it and something may not. It is the work itself, each movement, that is the point, that is the joy, and I see where it is all right. I do not know if that is just what she anticipates; I hope that is how she will see it.

I have no right to hope anything for her, she has her own goals. She has become more sure of something, and perhaps it is herself.

She is getting dark, like me. She wears shorts and a halter top most of the time, or else her bathing suit, and she lies out in the sun, reading. Once, after the incident in the garden, she tried to help me gather in firewood I'd cut. I asked her if it were something she really felt like doing.

"Not really," she answered, "but it seems like such a lot of work for one person. I don't mind helping."

I sent her back to the lawn and her books. "I want to do it," I told her, "and you don't." I don't know if she understood, but I think she is learning some sense of freedom. I hope so.

I have no right to hope anything for her.

It is not even as if she is my daughter. I don't have any reaction to the word "daughter." But there is a connection between us.

I felt it also with my own mother, that there was something between us — a current of common experience? I know that

Katie is testing the word "mother" on me, using it to see if it fits, and I think that's how she sees it, that we have a connection because she can use the word more and more comfortably. I don't think that's it. Katie was a little girl; now she's a young woman, and I was not part of most of it. And yet something has grown between us, a special affection that does not necessarily reflect itself on the surface of our talk. All that we have in common, apparently, is our blood background and our femaleness: is this what creates the connection?

Katie, seeing me now as Mother, asks questions, like a five-year-old, peppering them at me, demanding that I have answers, except that they're not five-year-old questions, they're not so easy, and the answers I know, I can't give her.

"It's funny," she says reflectively one night at dinner. "When I'm here, with you, I'm one person and I feel as if I'm being honest. I don't think I'm putting anything on for you. Then I go back into town to the hotel and somethings happens on the way, something tightens up, and by the time I'm there I'm somebody else, I'm smiling, charming, whatever, and I get terrific service, everybody knows me and they take care of me; except that they don't see me. Do you see what I mean?"

I nod. I know. I think of dinner parties and selling dresses.

"I'm one person with Daddy, another with Jean (who is his younger red-haired wife who is very calm, like Stephen,) and when I'm with the two of them together, I'm somebody else altogether. Elliott thinks I'm really flighty and silly, and it's my own fault because when I'm with him that's how I am; he's so solemn, he brings it out in me. I haven't been myself with Elliott for — years. Some of my friends are serious, so I'm serious with them, and some of them have a lot of fun, so I turn into a kind of ring-leader. It's scary, you know, it really is, I sit there and I think, "Okay, which one of these people am I," this is when I'm alone of course, and I guess I'm all of them, except none of them feels right, none of them is me, dead-on. And yet up here with you I feel like I'm being me, and I don't care because I trust you not to hate me, whatever I do." She stops, and I nod again and smile.

"I suppose that's it, isn't it," she says finally. "I don't trust them not to hate whatever it is I really am. That's weird, isn't it?

179

I know so many people, and I guess I don't trust any of them. Why do you suppose that is? I wonder what I'm afraid of? They're all nice people, Daddy and Jean and Elliott too. What am I afraid of?"

She goes off thoughtfully, and we do not talk about it again. I think maybe she is figuring it out; perhaps it will be different, now, when she goes back.

Would it be different if I went back?

Another time: "I wonder how come you're the one I trust? Of all people, you're the one I should trust least." This, in a bitter, resentful stage. I advance tentatively my own questions about blood-bonds and femaleness, but she doesn't accept that.

"There's no reason for me to like you," she says. "I should hate you because you copped out and dumped it all on Daddy and Elliott and me. Why the hell should I care about you?" Defiant now, daring me to tell her; which of course I can't, because there is no reason at all.

"As for femaleness, I think that's crap. There are plenty of females I've got no bond with, there's nothing there. So that doesn't make any sense." I have no answers to any of it. She waits for a moment, her eyes glaring into mine, her face stiff with angry hurt, or hurt anger, or one of those very painful emotions. And then her face starts to relax, the eyes begin to soften, and soon she laughs.

"But it doesn't matter, does it? You know that, you just sit there waiting for me to figure it out. I suppose that's why I like you so much — you know it but you wait for me." I do not want her to think that.

"No Katie, you're wrong. I don't know anything at all. I can feel some of it, but I don't know it. Sometimes you come to the same points I have and sometimes you don't. It doesn't mean we're right or wrong, it's just that sometimes we're together and sometimes we're not. It's not so important." I shrug.

It is that, that attitude of "it's not so important," the shrug, that she is least able to deal with.

"That's the whole trouble with you," she storms, "you don't care about anything. You just sit there and smile and nod and think, "I'm okay," and you don't give a shit about anything. Sure you're okay, you don't have anything to *deal* with. You try

180

coming back into the *real* world and see what happens. If you don't care, you're just a vegetable, you're just like your cabbages out there, sitting around waiting for the sun to shine or the rain to fall. I can't believe it, you just knock me out, the way nothing matters to you.''

Except, of course, she's looking at it from the angle of her world, and I am quite willing to admit that she has caught my life precisely. I am indeed just like a cabbage, sitting around waiting for the sun to shine or the rain to fall. I smile and nod, check myself because of course that's what she finds so irritating, and say gently, ''What is it that makes you think my world is less real than yours?'' I think, ''if she can begin to understand what is real in my life, maybe she'll be able to let go. And maybe she'll be a little more free herself.''

''Because you don't have to cope with things. You don't have to juggle people, or give anything, you can just sit here and do whatever you bloody well feel like doing and not worry about anybody. That's not real; that's not the way it is for anybody else.''

''Did you hear what you said, Katie?'' We are lying sprawled on the lawn beside each other. I am on my back, my hands behind my head, and it is very hard not to smile. Katie is lying on her side, looking at me, balanced on one elbow, one hand holding up her head. The other arm, the free one, is gesturing violently; she is very earnest and tense.

''What?'' she asks, surprised. Then indignant. ''I suppose whatever it was, you're going to turn it on me.''

''Maybe, if you see it that way. You were saying that I'm free, that I don't have to *worry* about other people, I don't have to *juggle* them, I don't have to *cope*. Is that what it's like for you, out in your real world? And if it is, tell me the good things, tell me what you value about it.''

There is a long pause before she smiles and answers.

''All right then,'' she says, ''I'll tell you. I like the idea of coping, it's like a game and I'm very competitive. I enjoy dealing with problems and being responsible. I like being able to plan and have a good time. I don't know how you can stand living alone; people are what make life worth living, and sure some of them are shits, but others aren't, and it's exciting to

181

make friends and feel good about them. Okay, I admit I had to think about that for a minute; and I'll grant you that what I said the first time sounded negative, and maybe that's the way I feel about it sometimes, but it's not all the time. On the whole, it's good. It's just not all good.''

I don't say anything. Not because I can't, but because it isn't the time yet; and I am only now beginning to see it myself, from this perspective as an outsider to all lives, including my own. What is real this moment is that I must cut today's wood, and so I stand, pick up the axe and head off toward the woods.

When I get back, I find Katie has dinner ready; she is also angry, because she thinks I went off without answering her because I think she is stupid. I find her demands that I cushion her insecurities occasionally wearing.

"Obviously," she says coldly, "you didn't consider what I said worth answering. Maybe you'd like to explain what you believe."

I sigh, swallow a smile. Why is it that what she says makes me want to smile? The contrast?

"Oh Katie. I don't 'believe' anything. You know that, it's what you keep fighting. It's not that I didn't think what you said was worth answering; it's just that I couldn't give an answer. What I've learned is inside me, and there's just no way I can translate it for you.

"Look, you can sit here and tell me every moment of your life that you can remember, and you can analyze all of it and tell me what each moment meant to you; but there is no way that I'll understand exactly because I haven't had the experiences. And I can't explain to you how it is with me because you haven't experienced what I have. We can get a sense of each other, but we can't know each other, we can't really understand. That's not so terrible; it seems to me that the sense we have of each other is quite a lovely thing. There's no need to force it into being something else.

"Katie, you'll leave here and go back to the city, and things will happen to you, you'll go to school and meet new people, maybe you'll get married next year, or be out on a dig, and each thing that happens will add new parts to you. Maybe at some point they'll all come together, and you'll think, 'well, so that's what it's all about.' I have no doubt but what it will be different from what I've found; that doesn't bother me. It's good for me, probably all wrong for you. All I'm saying is that you seem to want me to tell you what to think, even if it's just so you can tell me I'm wrong and irresponsible. I'm not willing to do that. I can be wrong to you and right to me, and there's no point in trying to bring it together. It's impossible. It might just as well be skipped, because it doesn't take us anywhere."

Her face is angry, taut, pleading. "Then that pretty well makes it a waste of time trying to talk to you, doesn't it? I mean, you don't want to talk about anything important, you don't want to share anything, so why don't I just leave? I guess that's what I might as well do, isn't it?"

She is begging me to tell her to stay; what strikes me is that when she says the words, suggests she could leave, my stomach seems to lurch and I want to reach out and hold her from going. I haven't seen until now how much I depend on her.

For youth? For old ideas brought again to my attention? For simple human connection? Am I lonely? All this will have to be understood. I am falling back into a trap she has set without intending to; or maybe that is wrong, and it is what she has intended all along; but first I have to stop her.

"No Katie, that's not the point," I say swiftly. "Surely we can be together and learn without having answers. I gain something from you, maybe you gain something from me?"

"Perhaps," she says. There is a triumph about her. "I suppose you're right. Anyway, I think I'll go back to the hotel now. I'd like to rest. I'll be back tomorrow."

And so I have had to consider: what does the expectation of this young girl who is, or was, my daughter, mean to me? Why do I watch for her? What is it I am expecting from her? I go to sleep with the questions still in my mind; there is no logic to what I am feeling. No, the clues must be in the feeling itself, but I do not have a label for it, knowing that love the way I remember it does not fit. I keep wondering what the lack has been here that I did not see, and that Katie has now arrived to point out or to fill.

I dream. I dream that in the morning I wake up to a huge explosion. The earth is rocking, the cabin is swaying, and what

I see out the window from my bed is just dust, dust everywhere, swirling, obscuring everything. I get up and make tea and wander around the cabin, holding the cup, looking out various windows, trying to see through the dust. It is as if the windows have been painted rusty-beige, there is so little to be seen through them. It would be like that except that it is possible to see the movement, the restless whirling of the dust particles, each separate and impenetrable to the eye.

I go to the kitchen to have breakfast. There is no point, I have decided, in going outside into this cataclysm; it is warm and safe inside, obviously dangerous and painful out there. Later I walk again, still trying to peer through the dust, but it is impossible; it seems, however, that the particles are slowing, moving in larger sweeps, more graceful than frenetic. I assume they are subsiding, that everything will be all right shortly, and then I will be able to go outside. I wonder how deep the dust will be, once it settles on the ground. Will I sink into it? What will it have done to the garden? I worry about the birds and squirrels, and think that the stream must be choking with it, clogged and muddied so that the water striders will be trapped. The dust seems as if it must suck up the water and the air both.

Suddenly it is gone; no, because I peer out the window and see that it hasn't disappeared, but is lying all over the ground, and it is almost to the level of the window sill, so deep. I will have to wade out into it, I want to see what it is and what it has done. And I remember the explosion, and wonder what that was. An earthquake, perhaps?

I open the door and the dust, all rusty-beige, is piled at the entrance above the level of my knees. The air is very still. The dust seems to have formed into a wall, because when I open the door none of it drifts inside, but clings together vertically as if the door were still against it. I think, "it must be solid then," and step high up to the top of it. But it isn't solid, it's just dust, and I fall into it, come down too hard, and I am choking, the dust is flying around me, in my eyes and my nose, I can neither breathe nor see. Eventually I struggle upright, choking, and am very still until all the dust settles again and my eyes and nose are cleared.

There is nothing to be seen but the dust. It is hanging like a

184

shroud on the bushes and even the willow. Their shapes are my landmarks, but their familiarity is gone. I follow the way to the stream and see that it has dried up, is filled with the dust, and it is as if the stream has never existed. I look around, re-check my position, and am certain I am in the right place. I turn away, toward the garden. There is no longer a garden, it is buried and there is no sign at all.

The path back to the pasture is also gone, but I know the general direction and can follow along, glancing back now and then to check where I am against the cabin and the willow. It is not hard to walk through the dust. It is very light and there is not much pressure against the legs. As I move on, it closes in behind me, so that there are no footsteps. There is no wind, and so I do not know how this happens.

The pasture is the same, and I search fruitlessly for the groundhog holes, certain that the animals must be suffocating, but I cannot find them, they have been too cleverly buried, and there is nothing I can do; there is no way to shift aside the dust.

And so I continue toward the woods, thinking that if it is no different there I must try to go for help, at the next farm or in the town. It seems to me that the road will be clear, that this is a very local circumstance, all mine. I wish I had looked, while I was in the pasture, into the next fields to see if they were also covered.

In the woods, all the trees are coated in the dust, which reaches high around their trunks from the ground. I am astonished to see an enormous log, not one I have cut, far too big for me, lying ahead of me on the surface. The dust is holding it up, and yet it does not support me, and I go closer to see why. As far as I can tell, there is no reason for it. I stand beside the log, my thighs touching it, and I am sunk deep and it is still on the top. I begin to tug the log aside; I want to see if it is supported by something solid beneath.

It is terribly heavy; it is a long struggle before I manage to budge it, even a little. Then suddenly it becomes easier, then easier, and everything begins to move, the dust is all sliding, coming toward me, and I have to work to stay on my feet. It is not flying in the air, simply moving toward me along the ground, slipping easily, in place, from the trees; and then I can see it isn't coming at me, but to a great chasm under the log I

185

have shifted, everything is going into it, like a waterfall of dust, and I think, "how lovely to be below and see it falling," but at the same time I am fighting to get clear of it, so that I won't be carried over. I reach a tree and cling to it and watch while all the dust, a great endless rusty-beige mass of it, every particle in place, moves to the edge of the chasm and then slips over the edge, down, down, there is no hurry, every piece seems to know its place and moves in harmony. It seems as if there is an endless resource of dust, that it will never come to an end.

And then, suddenly, it is finished. I have not noticed that the last of it has come to the edge, but now every particle is gone and the woods are green again. For a time it is very silent; then I hear a bird, an answer, a call, then a chatter of a squirrel and the skitter of another coming to join it, and then everything is in order, all the sounds are back, there is a breeze and the leaves on the trees are rustling. I leave the tree I have been gripping and walk to the log. I look down, beyond it. The chasm seems to have no bottom, there is no sign of the dust, it has all gone down, far out of sight, perhaps it goes on forever. "It would be a dreadful place to fall," I think, and push at the heavy log until the pit is covered again.

Then I begin to walk back. It is over. In the pasture there is no sign that anything has been disturbed; I look into the holes of the groundhogs and can see nothing, no traces of either the dust or the animals. I go on. The path has reappeared, I follow it along and see ahead the willow and the cabin, both free now, and after a while I cut over to the stream. It is quite clear, running openly, no traces of mud or dust, and the water striders slip over the surface. I stop further on and examine the garden: everything is green and fresh, healthy and growing.

I go back into the cabin, make a cup of tea and wander through, looking out the windows. The colours of the growing things are very bright.

Then I rinse out the teacup and go back to bed. I have been wearing my outdoor clothes, which are clean, no signs of the dust. I pull up the covers and put my head on the pillow. And then I wake up.

I am astonished by the remarkable clarity of the dream and the vividness of the colours. I begin to retrace the details, but as I try they slip away, I can't quite remember, they are fading, the whole dream is going.

It comes again several nights later, and again after that. I have never before had a recurring dream, and now I remember it clearly and it stays in my mind.

Katie says to me: "Why is this better than what you had before? Why do you prefer this?" She has stopped asking, "Why did you leave?"

"Because I belong here." She waits for me to go on, but I have nothing to add.

"But surely," she presses, "you can say what you didn't like about the other way, why you felt you didn't belong there."

"No. You see I didn't know then. I cared for all of you, the idea of belonging never occurred to me. Until I saw this place, and then it was too late. And now, because everything has changed so much, I can't quantify it, I can't say this is better, that was worse."

(Why do people want to do that? This is a better job than that one, this is a better person than that one, I am better than I used to be, what is all that about? I think if I went back, I would surely be able to let it be, and suddenly there is a twist of excitement, long unfelt, at a challenge, a change, and maybe it would be possible to go back.)

But whyever would I?

Maybe to be with Katie, to watch her freshness, see her change and maybe grow, watch what happens to her. I would be an observer, I see myself sitting placidly, watching Katie dance in and out with her life, feeding off it. A cannibalism. And yet I will miss her terribly when she leaves, a retribution, in a way, for the pain that was left back there.

She says, challenging again, "What are you afraid of? Why don't you come back and see what it's like? It would give us more time, too. We don't have much left, unless you come."

I am selfish, desperate with the idea of fading time. "I have another idea. You're right, we haven't had enough time, but it seems to me we're on an artificial schedule. You're eighteen years old, you have years yet, years to spare. Why don't you stay here, get an apartment in town for a while, and go back to school next year."

I am ashamed, now, that I ever reached a state in which I could say those words, attempt that kind of manipulation.

And she knows and is disappointed. She chooses not to blame me.

"All right," she says sadly. "I see your point. Of course I don't want to disrupt my plans; I should have seen that you wouldn't want to, either. I'm sorry, I was asking too much."

I think. Is it too much? If there is doubt, and there seems to be, is this place still right? I am very stubborn about holding onto it, but why? Isn't it possible its time is over? Should I at least go out there and see?

Later I try to open it up again.

"Look Katie, I want you to know I've been thinking about going back with you. But it's a hard decision, and I don't know what will come of it." Her face brightens. Why does she want this so badly?

"If you came with me, would you sell this place?" Her enemy.

"No. I'd need to know I could come back."

Suddenly we are talking about it, very seriously. "We'd have to get a two-bedroom apartment," she says. "Daddy's giving me some furniture from the house, you wouldn't mind that, would you? And he said he'd pay the rent on the apartment, because he understood how I wanted my own place now and I'm old enough. Of course, maybe you'd want to pay some of it yourself, I'm not suggesting it really, I just thought maybe you wouldn't want to be living in a place Daddy was paying for. I don't know how you feel about things like that, or about him, for that matter."

"Oh no," I say, forgetting the real issue in this stream of details, "of course I'd want to pay my own rent. It would be terribly unfair to take his money."

She giggles. "You're funny, both of you. You're always talking about what's 'fair,' he does it all the time and you always say what a fair man he is. What does that mean? It always sounds as if you're both on a bed of nails and don't think it's right to get off in one direction or the other, so you just keep sitting there."

"Fairness," I say quite pompously, "is just a matter of

188

respecting the ways of someone else. It's recognizing that someone else has the right to be different."

"Oho," she says, some glee in her bitterness, "you're one to talk about that."

"Oho," I say drily, "I am that."

It seems to me that everything is splitting, my life has shifted into three parts. There is being with Katie, which is infused now with a possibility of change, of moving on, with a sense of rootlessness and bewilderment. I feel sometimes with her like a child, a baby, quite helpless, being guided into things in which I have no choice. There is a kind of anticipation about it, but no control.

And the old ways, for all those jobs still have to be done. Out in the garden, tending the vegetables, I can feel it coming back. I can still get lost in it, move into it, and there is peace. And off in the woods, hauling back the wood for the winter, although I do not know if there will be a winter here for me, it feels right, there is no disturbance. I move back and forth between them, from my world to the other one, guided increasingly by Katie, although she does not do it consciously or on purpose. It is happening because I am weak, and there is that knot of excitement and of something on the verge of occurring. The two worlds are very distinct, the differences clear-cut.

The dream keeps coming back, although not every night, so that I see so often the dust, rusty-beige, moving inexorably toward and into that chasm, leaving behind it everything fresh and green. That dream is my third world, as real as the others, and it is rooted in my mind now, although I do not know what it means.

I drift from one world into the next, not understanding what is happening.

The strain between them grows. I feel that if I do not do something, take some action very soon, I will fly into pieces. I need, at least, to slow it down.

I ask Katie to stay away for three days. Three is arbitrary, a compromise. One day would not be enough; a week would take away too much of the time she has to be here. So I choose three, as something in the middle that likely will suit neither of us.

She protests. "But Mother, I've only got a week and a half

left. You say we don't have enough time, and then you take some of it away. Three days is ages.''

I suggest she go back to the city and look for an apartment during the time; she will need to do that anyway, but she points out that she can't take one until she knows if I will be with her.

I take the days anyway, leaving it to her to figure out how she will spend them. She leaves angry again, accusing me of being selfish; it seems that what we have developed is wrecked by my need for those days; she is back at the beginning of her resentment and rage. I regret that, but am relieved that I am still strong enough to risk losing her for a need of my own.

I spend a day of my precious time in bed. I sketch a little, write a lot, think about this position I am in, try to decipher the conflict. Occasionally I drift off to sleep and into the dream again.

I can see that it is saying something about my choices, but I can't tell what. I try to write it all down, naively of course, I should know better. I am like a childish decision-maker, writing columns divided into 'pros' and 'cons'.

But is anything so simple? The facts, the conflict, are apparent here, the decision should be. But.

I am drifting, quite detached, from one argument to an opposing one. It is as if I am not involved.

I do not think I am trying to recapture motherhood. And yet Katie means something, and again I cannot think of a word for it, but I do not want to be without her. Although it would be difficult to live with all her rages, resentment, bitterness, tenderness, freshness, openness, confusion and adolescence.

But of course: now it is clear. Katie is my opposite, and each of us is being drawn achingly to what we do not have. Katie is passion, all fire and love; I am peace.

Well, no wonder then.

I can get out of bed now. I eat dinner, work in the garden during the evening, in the coolness. No decision has been made, but I feel the recognition has quietened me. The plants are a little wilted, it has been a very hot, dry day and they have not been cared for. I see minute changes that show these few hours of neglect. I feel badly about it, and sprinkle some water from the stream over them, so that they will be better tomorrow. I go to bed early, despite all the rest I have had, and sleep easily. The dream comes again, but when I wake up I am pleased to find that it has not disturbed me.

I wake at dawn, have breakfast and go to the garden. Many of the tomatoes are full and red and need to be picked immediately. The green peppers also, they are a deep green; the whole area is bounding with abundance and readiness. I must catch up with it.

I pick the vegetables that are ready, water those that are left, turn over the compost pile so that the things that are already broken down are exposed to air outside, and whole things can rot in the heat of the centre. The pile stinks; it is a good smell.

I have great heaps of vegetables now on the kitchen table, on the counters, in the sink. I go back outside, not bothering with lunch, and into the woods with the axe.

With all my practice I can now split a log with three strokes. There are several there waiting to be dealt with, and they will add considerably to my winter woodpile. There is one more dead tree to be cut down, and I do that as well. There is an excess of energy in my body, the muscles almost working ahead of the mind, eager to stretch and contract, pushing me forward. I feel my body full of a juice that is like a desire. I attack the wood, not viciously but with all my strength, and the sweat pours. I strip branches off the dead tree with the axe, and break them up for kindling. I have a great pile to take back to the cabin. I load some of it onto the sleigh-affair and haul it back. I return and take another load. I am not thinking; I am moving and doing, and sweating and straining and pulling.

I have a quick dinner, a salad that is not enough to replenish what I have lost in energy, but complete. I get out my biggest pot and set water in it to boil. I blanch tomatoes, green peppers, green and yellow beans. Slowly the piles on the table, the cupboards, the sink, go down and finally are gone. In the freezer the piles are high and satisfying.

My body is aching; I feel, now that it is over, the effects of the day's work. I have a very hot shower for a very long time, and the heat strikes the flesh, is absorbed into it, into the muscles and the tissues to the very centre, and all of it is washed clean. There is great weariness, a deep heaviness in sleep. If the dream comes, I do not remember it.

When I wake, it is the third day, but I have forgotten that.

Time is gone again and today I will walk. There is a certain amount of anticipation about it, and I make a sandwich to carry with me for a lunch.

It is less hot today, and there are some clouds; it looks as if it may rain. It is good for walking, when the weather is not intolerably piercing.

I go down the lane to the car and start it, run it for a few minutes. Then out and down the road, slowly, kicking pebbles of gravel like a child, a little game; some plants are turning brown from the lack of rain, I see, and so it will be a good thing for them if the clouds do turn into something. There is almost no water in the ditches beside the road. I leap over one from energy, not from need. The skies are becoming more overcast.

I can feel a perceptible change in temperature as I climb the fence into the woods. Here, where the earth is utterly shaded, it is cooler, a little damper, heavier. I see toadstools lying flat against the ground, hugging the rotted meals of other years' leaves. There are patches of small blue flowers, I have no idea what they are called, but they are very pretty; it seems that flowers that grow in the woods are less flamboyant, more subtle than the brilliant flaring things of the sunshine. I see a rabbit, but it also sees me and bounds off in great powerful leaps out of proportion to its size. I sit on a broad tree stump, one of those, perhaps, that I have left here in some other time, and am very still. There has been a silence since I climbed the fence; I feel watched, and stay quiet. Gradually there come sounds, then more, then with growing confidence there is movement; birds are calling in the trees, and the squirrels and chipmunks are bold again, chasing each other, looking out for food, still watching with part of their attention, but relaxing. After a while I am a breathing stone. I feel rooted in the woods, far into the smells and sounds, the combination of dankness and freshness that is here.

I do not know what breaks it, but I am standing, moving, walking on, ready for the next place. I am at the edge of the woods when I feel that it is raining, very fine, very gentle so far, but I can see from the sky that it will get stronger, there is much rain in the clouds. I hold myself up to it, lift my face, feel it striking me. It is soft, slow rain, very pleasant, but at last I feel chilled, my clothes have been soaked through, the rain is coming harder, and I return to the woods to look for shelter.

Under the darkness of the trees, there is little rain. I hear it striking the leaves far above, but only a few drops penetrate to the ground level where I am. I unwrap my sandwich, shivering, and eat, waiting for the heaviest of the downpour to be over. The woods are full of shrieking, the birds are excited, flying in and out of the trees, out to the pasture where they get the worms that come to the surface for the moisture.

It is difficult to tell from there if the rain is ending. The chill has worked into my body and I decide to make a run for it. At the edge of the woods, I see that the rain is pattering down softly again, and it will probably be like this for the rest of the day, for the sky is still full of rain and the earth is thirsty. I clamber through the ravine and over the fence and run clumsily, wet, across the pasture, down the path toward the willow and the cabin still in the distance, coming closer, until I am on the porch, now inside. I strip off my clothes and shower, but still I am shivering, even later, after tea, and I wrap myself in a winter robe. I know I must not be sick now, and I set up an electric heater in front of the couch, lie down wrapped in a quilt, and wait for it to be over.

I feel well enough by evening to eat something, some soup and bread, and I know I am not ill. I sleep heavily, and I do not have the dream, at least not that I remember.

Early the next morning I am back in the garden. There will be more vegetables to deal with tonight for the freezer, more wood to cut today, and it is as if my body is all mine again, familiar, stretched, sturdy and able.

I have forgotten Katie. I am startled to see her by the cabin. How could I have forgotten? What happens to me here, that I forget so easily?

"Well?" she asks, defiant and anxious.

I do not know what she means.

"Well, what have you decided?" she demands.

"Decided? I don't know that I've decided anything." I am still puzzled; it is remarkable, how I forget.

She is annoyed. "But I thought that's what the three days were for. For heavens sake, you must know by now whether you're coming back with me or not. What have you been doing, anyway?"

"Oh, gardening and freezing and getting wood and walking." I remember now what it was all about. But what was so important about it? I can see that the girl is furious with me, and I feel badly about that. I am seeing with astonishing clarity this morning, I think, almost as I do when I have a fever. The colours are very bright, the girl's expression clear, and it is all pounding into me with unusual force. The trouble I am having, it seems is that things are not coming together inside my mind; they are each staying separate and sharp, which is difficult.

I feel a little helpless. I shrug, and her mouth twists.

"Oh," she says, and the voice is frustrated and angry and very close to tears. "You are the most — *selfish* person I've ever met. I can't believe the time I've wasted up here with you. Do you have any idea what's been happening to me in the last three days, while you've been happily playing with your vegetables? I haven't slept, I haven't eaten, I've been terrified you'd turn me out when I came back. I was so scared you'd decide to stay here." She stops, takes a deep breath. "Well I bloody well hope you do stay. You're not human. For the rest of my life I'm going to stop before I do anything and think, "is this something *she* might do, and if it is, I'm not going to do it. I wouldn't be like you for anything. You're crazy."

It hurts. I feel battered. I have nothing to say to her. I stand here, watching her, and she is clenched and puffed with rage. I catch her vision, and what I see is a middle-aged woman with chopped gray hair and brown withering skin and bewildered eyes that are quite mad.

I am pummelled by her anger and her vision. I am removed from my self, and I see what she must see; and yes, of course, this isn't me. Years roll back and I am shocked, I am the old Abra looking at this one. I am mother and wife and this apparition of the Abra who has come from that is more than horrifying.

I feel very meek, very wrong and child-like. I am dazed, unsure where I am, who this person is who watches me so full of rage; relationship and place disappear in the terror of seeing the person I appear to be.

I think, "my God, I must put myself together, straighten my hair, put on new clothes, I can't let people see me this way." I am quite frantic, patting at my hair, pulling at my jeans and blouse, dirt-streaked from the garden, trying to hide, trying to make myself presentable.

"Well?" she asks again. More gently this time, a little frightened. She sees now, as I do, that the label for this is madness, this is what is wrong. I can see that, of course. I see that.

I must try to make it right.

"Will you take me with you?" I sound plaintive, begging; she must take me, I have nowhere else to go, and no one else to make me sane. She must.

But now she is hesitating, seeing the burden, thinking, "but what can I do with a mad woman?" She is quite right.

It is her desire to be good, to do good things, that wins. She smiles bravely, kindly, and says, "Of course, when do you want to go?"

"Right now, if you like." It is urgent, it seems that I may not survive if we hesitate. And yet I must do what she wants.

She is more terrified, by the immediacy of what she is taking on, but again she copes. "All right then, let's go get you packed."

We walk together to the cabin, and she puts her arm around my shoulder. It is there with some hesitation, with responsibility rather than with caring, as if I have become something rather frail and vulnerable — old. There is a fleeting distaste in me, I want her arm off me; but we both endure it, into the cabin.

I look around. What should I take? Katie begins to wrap dishes, apparently planning to be thorough. I feel panicked, fearful of not getting away, and make her stop. "Let's leave those things, just take what I absolutely need. We can come back for the rest some other time."

She is humouring me, not wanting to upset me more, now that I am labelled mad and therefore dangerous. Or maybe I am wrong, I am not understanding clearly, and what she wants is simply to please me and make me calm.

We shovel a few clothes into a suitcase; I have so little, even I am surprised, just some slacks and underwear and tops, a coat and boots for winter, shorts for summer; it seems pointless to bother with any of it, none of it suitable for another kind of life.

But of course I must take something. I can hardly go back to the world utterly without possessions.

Katie is tense and jumpy, worrying about details that keep her mind off the cataclysm of what is actually happening, the difference I will make in her life, the load that a generous impulse has lumbered her with. She asks about the bank account, should we close it out on the way through town; should we nail shut the windows so that no one can steal all the things we are leaving behind; are there spare keys hidden around that should be retrieved; is there anything besides the clothes, so poor, that I want to take. I tell her "No, no, nothing, let's go, we can come back." I don't look, don't consider if there is anything else I should take, because it is urgent to get it over with, get away from here, stop being mad.

There is pain in every moment, a stiffness, an independent will in my muscles, and a combat going on in my mind, ordering the muscles, commanding, barely controlling them, to keep going, do what must be done.

Katie, who carries the suitcase, locks the door behind us. I walk steadily, do not turn around, there will be no good-byes, there is no point. Surely the place must disgust me, it must reflect the disgust there is toward something mad. I do not see the lane, the trees beside it in two rows, the ditches almost dry from summer. I do not see, my eyes are open but I cannot look. Katie's car is parked at the end of the lane, beside the lean-to shack where my own is kept, and my eyes are fixed on it, each step closer to the end, the end coming nearer, a little gold-coloured car, compact, efficient, the goal. Katie walks just behind me, I can hear her steps, cutting off the past behind, and in front of me her car. I am marching on and on to that car. I do not, can not, comprehend that there is anything beyond that car, which is very clean, seems pure, shining yellow in the sun.

We walk forever and for a moment. The lane stretches infinitely before me and the car seems so close I might reach out and touch it, the centre of my vision.

But when we reach it, when I can touch it, it is unreal, as if it

196

should have receded again into the distance. I am confused, turn to Katie, who is very efficient, unlocks the passenger door and puts my suitcase in the back seat. "Well, we're off then," she says. "In you get." I wedge awkwardly into the car. "I'll show you how to use the seatbelt, it comes down over the shoulder and fastens over here like this." She is reaching around me, pulling at a leather strap, and something clicks and when I try to lean forward I can't. One part of it reaches across my chest, the other across my lap. I am trapped. I pull at the strap, but it holds me tight.

Katie is walking around to the driver's side. When she looks in, her face changes, she stares at me and her eyes are wide. I do not know exactly what I am doing, except that I am struggling, fierce now and full of fear, not just panic but far-deep fear, to get free.

I need her help. She has put the strap on, she can let me out of it, she must know how, I am suffocating in it. I beg. "Katie let me out of here, get me out," and I am crying with so much fear. Her face disappears and then she is beside me, saying "calm down, Mother, it's all right, it's just the seatbelt, you're supposed to wear it but if it bothers you, you can leave it off, it's not serious," and she is crying too.

It takes some time. I am struggling and she can't find the button to push, but finally something goes click again and Katie is pulling on the harness. My arms are thrashing and she has trouble getting me untangled; everything is panic and confusion. And then my body is moving again, it is free, and all that is left is a terrible trembling that will not stop.

I can see Katie and yet she isn't real; the road is there, but it is not real, none of it has form, it feels as if everything will melt if I touch it. I want something to be real, I want to reach out and touch something.

I push Katie aside and scramble out of the car. There is a moment when I look around and don't understand. Nothing is familiar, there is no direction, no space, nothing I can focus on, nothing that will absorb me, or that holds anything of me.

It is a blurred vision, and suddenly it clears. I can see it all, and I know. I think, "what have I been doing, what can I have been thinking of?"

I push back past the still-bewildered Katie and reach into the back seat, pulling out my suitcase. I stand, panting, until gradually my breathing slows and I can look around and see what is here. I know again; the rest has been an aberration. I go to Katie and put my hand on her arm. She is trembling now and I feel her pull back just a little, although it isn't a conscious movement; she is finding me repulsive, and maybe frightening. I feel very calm.

My voice, when it emerges, is remarkably even and tender. It is my own voice again. "Dear Katie. I'm so very sorry you've had to go through all this. I'm sorry you've had to suffer because of me. I'm sure you know already that it will be better without me."

She will not look at me.

"I can't expect you to understand. I've seen myself as you must see me, and I know it looks dreadful, crazy. I was taken in by that for a while. But it's really not like that at all, not to me.

"A long time ago I looked at what I had done, leaving you and Elliott and Stephen and coming up here, and I thought, 'I've had a breakdown.' But then I realized that wasn't a bad thing, I was so used to trying to decide if something was good or bad, I still had that, and I thought, 'well, it wasn't a bad thing, it was a good thing, because I've taken what was broken down and put it back together, and altogether it's very much better for me.' You see? No, that's stupid, you can't see, not yet. Maybe someday.

"In here," and I pound my chest with a forefinger, trying to make her look, but she won't, "in here I am well. I know."

I tip her chin with my hand and hold it, making her look at me. She is crying, tears trail down her face; they do not stop and she does not move to wipe them away.

"Someday, if you ever feel like it, come back and see me. I've felt very close to you. I am grateful that you came. I know that right now, and for a long time, you will hate me, but maybe that will end and you will feel like coming back. If that feeling ever comes, please do."

I lean forward and kiss her on the cheek. She does not flinch.

"Thank you, Katie."

I turn away then, pick up my bag and begin to walk up the

198

long lane. There is nothing at the end that is a goal, nothing to fix my eyes on, just the lane, and at the top I see the cabin and it is home, again.

I unlock the door and go in slowly, looking around, absorbing it. In the bedroom I dump open the suitcase and put away the clothes. I go to the kitchen and make tea.

I hold the cup while I walk through the cabin, looking out each window, seeing the grass, the bushes, the wild flowers, the weeds, the willow, the garden, a little further off the bank of the stream.

I wash the cup and go to bed. I am very tired. I do not dream.

The next day I weed the garden and pick more vegetables, chop and haul some wood, eat dinner and spend the evening again blanching and freezing for the winter. There will be plenty this year, no problem.

I am very tired. I go to bed. The dream does not come back.

The Women's Press is a feminist publishing house. We aim to publish a wide range of lively, provocative books by women, chiefly in the areas of fiction, literary and art history, physical and mental health and politics.

To receive our complete list of titles, send a large stamped addressed envelope. We can supply books direct to readers. Orders must be pre-paid in £ sterling with 60p added per title for postage and packing (70p overseas). We do, however, prefer you to support our efforts to have our books available in all bookshops.

The Women's Press, 34 Great Sutton Street, London EC1V 0DX

Joan Barfoot
Duet for Three

Aggie is eighty, and dying. Helpless, unwieldy, incontinent, her body is slipping out of control, and she can only remember the heady independence of those happy years after the death of her husband. Now she is dependent on her ageing daughter June, a woman who can neither accept nor offer love. Her consolation is the passionate love she feels for her granddaughter Frances, a free spirit whose dreams and desires, this time, will perhaps not be destroyed by the forces of circumstances and convention.

"A marvellous book about mutual dependence, written in Barfoot's tense and urgent style." *The Sunday Times*

Fiction   £3.95
ISBN: 0 7043 3981 1